searching for

Other books by Nyrae Dawn

OUT OF PLAY (WITH JOLENE PERRY)

Writing as Kelley Vitollo
for adult readers

LUCKY BREAK
LUCK OF THE DRAW
JUST MY LUCK

searching for beautiful

nyrae dawn

Entangled Publishing, LLC
2614 South Timberline Road
Suite 109
Fort Collins, CO 80525
Visit our website at www.entangledpublishing.com.

Edited by Stacy Abrams
Cover design by Pamela Sinclair & Kelley York

Print ISBN: 978-1-62266-148-0
Ebook ISBN: 978-1-62266-149-7

Manufactured in the United States of America

First Edition March 2014

To my girls, Mckenzie and Kelsey. May you always know how beautiful you are, without having to wait for someone to tell you. Real beauty comes from the inside and you're capable of creating your own beautiful. I see it shine from you every day.

Chapter One

One, two, three, four. I focus to slow my breathing. In, out, in, out, trying to make the breaths stretch slowly, closer to tortoise rather than hare, like they're rushing right now. My palms sweat, making my hands stick to the steering wheel, almost like they're in clay on my pottery wheel.

Why am I so nervous? I shouldn't be. This is Jason and he loves me. How many times has he assured me I can tell him anything? That we're connected...soul mates, who were lucky enough to find each other in this crazy, screwed-up world we live in.

More than that, he likes it when I talk to him, when I tell him what's inside me. Because at home, all he has is ugliness. Fighting parents, a dad who is always putting him down and calling him names.

I'm his haven. His beautiful.

Funny how out of all the billions of people in the whole wide world, I found him. That he calls me his beautiful when that's what Dad always called Mom. Not in the same words—la mia bella signora is what Dad used to call her. My beautiful lady. That's how I knew Jason and I were meant to be. It was a sign that I'm destined for a love just as true as my parents had. Just like I always felt it was destiny for them to adopt me. She was meant to be my mom.

My heart starts to calm at the memory of Jason whispering those words to me. Of his breath against my ear. His body wrapped around mine. *We love each other,* I remind myself, so I shouldn't be scared to tell Jason. Now the rest of it? That makes my stomach turn and my head pound. Dad is going to freak.

After pulling the keys from the ignition, I get out of my car, running my hands down my red dress. It's the one I wore the night we met.

If red wasn't my favorite color before, it definitely is now. He'd touched my hair, the red that surprises everyone, since Dad is Italian. But then, it's not as though I would look like him.

That quickly, it had been like Jason and I knew each other forever. Did he know then? Feel the draw he told me about later? Feel the same spark with me that Mom always talked about with Dad? I hadn't at first. I didn't want to feel anything when I met Jason. Caring hurt, and I had enough hurt to last a lifetime.

I love him now, though. That's what matters.

Red hair…red dress, and now red cheeks. I never knew

tinge

nyrae dawn   3

blushing could be so damn sexy...

Half of me wanted to laugh at him. I mean, really? How dumb did he think I was? At the time, it was obvious his words were lines, but instead of laughing, I talked to him. He talked back, and nothing's been the same ever since.

Smiling, I start to walk toward his brother Sam's house. Luckily, he's always out of town, so we never have to worry about seeing him. It's the perfect place for Jason and me to meet.

The front door swings open before I get a chance to knock. Jason's there, his blond hair messy like always. He's wearing a pair of shorts, no shirt. Even after the past three months, I still shiver seeing his toned body. The ripples of his abs and firm arms. He works out like crazy.

"Hey, babe. About time you got here. Sam will be home soon, so we don't have much time to hang out."

As soon as he pulls me inside, his mouth is on mine. So recognizable, that mint tinged with smoke. I've always hated smoking, which is why he sucks on the mints. But still, the mixture is him. I would know it anywhere. It's not that I necessarily like it, but it's familiar. And familiarity is important.

Tell him, tell him, tell him. The words creep into my head. I try to slam the door on them, but they're like his smoke, floating under the door and filling the room until I'm almost suffocating on them. "Jason..." I pull back a little bit. "I want to talk to you, remember? I have... I have something to tell you."

He smiles, threading his fingers through mine before

pulling me farther into the house. Into the living room. "Sorry, I just missed you. You know how irresistible you are to me."

I feel the heat burning my cheeks.

"Ah, there is it. Love that blush."

Somehow, it's those words that give me the courage I need. He loves my blush, my laugh. How many times has he told me he loves everything about me?

Love will make it okay.

"I…" I grab his other hand, too, needing to touch him as much as I can, wanting to look him in the eyes when I speak to him. "I need to tell you something important."

He cocks his head a little, his hands tightening. "What is it?"

"I'm…" *Push the words out, Brynn.* They've been eating me alive for weeks and now I just need to *say* them. My hands start shaking and briefly I wonder if he can feel it. My throat feels clogged, like words or breath can't get through. They're trapped behind a barrier of fear. *Do it!* "I'm pregnant."

The sentence somehow sucks all the air out of the room. It's suddenly hard to breathe again. Jason's hands grip mine tighter and tighter. I steady myself, proud of how I'm handling this. I spent two days crying before today, freaking out. I promised myself I wouldn't freak when I told Jason.

"Excuse me?"

"I'm pregnant…with a baby. Duh, of course it's a baby, but your baby…*our* baby." I step closer to him, but he pulls away. His hands jerk out of my grasp.

"How the fuck are you pregnant, Brynn? It sure as hell can't be mine. I've worn a condom every time we've been together. Every. Single. Time." His words make me flinch. They're like a whip biting into my skin.

Tears blur my vision; anger tries to block them. I'm shocked that Jason could accuse me of something like this. Then I remember the stories he's told me, the anger he lives with every day. I promised Jason I wouldn't be like that. *We* wouldn't be that way.

But he made *me* the same promise, too.

Locking eyes on him, I notice his face is red, see the angry set of his jaw as he crosses his arms. Who is this? Jason has never yelled at me before. "I don't know… I don't know. But I'm pregnant. I swear. I've heard stories about girls getting pregnant even with a condom. Maybe it, like, had a hole in it. This isn't something I would lie about, Jason. I've never been with anyone but you. Only you. You know that."

My hands shake. My heart, too. I love him. *But he thinks I would cheat on him.* The anger tries to push its way in again, but I swallow it down until it creates this sort of vacuum inside me instead. Blood rushes through my ears, making it difficult to focus on anything else.

"Hate to break it to you, Brynn, but if you haven't been with anyone but me, you wouldn't be knocked up right now."

A chill sweeps over me. The air conditioner? Whatever it is, it feels strong enough to knock me over. No, break me apart, blowing pieces of me around the house. I shake my head, trying to make sense of what he's saying. Trying to swallow down the need to vomit. "How can you say that? You know I love you. I'd never. I love *you*, Jason."

He laughs. I used to love the sound, and now it's beating me into the ground, sounding so different from any of his laughs before. "Didn't you tell me your little boyfriend broke up with you the day before we got together? I'm sure you loved him, too. Grow up. I swear, you're so naive."

How many times have I told him I never loved Ian? The only other time I thought I was in love, I was a dumb kid... Kid...

This can't be happening. Jason can't be treating me this way. Not when I'm going to have our baby. A *baby*. I clutch my stomach. The word suddenly starts repeating over and over in my head, blurring and mixing with Jason's angry accusations until it's all I can hear or feel.

"Jesus, I'm such a fucking idiot!" He runs a hand through his hair. "How long have you known? Who told you? Figured you'd try and trap me, did you? Hate to break it to you, but it's not going to happen."

"What?" The word manages to tumble out of my mouth.

He's pacing now, and my eyes dart around the room, following him. It's a struggle when I can't stop his voice in my head or the nausea in my stomach.

Hate to break it to you, Brynn, but if you haven't been with anyone but me, you wouldn't be knocked up right now.

"This isn't a game, Brynn. This is my life. I could go to

fucking jail over this shit. You have to get rid of it. I'll give you money or whatever, but you have to get rid of it."

Dizziness twists and turns around me, pulling me in, dragging me under. *Jail... Get rid of it...*

Oh, God. I'm pregnant. I'm sixteen and pregnant. He wants me to get rid of our baby. My dad will never talk to me again.

With Jason by my side, I thought it would be okay. Thought we could make it work. I'd have someone else to love.

My eyes flutter and my legs go weak. I crumple to the floor, not sure what else to do. "Shit," Jason curses from above me. An eternity later, he joins me on the floor. "Shhh, Brynn. I'm sorry. I didn't mean... You just freaked me out. I... Shit, baby, you can't tell anyone. I love you so much and hate to say this to you, but you can't tell anyone. You have to get rid of the baby and no one can know it's mine."

He wraps his arms around me, pulling me to his lap. God, I want to feel safe here, the way he's always made me. This is the Jason I know. The one who's calm, sweet, and loving, not this man flip-flopping between anger and affection that I'm seeing now.

"Shh...don't cry. I'm sorry. I love you. I just... I wanted you so much, that I couldn't stop myself from lying. One look at you and I was a goner. When I found out how old you are... I did it for us."

You can't tell anyone...

"I couldn't lose you, but don't you see? This is serious shit. You don't want me to go to jail for loving you, right?" His words are a blur, a muffled echo in my head.

You have to get rid of the baby and no one can know it's mine.

My mom died, and now he wants me to kill our baby. Don't know if I can do it. *Baby… Pregnant. No one can know it's mine.* "What are you talking about?"

"Oh, Brynn. You're so beautiful. Stop crying. I can't handle hearing you cry. I'm so sorry, but you can't be mad at me for loving you. That's why I did it. You love me, too, don't you? If you do, you have to get rid of the baby and not tell anyone. I'll pay for it. I don't want to lose you."

If Jason can't accept what happened, how can I expect Dad to? He'll hate me. Be disappointed. He's already broken because of Mom. "I love you, too," I whisper. "But…" I don't think I can do it. Kill my baby? Kill our baby?

"How far are you?"

"Seven weeks…"

"It's okay. It's not a baby yet. You can do this, Brynn. Do it for us."

My stomach cramps. I just want to go to sleep. Want this to all be some kind of dream.

"I'm not mad that you knew," he continues. "People sometimes lie when they love someone so much. That's why I did it at first. We can keep on pretending like we have been. Keep being happy. I'm only twenty-three. It's not like it's that big a deal."

Twenty-three, twenty-three, twenty-three. The urge to throw up climbs into my throat again. Dizziness sweeps through me. "Jason?"

"Red, you have to trust me. It will work out. You're

my beautiful. My beautiful, Red. Don't take that away from me. We'll be okay… It's not a baby yet, anyway."

Each and every one of his words stabs into me at once. I don't know which to focus on. Can't make myself pick any. Love mixes with lies and there's a part of us inside me and he says it's not real. He wants me to get rid of it.

My body takes over and I'm scrambling away from him.

Jason walks toward me, but I can't make myself back away any more. "Don't pretend you didn't know, Brynn. How could you not? I played your game because it made you feel better, but you know who I am. You always knew how old I was. Everyone else will know it, too. They'll know you wanted to trap me. Or they'll think you lied about your age. You wanted an older guy because you were messed up after your mom died. It happens all the time." He shrugs.

"You'd tell them I lied?" He said he loves me, but now he'd tell them I wasn't honest about my age…

It hits me, knocking the air out of me, how much I don't know this Jason, when he says, "Get rid of it and I won't have to." He's so to-the-point. So cold that I don't know if I want to keep crying or hurt him. I can't believe I fell for him.

"I hate you!" I yell. They're the most immature words in the world, but they're all I have. "I *hate* you, Jason!" Stumbling, I run toward the door, but he grabs my arm. A pain shoots through my stomach. My eyes water. My ears feel full, almost echoey.

"You'll break your dad's heart. He'll know his little baby is sleeping around and got knocked up. That you lied to sleep with a local baseball player. After losing your mom, can you do that to him? Everyone else will hate you for trying to trap me, too. Do you want that? Do you want everyone to know you're a slut?"

I rip my arm away from him, covering my mouth with a shaking hand. He's right. I know he's right. *Everyone will hate you.* Haven't I lost enough?

It'll be my word against his.

Jason… I love him, but he never loved me. How will I tell my dad? How will I be a mom?

"Be smart, Brynn. I swear to God, you'd better be smart and get rid of it."

Ignoring his words, I run from the house. I don't remember driving home. I don't remember starting a fire in the woodstove and throwing in that stupid red dress. All I remember are his words. He doesn't love me. Never loved me. He saw someone young and naive and he used me. He wants me to kill the baby.

I know I can't, but I never get the chance anyway. The cramps start in the middle of the night. The rush of blood quickly afterward.

Dad hears me crying.

He takes me to the hospital.

His anger came the next day. The yelling, the disappointment.

He hasn't looked at me the same ever since. No one has.

Jason was right.

Chapter Two

Before

"So, you and your mom were close?" Jason slips his hand into mine, interlocking our fingers. My heart's mixed up, not knowing if it wants to jump for joy at the contact or break in a million pieces because he brought up Mom. It's been two months, and it feels like two decades and two seconds at the same time. How can she have been gone this long? Time feels like it's never-ending.

So many conflicting feelings, but none that I want to focus on, so I give my attention to Jason instead.

"Yeah...she's..." I can't bring myself to speak the word "gone." It's wrong...bad, the worst thing she can be. "We were very close." Ugh. How can "were" suddenly be a bad word, too? "She was my best friend. Everyone loved her." I feel myself smiling, which is a miracle. I haven't smiled when it came to Mom since it happened. Dad is in his own world and even if he wasn't, I'm not sure I could go there with him.

Ian, my ex-boyfriend, doesn't understand. He's too busy with sports and having fun to take time to care about much.

Ellie and Diana try, but they don't understand, either. When you haven't experienced it, it's easy to think you fully get it, but you don't. It's hard with them, because they knew her so well. They loved her so much. Not nearly as much as me, but as much as best friends can love another mom. She had that kind of power, though. My friends were jealous she was my mom.

Maybe that's why I can't talk to them about it—she was the one thing I had that they didn't, and in the blink of an eye, she was taken away from me.

My chest starts aching again.

"I'm sorry." Jason uses his other hand and pushes a strand of hair behind my ear. "It's so hard to lose someone close to you. I lost my grandma. When I was young, I always wanted to be at her house because it was calm there. I could be happy. She was more like a mom than mine is—I loved her more than anyone else. Nothing's been the same since she's been gone. Just another thing we have in common." He gently squeezes my hand.

"Just another thing," I repeat. Jason knows what I'm going through because he's lived through losing someone he loves. I hate feeling comfort in that, because it means he lost his grandma, but he makes it so I don't feel alone.

"We can talk about her if you want. Or we don't have to. It's up to you. I don't want to push you, but I want to be here for you, too."

That's exactly what I need. Everyone else tells me how to feel. But Jason lets me go at my pace. Feel what I feel and talk when I want to talk. It's like he's filled a void inside me I never thought would be filled again. Makes me feel when I never thought I would want to feel again.

I snuggle against him as he leans back on the old, bumpy tree. We're at our spot, the quiet, out-of-the-way piece of heaven where Jason likes to bring me. No one bothers us here. No one comes here. It's ours and only ours.

"You're amazing," I tell him, and I mean it. Sometimes I can't believe I found him just when I needed him. Maybe Mom sent him to me, to help me get by without her. She always knew the right thing to do, and I can't see this being any different. If she couldn't be here for me, I know she would find a way to send me someone who could.

"No, you are. I don't know what I'd do without you, Brynn. I need you so much." His words are so smooth, so perfect that I used to doubt them. But then, I could have seen Dad being like this with Mom. She used to reminisce about how he always said the right thing.

I turn to face him and Jason's lips come down on mine, so soft, *so* gentle. He takes the kiss deeper, pushing his tongue inside my mouth. It goes straight to my head. *He* goes straight to my head, making my heart tap-dance and my stomach flutter.

I shiver when his hand edges under my shirt. His fingers tickle my stomach. My heart goes even wilder, but now for a different reason. Nerves push their way through, threatening this perfect moment between us.

Relax, Brynn. Calm down.

His fingers tickle my belly before going higher... higher, and then they tease the edge of my bra. It's almost like an electric shock, making me jerk away. It feels weird to go from thinking about Mom to getting felt up.

Jason lets out a heavy breath and I automatically feel guilty. "I'm sorry...," I whisper. He's here for me; I should be able to do this for him. It's not like it's a huge deal.

He curses beneath his breath, but then looks at me and gives me a tight grin. "It's okay. I don't want to push you. I never want to push you, Brynn. You know I love you."

The words cover me like a comfortable blanket, filling more holes and voids inside me. Pretty soon, he might have me all patched up.

"I love you, too."

He stands and holds his hand out for me. I let him help me up. "Do you want to do something?" I ask. "Maybe see a movie or go out to dinner?"

He shakes his head. "I asked Sam if we could go to his house. He'll be out for a bit today. I just want to spend time with you."

I feel like I'm floating. I love that Jason wants to keep me to himself. That he loves spending time with just *me* because I'm that important to him. For me, he's perfect.

Chapter Three

Late June
Now

"I don't want to do this." They're the first words to spill out of my mouth all morning. It's not the first time I've said them, but I'm hoping this time, they'll matter.

Dad finishes parallel parking. He's an expert at it, but I've never been able to do it. The whole pulling in backward thing freaks me out. I'm lucky I passed my driver's test.

Once he kills the engine and lets out a sigh—one of the many he's let escape the past couple weeks—he replies. "It's for the best, Brynn. You might not see it now, but it's true. I... It's just the right thing. We have to do it." I'm not sure if he's trying to convince me or himself. Still, it's the longest string of words he's spoken to me at once since "the incident," so maybe it's progress. It's not as if he ever spoke much anyway—Mom was always the vocal one — but words never seemed painful to him before.

Now they're agony.

I hate that I did this to him. That the love of his life died from a stupid aneurysm and now the daughter she loved so much is breaking him again. Is he wondering what she would think? Wishing she had to deal with this and not him? Thinking that she never would have screwed up this badly? Or even worse, I worry that he wishes they didn't adopt me. Maybe if he had a real daughter, she wouldn't have screwed up as badly as I did.

"I'm scared." My eyes dart down, suddenly interested in my lap. In the swirl of the blue fabric of my jeans.

Another sigh. "Me too, *dolcezza*."

I can't help but look at him. I haven't been his sweetie in years. I'm not sure if it's my fault or his; I thought it made me sound like a baby, and he never pushed it. He hasn't pushed anything in so long. Until now.

"The right thing," he mumbles again, climbing out. "Come on. Let's go in."

The slam of the door makes me jump. Then I get out of the car and follow him into the office of the lawyer he hopes will get my ex-boyfriend thrown into jail.

• • •

"So we have Jason Richter saying Brynn lied about her age. That she told him she was eighteen. We have her friends, who say she bragged about her new boyfriend. About how much she loved him. More than one of them says she told them *she* didn't want anyone to meet him yet. That even though Mr. Richter wanted to meet her friends, she wanted to keep him to herself for a little longer."

"He's older than her. It's obvious he lied. Brynn making up stories about their not being able to meet him was just a silly thing kids do."

Just like Dad's been so fond of doing lately, our lawyer sighs. "I understand that, Mr. De Luca. I do, but you have to look at it from the outside. We're going to tell people she lied then, but ask them to believe her now. It makes her unreliable. With her friends all telling the same story and Mr. Richter saying she lied to him, it doesn't look good.

"We have a girl who's lied—" the lawyer continues.

"But—" Dad cuts in, but Mr. Rogers holds up his hand.

"I'm playing devil's advocate here. We have a girl who's admitted to lying. Who started acting strangely to her friends."

"Her mother *died.*" This time, Dad doesn't let himself be cut off. "That has to count for something."

"It could account for her lying about her age to impress a boy, too." The lawyer almost looks sad as he continues. "*She* spent months with Mr. Richter in secret, which they can very well argue she did because she didn't want him to find out how old she really was. We have her ex-boyfriend Ian, who says she stopped calling him and then flaunted Mr. Richter, bragging about her new boyfriend. Which again, they will say is proof she knew who he was. She's kept secrets. Lied over and over, and that's what people are going to focus on."

And I had. I'd lied about a lot to be with Jason.

"We also have a small-town boy makes good. The kid from the wrong side of the tracks who worked hard and made it to the minors, despite his felon father."

He's right. Maybe I deserve this somehow, because of Mom and how I treated my friends after she died. Even before Jason, I'd pulled away.

"Being frank with you both, I'm not sure we could get a conviction. I'm not saying I wouldn't try. I'm saying it will be hard, maybe impossible." He pauses and then turns to me. "I'm saying it's going to drag out any little blemish they can find to ruin your character. I'm saying there will be nasty things said about you. I'm saying you have to really be sure it's what you want before we decide to go there."

Leaning back in his chair, Mr. Rogers pushes his glasses up his nose. "Can you do this, Brynn?"

No, no I can't. "Daddy?" I turn to look at Dad. This time, I'm the one using a name that's been lost to us for so long.

"I'll give you guys a minute." Mr. Rogers stands up and walks out of the room. Dad's eyes never leave mine. There are more wrinkles than there used to be. Dark circles. And they look broken. So broken, and I hate that I'm the one who made him feel this way. That I saw a boy behind his back. That I had sex and got pregnant at sixteen. That he has to deal with all this stuff that makes him so uncomfortable, because he's all I have. Because they chose to adopt me and I screwed up so royally. I'm even sorry for Mom, because maybe if I'd let her rest, maybe if we hadn't fought, she'd still be here.

I'm also sorry that he has to look at me and wonder... am I the liar? Am I the one who really tricked Jason instead of the other way around?

"God." Dad leans forward, elbows on his knees, and hands covering his face. He's quiet for a few minutes before his shoulders start to jump up and down. Cause and effect. Tears start filling my eyes, too, playing follow the leader down my face.

"I don't know what to do, Brynn. I don't know what to do. What's right. How to fix it."

What he means is how to fix my screwup. How to fix me.

"Your mom would know what to do. If she were here, this probably never would have happened."

This meaning my colossal mistake. The lies that put us here. Why did I ever trust Jason? How could I have been so stupid to believe all his practiced sincerity? Why couldn't I have leaned on my friends instead? "I just want it to go away. I want to forget it. Forget him. I just want it to get better." I pull my knees to my chest, not caring that my Chucks are probably getting dirt on the chair. "Can't we just forget about it? I can't..." A ball lodges in my throat, and the words won't come out. The knees of my jeans are wet with tears. "Please, Daddy. Please just let me forget about it all."

"Shh. It's okay, *dolcezza*." Dad's hand cups the back of my head. His arms wrap around me. "Shh, we'll just forget it ever happened. It'll be okay. I won't make you go through with the charges. It's over."

I'm so relieved when he says it. But Dad is wrong. So wrong.

It's only just beginning.

Chapter Four

Before

"You seem happier." Ellie gives me a thumbs-up.

Happy. It's been such a foreign word lately. But I do feel…happier. I'm not there yet. It doesn't seem right to be happy without Mom, but I'm getting closer, because of Jason and how he makes me feel. Like I'm normal, when I haven't been for so long. "I'm trying." I shrug.

Diana lays her hand on my shoulder. "It's good to see."

"Thanks."

"What time are the boys getting here?" Ellie asks.

My heart drops at that. "What? You guys didn't tell me they were coming with us." It's okay when Todd and Kevin are with us. They're Ellie's and Diana's boyfriends, but where they are, Ian almost always is. My ex-boyfriend isn't too happy to be around me anymore. I'm pretty sure he hates me, though I don't fully get why. I wasn't the one to dump *him* after he lost *his* mom.

"They always come, Brynn. I figured you knew they'd hang out with us." Diana moves to the mirror and puts on her lip gloss.

I figured they would realize it was awkward. "Maybe I shouldn't go."

"What?" Diana asks. "No, we miss hanging out with you."

"We can tell them not to come over," Ellie adds.

The truth is, I know they would. But I know they don't want to. They want to hang out with their boyfriends and they want things to be the way they used to be. I do, too, but I'm not sure how to get there.

"No, no. It's fine." It wouldn't be fair to make them cancel. Before anyone else can speak, Ellie's bedroom door pushes open and the boys come in, laughing.

"Hey." Kevin waves at me.

"Hi," Todd says before each of them go to say hello to their girlfriends. Ian pushes his way past me without a word. Nerves kick up my heart rate.

"What time does the movie start?" Ian collapses onto Ellie's bed.

Diana tells him and then he says, "Cool. I need to text my girl to tell her when to meet us."

Even though I try to stop myself, I still whip my head his way. Ian has a girlfriend? Not that it matters. I mean, I have Jason. Still, I didn't know.

"Um, thanks for telling us you were bringing her." Ellie gives me an *I'm sorry* look.

"I didn't know I had to," Ian tosses back at her.

Todd and Kevin try to pretend they aren't paying attention, but Diana doesn't. "Why don't you invite your new boyfriend, Brynn? That way we could meet him and it'll be all couples."

My stomach drops somewhere near my feet. All I can do is wonder what Mom would do, what she would say. She always had the answers. Without her I teeter between decisions, unsure all the time.

"You really *do* have a boyfriend, right, Brynn?" Ian laughs.

"Of course she does." Ellie steps closer. I don't miss the look she gives Diana. These girls have been my best friends my whole life, yet they don't believe Jason is real, either. My cheeks heat and I dart my eyes away.

"I wouldn't lie about having a boyfriend. That's stupid."

"We'd love to meet him," Diana says. I shake my head.

"So he's embarrassed to be seen with you?" Ian sneers.

"Hey, man." Todd hits his arm. "That's not cool."

"No," I say, "but maybe I don't want him to meet *you*." The words fall out of my mouth, unplanned. Ian looks shocked. Even though it's wrong, it fuels me forward. "He actually asked to meet you guys." *Shut up, shut up, shut up.* Still, my mouth keeps going. "I just…" I look away. "Want to keep him to myself a little longer."

This isn't what Mom would do. The whole time I stand here, I realize that. It does nothing to stop me, though. I'm mad and disappointed in myself.

"Yeah, right." Ian stands up.

Words struggle to form clearly in my mind. How to

relate to my friends right now, how to be a part of them *and* Jason. But as my eyes scan the room, seeing the way no one will look at me besides Ian, I realize none of them believes me. It hammers home how we're suddenly on opposite sides when we never were before. The urge to look away hits me, too, to find a way to erase their doubt. Without another word, I storm out of the room. None of them try to stop me.

Chapter Five

Now

"Oh look, your friends are here," Dad says when we pull into the driveway. My heart stutters at the sight of Diana and Ellie standing on my porch. Ellie's hair looks blonder, like she's been spending every second in the sun. She bleaches it sometimes, but I never really thought she had to. It always looks shiny and perfect, hanging down her back.

Diana's dark hair is in all those tiny braids she wears every summer. Her "summer look," she calls it. I see little hints of purple and know she must have weaved some of her favorite color in. Diana has these awesome bright-green eyes that everyone notices. Her already-dark skin is even darker, telling me that they probably *have* been out and about all summer.

Without me. And I deserve it.

"I forgot, I need to pick something up for dinner at

the store. Why don't you go and visit for a bit? You know, get back to normal. I'll be home in a little while." Dad pats my leg. He's trying to be helpful—I get that—but he's not. I'm scared to be alone with them, because I know they're upset with me. They don't get what happened, but it's hard to talk about it. Even *I'm* still trying to make sense of it in my head.

"Okay." I stand on the street until Dad's car is out of sight, hoping the reprieve will kill my nerves. I study our last name, De Luca, on our mailbox. I never got that, why people put their names on their house or their mailboxes, announcing to the whole world who lives there. Mom loved it, though. She was so proud to be married to Anthony De Luca. For her and Dad to give me all the things she never had.

When I know I can't stand here any longer, I turn and walk up to my porch. "Hey." The three of us stand there for what feels like an eternity, looking anywhere except at one another.

"Hey," Ellie finally says, shuffling her feet.

"Hi," Diana adds afterward.

Neither of them can meet my eyes, and I wonder if it's because they feel guilty or if they're just too angry at me.

"You guys wanna come in or something?" I ask. *Please let them say yes. Let them come inside, hug me, and tell me everything will be okay. That they know Jason is a jerk. That they believe me. That we can be friends again and they forgive me for everything I've done.*

Diana bites her lip, looking at the porch, the swing,

anywhere except at me. One of the black-and-purple braids hangs over her shoulder and I concentrate on that as she speaks. "Are you really pressing charges? That's what everyone's saying. I mean, you *wanted* to have sex with him, right? He didn't force you?"

Everyone? Of course everyone knows. That's how it goes in a small Oregon town like ours. "No, he didn't force me...I loved him." It's true. I wanted to lose my virginity to Jason. At first I was nervous, but I thought he loved me. I thought that was the way to give him back a little of what he'd given me. "But—"

"And now you're trying to get him thrown in jail?" Ellie asks. "I don't understand that. I mean, if he forced you—"

"No. No, I'm not. We're not pressing charges. It was my dad's idea, but I told him I don't want to." I lean against the door, playing with the gold doorknob just because I need something to do, anything to help me block out the thoughts in my head. I did *want* to have sex with Jason but that doesn't make it right. He was still older. He still lied.

"What happened to you?" Diana whispers. "I mean, I understand about your mom, but it's like you're a totally different person. Why did you cut us off? We've been friends forever and you ignored us. You lied to us. And Ian... You broke his heart, Brynn."

"Ian broke up with *me.*" That's the one thing they all got wrong. Not that I don't understand why he did it, *that* time. I'd blown him off and didn't pay any attention to him, but still. Out of all the replies I can give to her accusations, I know it's the least important, and I want to take it back immediately. But it's true.

Ian and I were always breaking up and getting back together. Most of the time he did the dumping, too. Our relationship was never like Mom and Dad's. Like Ellie and Diana have with their boyfriends. I never thought he loved me like I did Jason. "And I'm sorry I lied about some of it. It's not all what you think, though. I didn't lie about—" My voice cracks. A slight wind blows, making the leaves on the tree in my front yard rustle.

"Now you're sorry? When everything falls down around you? How are we supposed to believe that? All you've done is lie lately. You didn't want us to know about Jason. Why would you do that if you didn't know how old he was?"

My heart starts to thunder. One lie. I don't know what to do or say. If I tell them I didn't know, it just looks like I'm covering. "He told me no one could see us together. He said he couldn't meet you guys and I couldn't tell anyone about him."

"Pfft, but you did. You told us *all* about him. *You* told us you had this awesome guy who you weren't ready to introduce us to!" Ellie shakes her head.

It was stupid to lie. Stupid to be so insecure. I get that. Dropping my head back I close my eyes. I need to make them believe. I *need* them.

"I lied, but not for me. For him," I say. "Don't you think I realize how stupid that is now? Don't you think I've lost enough?"

"*You* dropped us. You started to pull away, and then it

was all about him. We were best friends, Brynn. It doesn't make any sense."

Diana adds, "Regardless, it was *us.* We shared everything. There were so many secrets between the three of us, but as long as it was only in our circle it was okay. Before, you wouldn't have hesitated to tell us something, even if some guy didn't want you to. Our friendship was more important than that."

Everything Mr. Rogers said is happening. And they're right, too. It's not like I can expect them to believe me. I just want to go back in time. To go back to the day Jason called me Red and this time, tell him to fuck off. To walk away from him and never think of him again. I want to go back to after Mom died. No, to before she died. I want her back. My life back.

"We all went to one of the Storm's games last year, Brynn. How do you expect us to believe you didn't know who he was?" Ellie almost looks like she's pleading with me. Like she wants me to give her an answer she can believe, but all I have is the truth.

"What?" I push off the door. "That happened way before I met him! Did you know who he was? If I said the name Jason Richter, would you automatically know he's a baseball player? We couldn't have cared less about that game. The three of us only went because the boys wanted us to. While Ian, Todd, and Kevin watched that stupid game, we painted our nails! We freaking Facebooked on our phones. Plus, it's not like there aren't a million Jason Richters in the world." *I'm sorry I lied. I'm sorry I couldn't deal with Mom better. Sorry I still don't know how to deal with any of this.*

Even though Ian and I had been off and on, it had always been the six of us. The only difference is, before the end of seventh grade, we had Christian instead of Ian. But then Mom died. Then I messed up the balance when I met Jason; I kept myself apart from our little group.

"Pretty big coincidence." Ellie isn't pleading with me anymore. That's always been Ellie. She doesn't take crap from anyone. She's strong, and I've always wished I could be more like her, but now I'd love for her to not be the type who is willing to walk away. To understand and give a second chance, because I don't know how I'll deal with this if I lose them for good. "And speaking of Facebook, what about his page? It would have said he played baseball."

"He told me he didn't have one. Why would I assume he lied about that?"

"Whatever. That doesn't explain the rest of it. I thought we were friends." Diana shakes her head. "I guess all these years meant nothing to you if you can't tell us the truth. We don't even know who you are anymore, Brynn." A single tear leaks out of her eye.

With that, they turn their backs on me and walk away.

I don't know who I am anymore, either.

Chapter Six

Before

"We should go out tonight. I don't feel like being in the house." Ellie looks at me from my computer chair. I'm curled up on my bed in my pajamas. It's Friday night. We love hanging out on the weekends, but how can I ever go out again? They shouldn't expect me to.

"I don't feel like it." I trace the pattern on my headboard with my finger, every curl of green leaves and vines. All the delicate flowers Mom spent hours painting for my birthday this year. It's still here and she's not. She hasn't been here for a month now.

I wish I could make something, the way she did. I used to be able to. But I haven't touched my pottery since she's been gone.

"I think you should," Ellie adds. "Even just the mall or something. You can't spend all your time locked in the house like…"

My father?

A hermit?

The loneliest person in the world?

I feel like them all. I don't think there will be a day when I don't feel like I'm all of those things. Maybe that's the way it should be. There isn't an answer book to this type of thing.

"What about Ian?" Diana adds. "You've been ignoring him. All he wants is to be there for you, Brynn. We all do." I know it's true; I do, at least with her and Ellie. But knowing and reacting are two different things. I can't make myself do the latter.

My lips stretch into a half smile to placate them. I don't tell them Ian is calling me less and less. That I'm not calling him at all, though I'm sure they know that part, since I'm not calling them, either. "I'm tired... I don't know..." *My mom is gone!* I want to tell them. My best friend in the world is gone and I hate the way things were left between us. Why can't they understand?

"Okay, so you relax tonight, but you have to go to Ian's birthday party tomorrow. That's, like, a girlfriend duty." Ellie comes over and sits next to me on the bed. "I know you miss her..."

If she knows, then why is she talking to me about girlfriend duty? Parties and movies don't mean anything to me right now.

"God, she was the coolest, right? Your mom was so awesome. I always wished she was mine." This from Diana.

"Oh, you remember that one time..."

They launch into stories about my mom. Stories about her like she was theirs. Like they miss her as much as I do. Like it's okay to sit here and talk about her as though it's not a big deal that she's gone. It *is* a big deal. The biggest deal, and they're laughing and talking and I hate that I can't do it, too. I hate that I'm mad at them for it.

They go straight from that into Ian's party and what they're wearing and, *oh, Brynn, I think you should wear*, and I nod when I'm supposed to and reply when I'm supposed to, but somehow their words leave me feeling more and more empty inside.

For some reason, I don't want to share my thoughts or memories of her with them right now. I don't want anyone else to talk about her.

That's a lie. I want *Dad* to talk about her.

"Brynn? Did you hear me?" I snap out of it and look at Diana.

She frowns and grabs my hand. "You didn't even hear any of that, did you?" She doesn't give me time to answer before she continues. "I know you're sad and we get that, but we can't help if you don't talk to us. Talk to someone. Your mom would want that."

It's those words that shove me over the edge. I can't believe they would tell me what my mom wants. That they think they can say to talk it out and I just can. She didn't have to find her mom dead.

Clay mixes with water down the drain as I wash my hands. I'm still frowning, still annoyed at Mom, but my eyes keep flashing to the vase I just made and I can't stop thinking... She would love it. I love it, but I know she would even more. Mom's always been into thinner, longer designs and that's exactly how this one came out.

As frustrated as I am at her, excitement still skitters through me when I think of how she'll react when she sees it. Mom loves it when I create things. It feels good to make her proud that she picked me.

But she also had an attitude with me today for no reason. She's been on my back all day. Serves her right if I don't show it to her right now.

Deciding against telling her, I turn off the faucet in my pottery room and head for the door.

I count the steps from my room to the back door. Fifteen. Shaking my head, I giggle when I think of how crazy it is to count my movements as though that will make it take longer to get inside. I've already been out here longer than I need to be, so I finally just push the door open.

See her legs on the floor as I push it farther and farther.

My heart starts to jackhammer. What is she doing on the floor? What is she doing on the floor?

Her waist.

"Mom!" The door hits the counter as I shove it open.

"Mom!" My legs collapse from under me and I hit the floor.

She's not moving. Not talking. I'm afraid to see if she's breathing.

No, no, no. *"Mom? Please! Please, wake up." The words break apart as I speak them. My tears fall on her as I pull her head to my lap. Holding her, I struggle to get my cell out of my pocket. My fingers shake as I dial 911, my free hand running through her hair like she does with me.*

The woman who answers hardly gets out any words before I yell, "Help. Please. Help me!"

"Brynn?" Diana snaps me out of the memory. One look at her tells me she's frustrated. "We're going to go. Think about what I said, okay?" She stands and then so does Ellie.

"Do you want us to pick you up tomorrow?" Ellie asks.

"No," I manage to say, tracing the headboard again. "I'll meet you there."

"What time?" Diana asks.

"Umm…seven?" I feel like I'm on autopilot, saying what I'm supposed to and not feeling any of it.

"Okay, we'll see you then."

"Love ya," they both say.

"Love you, too…"

I can't make myself go to the party. I can't make myself answer the phone. And when I go back to school, it's a struggle just to hang out with my friends.

The worst part is I know they're right. Mom wouldn't want this for me, even if I did sit in my pottery room being angry at her while she was dying.

I wish I could be as good as she was.

Chapter Seven

My parents met at a high school dance. Mom used to tell me about it all the time, how Dad didn't go to her school but he'd been at the dance with someone else, and the second their eyes locked from across the room, she knew he was someone special.

She told me how he'd asked her to dance. How he'd called her *his* beautiful lady in Italian. She said when his arms wrapped around her, she felt dizzy, and in that moment, she knew she loved him.

Ever since the first time I heard that story, two things were true about me. First, I was a total romantic. I wanted a love like Mom and Dad's. I wanted to be someone's beautiful, maybe even fall in love just like they had.

Second, I've always looked forward to school. Don't ask me how I brought those two things together—maybe since it was a school dance or because I wanted to believe I'd find my true love at a young age. Or maybe it was because the first time I thought I fell in love, it was at school, in the seventh grade. But whatever the reason, I loved school. Thrived in it.

Now, the thought makes me sick to my stomach.

I can't stop staring in the mirror of my armoire, looking for some sort of sign that I've changed in the last few months. That spending the summer without my friends, alternating between the house and my pottery room, working to create something that just won't come to me, is enough punishment. That watching my dad try to talk to me, when he can hardly look me in the eyes, is enough of a prison. That knowing I once had life inside me—even if only for a little while—only to have it stolen, is enough torture.

I've paid for Jason's sins *and* mine, and now I'm not the same Brynn anymore.

I can't find those signs I'm looking for.

Nothing tells me this nightmare is over. That when I show up at school today, Ellie and Diana will hug me. Tell me they're sorry for not believing in me and that they want to be best friends again. That Ian will tell me I didn't deserve what Jason did to me, and that even though we have a past together, he wants to be friends, too.

We can't go back and I know that. I don't even want to, because I will never trust another boy with my heart or my body again, but I want back as many parts of my "before" life as I can have. Selfish, maybe, but true.

"Knock, knock," Dad says from my open doorway.

"Can I come in?"

"Sure." I shrug.

"How are you doing?" He's studying the white metal of my armoire, picking at the peeling paint as though he's never noticed it before. He's all dressed up in his suit for work. His black hair is thinning, and I can't help but wonder what Mom would say if she could see it. If she'd tease him like they loved to do or if she'd keep quiet because she'd have a little gray in hers. Or a couple wrinkles around her mouth. She probably wouldn't, though. It hasn't been very long, and I know Dad's aging is because she's gone.

"Okay." Picking up my brush, I run it through my hair, wishing my answer were true. I'm scared to death to show my face at school. Scared to see the looks from everyone else. Hear the stories of summer parties I missed. See my group of five that used to be six.

I have no doubt everyone knows. I can't help but wonder if even after a summer, it's just as fresh for them as it is for me.

"Are you sure?"

My eyes catch his in the mirror. He holds them, and it's like a time machine, briefly making me feel like nothing has changed. Maybe if we keep looking at each other like this it will make things easier.

"Yes."

Dad gives me his ten billionth sad sigh. "Brynn... do you want to do this? Maybe we can look into online school or something. I know they have programs like that now. You'd just have to go in once a week or so. That might be...easier."

Wow. It sounds like he already looked into this. The thought makes my palms sweat. If Dad's worried it'll be this bad, it'll probably be worse than I thought.

My first instinct is to jump at the opportunity—scream "Yes!" because I don't ever want to face my friends again. I don't want to see the accusation in their eyes. Watch as they run my lies through their heads and turn them into something more than they were.

My only other option is to keep wandering around here, though. To have to look at Dad through a mirror because it somehow gives him the distance he needs to really be able to do it. To *see* Brynn and not the daughter who got pregnant and lost a baby at sixteen.

No, thank you.

"I have to go back to school, Dad. Maybe it won't be that bad."

His eyes dart away from mine. "Okay. Call me if you need anything. I love you." And I know he does. He might not be good with words, even worse so with Mom gone, but Dad loves me. He loved us both. *If all this didn't change how he feels. If this didn't make him think choosing me turned into more hassle than I'm worth.*

With a kiss to the top of my head, he walks out. Love me or not, it's the first time he's kissed me since before.

. . .

Eyes follow me all day.

Whispers, but no one actually speaks *to* me. There's an invisible force field around me, keeping anyone from getting too close when I walk down the hallways. All my female teachers hug me. All the male teachers look at me awkwardly.

It's not like it is in the movies. People don't put signs on my back or shove mean notes in my puke-green locker. They don't cough while muttering "slut" under their breath or trip me in the hallway or anything like that. Mean girls and bullies would almost be better, because right now, it's like I don't matter enough for anything. I'm not worth the time to pick on, but I'm still the black widow no one wants to get close to. Silence sometimes hurts more than anything.

For the first time in my life, I'm an outcast.

I used to be Ellie and Diana's best friend—the girl who kicked ass at pottery. I was Ian's girlfriend. Runner-up to Diana for sophomore winter formal princess. I had friends. Tons of them, and now, just like with Dad, people struggle to look me in the eyes. No one knows what to make of the girl who got knocked up by the small-town baseball star, only to lose it all. Lose my baby. I squeeze my eyes shut, trying to block out the pain.

Unlike with Jason, it was always a real baby to me. *I lost my baby...* The thought makes my heart hurt but I struggle to ignore it.

I spend lunch in the bathroom. Yes, the bathroom. Only in southern Oregon would it rain the first day back at school. We usually have more time before the deluge starts, but I guess it's fitting. Since we have a closed campus, the whole student body packs into the cafeteria. There's no way I can be in there. Feel that many eyes on me at once.

Because I'm not desperate enough to actually eat in here, I shove my lunch into the trash. Like this morning, I look in the mirror, waiting, hoping to see something that isn't there. When I hear the door creak, I push away from the sink, scramble into a stall, and close the door. It's ridiculous, but I can't help it. It's easier to be ignored in a classroom of people than by one or two girls in the restroom who will be scared to talk to me, but unable not to look at me.

"I can't believe summer is over already!" Diana's voice mixes with the sound of the door opening.

"Right? I'm so not ready to be back in school," Ellie replies.

I listen as they talk and laugh, probably while putting on their makeup. We used to do it all the time. I started telling the boys it was our time to rejuvenate, and soon Ellie and Diana began calling it that, too.

A smile pulls at my lips with the memory.

Decide to be friends with me again! Decide I've suffered enough. Decide to talk to me. To believe me when I tell you the truth. Or, at least, say you miss me. Please, just miss me...

More laughing and talking and then another creak of the door and I'm alone again. Anger rushes through me. I'm not even sure where it comes from, but it's there, building higher and higher.

I miss them. Miss them so much it hurts. I know I told Dad I could do it, but I can't. Not today.

The second I stumble out of the room, I run into a cloth-covered wall. A pair of hands grabs my elbows as I fall.

"Whoa, speed racer. I'm pretty sure you just ran a red light there."

I freeze, ridiculously wishing I could stay in this moment because it's the first time someone has spoken to me normally in months. No accusation. No questions. No pity. No anger.

And it's beautiful.

With no mirror, no roadblock, his eyes meet mine, crisp and clean, the bluest blue in the whole wide world. A cloudless sky. The ocean in Corpus Christi where we went on vacation one year. Like a fresh coat of blue paint on a newly fired piece of pottery. And familiar...somehow familiar, though I can't place him.

Burnt-brown hair, a couple shades darker than his creamed-coffee brown skin. It's kind of long. Long enough that it curls behind his ears so it doesn't get in his face. For some reason, I want his hair to fall forward. For those too-blue eyes to look at me through the silky strands instead of dead-on. I'm not sure I'm good enough to be looked at with nothing between us. Maybe everyone else has it right and this boy who doesn't put a buffer between us has it wrong.

"You good? If I let you go, you're not going to bulldoze through me, are you?"

Normal. He's talking to me so normally. His voice

rattles me a little, squeezing inside me and passing barriers, like it's a road traveled before.

I smell something slightly sweet…sugary but twined with a light scent of Irish Spring soap. Jason used to smell good, too. I'm sure that was part of his plan, just another way to lure me in. Though I guess I can't really blame him when I let him do it.

"Can you speak?"

I jerk away from the guy when the bell rings. As though the sound opens the dam, a flood of students automatically fills the hall around us. I can imagine what everyone is thinking: *Oh, now Brynn's going to try to hook up with the new guy. Does he know she's been pregnant? That she screwed an older guy?* I'm sure they'll tell him soon enough.

I can't handle it. Without a word, I turn and rush away. I don't even have to push through the crowd because it parts for me, everyone sitting back to enjoy the show.

Chapter Eight

Now

For as long as I can remember, we've always eaten dinner as a family at the dinner table. We're not one of those fancy families with a long table, decorative lighting hanging in the middle of it and forks on each side of the plate or anything. Our dining room is small. The table could fit six if we put the leaf in it, but we never do.

Four chairs, used to be three people, and we'd laugh and eat either whatever experiment Mom came up with that night, or once a week, on Sunday, Dad made sauce. The De Luca family recipe, he'd call it. And I'd be the next person to learn it. I loved being a De Luca. I always knew it, but Sunday's sauce was a reminder. It used to be the only time we made it, but you could always count on it on Sundays.

He would get up early and start it, making meatballs and throwing in pork and Italian sausage, too. Mom loved

Dad's homemade meatballs. It was always her favorite part. Dad went for the pork, saying it mixed well with the tomatoes. I liked the Italian sausage. We'd each grab our favorite parts, except once in a while, Mom would tease Dad and try to steal his pork. When she did that, he'd follow suit and hijack my sausage, which left me to pretend I was taking Mom's meatballs from her.

The pot was huge, so of course any one of us could get up and grab more off the stove, but we never did. It was always a game. Maybe a silly one, but it was ours.

We still eat at the table every night, only two of the four chairs filled now. Dad doesn't make sauce on Sundays anymore. At first he was too depressed, then we talked about it and both decided it didn't make sense to do it every week. What was the point of making that much food for two people? Maybe once a month would be better. But it's been months and the only time we had sauce was when we went to Grandma De Luca's for Christmas. Now we either have takeout, or Dad and I take turns cooking hamburgers or steak.

Never, ever sauce.

Tonight it's Dad's turn to cook, but I go ahead and make pork chops and mashed potatoes so it's ready when he gets home. I have no doubt he knows I skipped the second half of my day today. Maybe the food will soften the blow.

My heart jumps when my cell rings. It hasn't really done that in so long. I mean, Dad calls, but that's about it. After letting it ring again, I pull it from my pocket. Not recognizing the number, I answer the call. "Hello?"

"I was right, Red. Wouldn't it have been easier just to listen to me? We still could have been together, you know. And now you're alone, aren't you? That's what you get for betraying me."

Before I can dislodge the fist in my throat, Jason hangs up. Dropping the phone on the counter, I lean over it, my arms on the granite surface. Heat and cold somehow battle each other inside me, both trying to take hold.

The cold makes me shiver. The mocking sound of his voice, and the fact that he just called to be hateful. To be an ass because he knows he was right. He knows me enough to realize how much being alone makes me feel like I'm disappearing.

But then that heat starts extinguishing the cold. Jason feels invincible. Like he can call and torment me, and I won't do anything about it. I let the anger wash through me, hold it in, because I'm where it belongs.

Because he's right.

Chapter Nine

Before

"Let me grab the chair for you." We're in Sam's dining room for dinner.

Jason told me to dress up, that he wanted to take me out, but we can't because he doesn't want it to get back to his dad. He pushes Jason so hard, and is so worried about a girl getting in the middle of the goals he has for Jason, that he's a jerk about dating.

So, Jason decided we'd pretend to go out instead. I'm wearing his favorite red dress, happiness dancing around inside me as I wait for him to pull the chair out for me. When he does, I sit down.

"It smells good," I tell him.

"I cooked." Jason winks before disappearing into the kitchen. He comes back with a plate of steak, potatoes, and a salad. He sets it in front of me before putting his on the seat next to me and sitting down.

The steak is perfect. Everything he does is. We eat and laugh and he asks me about school. He touches my leg under the table but doesn't try for any more than that.

We're finished eating when he says, "I'm staying with Sam tonight, so he said it's cool if I have some of his wine. Do you want some?"

He pours a glass and then hesitates with the second one. A knot forms in my belly. I want to drink with him. It feels…I don't know, *adult*, like we're married and this could be our house or something. But I still have to drive home.

"No, thanks."

Jason's forehead wrinkles. "I wanna have a drink with you. You trust me, don't you, Red? I won't let you get hurt. Half a glass and that's all. You'll be good by the time you drive home."

It's on the tip of my tongue to say yes, but I shake my head.

"Sorry. I don't want to push you. I just thought you'd like it, that tonight could be special."

He sets the bottle down.

Guilt rumbles around inside me. He tried so hard. Jason wanted this night to be perfect for us. He's made things better for me and disappointing him sucks. Especially when I know how tough things are with him and his dad. He's trying so hard to be someone different. It's one of the things I love about him the most.

"I got ya something." He kisses me and then walks out of the room, coming back with a bouquet of flowers.

"They're beautiful."

"Eh, it's nothing."

"To me it is."

He cups my cheek. "Then I'm glad I did it. Since we're done eating, wanna go outside with me?"

"Sure."

We go to the backyard, Jason bringing the bottle with him. I sit on his lap and when he asks me if I want a drink the next time, his forehead doesn't wrinkle when I say no.

We talk and he makes jokes that I laugh at. I love these moments with Jason—just talking and enjoying each other.

About an hour later, his cell beeps and he frowns when he tells me he has to leave.

"I'm sorry, Red. I'll make it up to you. I was hoping tonight would be the night."

My heart speeds up a little, but I fight to calm it. I want to have sex with Jason. I told him we would soon.

"Soon," I say.

He cups my cheek. "I love you so much. You're so special, Brynn. I can't wait to be with you."

A pleasant ache forms low in my belly. Suddenly, I can't wait, either. "I love you, too. I want— I want to be with you, too."

Jason smiles and then he kisses me. After walking me out front, he thanks me for spending the evening with him before I get into my car. Jason stands in the driveway and watches me until I drive away, hopefully wishing we were still together, like I am.

Chapter Ten

Now

My eyes squeeze closed. I can't believe it was all a lie. How could someone fake that? There were times Jason got angry or times I didn't get him, but we had those perfect, wonderful moments, too. Those were the ones I loved.

"Smells good." I jump at Dad's words. He steps into the kitchen in a T-shirt and jeans, having already taken off his suit. I didn't even hear him come in the house.

Just like the kids today stared at me, I can't stop looking at him, trying to figure him out. Is he going to be pissed about school? Will he finally be able to look at me? Will he call me *dolcezza* again and hug me, tell me that he wants to kill Jason for hurting me? That he believes me, because even though he's been by my side, he's never spoken those words.

"Thanks." I dish us both plates, words teasing my

tongue. *Jason called.* They should be so easy to speak, but if I do, everything will start again. Dad will freak out and we'll never be able to get over it. I want to forget.

Once we're both at the table, he cuts into his meat, takes a bite. Then another, flickering his gaze to me every few seconds but never holding it there long. It's so strange, seeing my dad so adrift like this. At a loss for words. There's a difference between someone who doesn't speak often and someone who doesn't have a lot to say. He's always been sort of quiet, but he always knew what to say when it counted. His words always meant something. It's another thing I feel like I've stolen away from him.

"So...I'm assuming you know I didn't go to my afternoon classes." I toss a life raft out to him, the way no one did to me.

"Yes, I spoke with the school before you went back. We decided it best if we keep in contact, at least in the beginning. We—"

"You what?" The fork tumbles out of my shaky fingers, clanking against my plate. So he had talked to someone about my doing independent study. Maybe I should feel thankful but somehow, I feel betrayed—like he didn't even trust me enough to come to me about it before he talked to the school.

"No one knows we're in contact, Brynn. We just want to make this transition as smooth as possible. Keeping in touch is the best way to do that."

Transitions. I'm tired of transitions, learning to live without Mom, dealing with betrayal, knowing I had a baby inside me and now it's gone. "No, you wanted to check on me. What? To make sure I don't have sex with other boys like I did Jason?"

Dad's face pales, making me wish I could snatch the words back. Shove them down my throat, like they never came out. Fear singes me. If I push him too far, maybe he really will regret adopting me.

"I…" No other words come out. He's struck mute again, but he's looking at me. Really looking at me, except it doesn't feel good. It makes my gut clench because I see what he's looking for. Guilt. Trying to look inside me and decide if it's true. If I did play Jason. If I'm the liar Jason said I was. Or even if I didn't lie, if I knew. If I thought it cool to be the sixteen-year-old girl sleeping with a twenty-three-year-old.

I hold my breath, hoping that will wrangle in my cry.

"That's not fair, Brynn." He rubs a hand over his face, tired…weary. I am, too. "I have no idea what I'm doing here. I'm trying as best I can. I just told the counselors you had a traumatic summer and I want to make sure you transition okay. That's all."

And I believe him, because I'm doing the same. We're both getting pulled under. Both swimming for the surface, only to get caught in a whirlpool and sucked under again. All because I loved Jason. And because even though he doesn't know if he believes me, I know Dad is trying to support me.

Dad's eyes pull away from mine, studying his mashed potatoes like they're one of the crossword puzzles he likes to do.

"I know it's hard, but no skipping again. If you make the choice to be there, you have to do it all the way."

I nod my reply and the rest of the meal is eaten in silence. Dad cleans his plate. I push the food around mine until he's done.

"I'll wash the dishes." Dad tries to smile at me when he says it, but he doesn't quite manage.

"I'm going out to get some work done."

"Have fun," he says.

If he'd taken the time to ask, he'd know I haven't finished a piece since Mom died.

• • •

Mom wanted me to try everything as a kid. She'd sign me up for the most random classes, telling me it was the only way to find "my thing."

It's because of one of her random classes that I found it when I was ten. Pottery. I took to it right away, like my hands were meant to be covered in clay. I wonder if God has a checklist. If there's a form he fills out, marking bubbles for each new baby to be born. This one will be able to sing, the other run track. Brynn De Luca? She's meant for pottery.

When I was fourteen, Mom talked Dad into building my pottery room. A girl deserves her own space, she told him. Without space, it's hard to grow, and Mom knew if she gave me the space, my talent would grow.

Dad would never deny her anything—either of us,

really—so I got my room off the back of the house. I have to go outside to get to it and it's not huge, but it's big enough. There's space for all my supplies, cabinets for me to fill with whatever I need. My pottery wheel and even a small kiln.

When I step inside, I flick the light switch next to the door. It looks just how I left it. Two six-foot-tall wooden cabinets against the wall, one on each side of the door. A few older pieces of my work on the counters. A sink and stereo. There are two windows, one above the sink, which is on the back wall, and one on the left side.

But my wheel is still empty, in the middle of the room. My wooden chair with the pillow Mom made for me, sitting on it. There's a small couch against the wall, where Mom or Dad used to sometimes watch me. It's been lonely lately, too. And of course, in the corner, my kiln, cold and dusty.

And I can't do it. Not in this room. How can I do anything here when I sat in that chair, making a vase while she was dying?

I turn and go outside again. Gasping, I suck in a mouthful of the rain-tinged air. I should be over this by now. Why can't I get over it?

"Enjoying your night?" a voice says from the other side of the fence, separating my yard from the neighbor's. The house has been empty forever. Apparently, it isn't anymore.

"Whatever, Peeping Tom." Shivers skate over me. Talking to spooky neighbor guy, who I can't see in the dark, definitely isn't a good idea. I turn to head back into the house.

"I'm crushed. Two times in one day you didn't remember me. In my defense, I'm not trying to be a creeper. Just wanted to say hi to an old friend."

I stop, the voice sparking something inside me. Memories that have nothing to do with having run him down this morning. Reaching inside his back door, he turns on the light. The fence is low enough to see his raised porch. Oh my God. I'm shocked into inaction, my mind riding a cloud back in time. To the seventh grade…

Chapter Eleven

Before

"All right, kids! This is the last slow song of the night. Enjoy!" The DJ's voice echoes through the room, each pulse of his words making my eyes flood with tears. I haven't danced with a single boy all night. This is my first dance. I've dreamed about this day since Mom first told me how she met Dad.

I wasn't supposed to be miserable. The boy of my dreams was supposed to see me from across the room and come talk to me. It was supposed to be perfect.

Ellie and Diana stand by me at the gym door, like my jailers. If not for them, I'll run and they know it. The three of us have always been on the same wavelength like that. We can read each other too well.

"Thanks," I whisper.

"It's just one dance." Ellie squeezes my arm.

"He'll come around," Diana adds.

"You guys rock." I seriously have the best friends in the world. "Do you want to—"

"Brynn!" A voice cuts off my words.

It's weird how one moment can stand out in your mind. I don't hear the music, my friends, or any of the other people. Just my name being yelled across the gym.

The rest happens in slow motion. I turn. Christian stands about fifteen feet away from me. His lips quirk in a half smile as he does the finger thing. You know, when a guy crooks his finger at you and says to come here.

Thump. Thump. Thump. My heart threatens an attack. When I don't move, Ellie or Diana—I don't even know who—gives me a slight push. My feet are heavy as I walk toward him

"Do you wanna dance?" he asks, his Hispanic accent coming out a little more than usual.

I can't find the words to reply, so I nod. Christian leads me to the corner of the gym. We don't talk as he wraps his arms around my waist, giving me chills. *Is this what Mom felt when she first danced with Dad?* I wonder. Maybe this will be the start to my very own love story with the boy I've had a crush on forever.

He smells sweet. Like candy. Still, no words come as I lock my shaking fingers together behind his neck. In the same slow motion, we move together, no sounds but the music and my friends cheering for me in the background.

When the song is over, Christian looks at me with his too-blue eyes and I know right then, I love him. I mean, I've crushed on him for months and months, but now I know it's love. Like the forever kind.

"Thanks for the dance, Bryntastic," he says. I don't know why he calls me that, but he's done it for months now.

Again, my reply is a nod. Christian smiles one more time before disappearing into the crowd. Me? I run. Run to the bathroom, Ellie and Diana right behind me. Tears pour down my face and they laugh and hug me as we spin around the girl's room, one of my most exciting moments spent with my best friends.

Just like Mom and Dad, I fall in love at a dance.

A week later, Christian and his family are suddenly gone and I never see him again.

Chapter Twelve

Now

Until now.

"Long time no see, Bryntastic."

"Christian," I mumble. It can't be him. He can't be back. I hate boys, and I don't want to hate him. I'm not dumb. I know I didn't really love him but still, he's a good memory. One you want to keep locked away so it never has the chance to be ruined because you know something like that will never happen again. "I have to go," I say, and for the second time in one day, I run away from Christian Medina.

. . .

"Hey, beautiful." Soft fingers brush the hair out of my face. Though my eyes are begging me to stay closed, everything inside me needs them open. I need to see the face that goes with the voice I love so much.

Prying them open, I come face-to-face with Jason, leaning in my car window. "Hey…sorry. I must have fallen asleep waiting for you." It's a shock I didn't wake up because of his car. It's his prized possession. Super loud and really fast. He likes speed.

"That's okay. Sorry I'm late. Something came up."

Laughing it off, I reply, "You're terrible about being on time."

"I know. I'm sorry, Red. I had to do something with my dad." His brown eyes never leave mine, so sincere. "You should come in with me. Since I'm late, we might be cutting it a little short. I want to spend some time with you before Sam gets home. It's our anniversary." Leaning closer, he kisses me. I immediately melt into him, savoring that mint and smoke taste. No one has ever kissed me like Jason does. Not Ian. Not Brian, who I kissed in that game of spin the bottle. Just Jason.

"I missed you," he whispers against my lips. "I want to spend as much time with you as I can." By then, he's already pulling my door open. Taking my hand and gently tugging me into his brother's house.

It only takes him about ten minutes to get my clothes off. It's only our second time doing it, but I already feel more comfortable than I did the first time. Jason loves me and I love him. Like he says, what better way is there to show it?

My eyes slip open so easily, I'm not sure if I was dreaming or remembering. Or maybe it's that they're so wet and full of unshed tears that it's too hard to keep them closed.

These memories make me feel like I'm drowning and flying at the same time.

I hate that I can't stop dwelling on them. On him. Jason. I still remember the rapid beat of my heart when he told me he loved me. When he called me his beautiful. It felt good. Real. So good I want to bottle up that old feeling and store it inside me. Deep inside where it will always be safe and where I can feel it any time I want to without any shame. Experience it like I did for a brief second when he called today.

Then there's the part of me grounded in logic rather than emotions. Funny, how before this I didn't realize I had those two parts. I didn't realize they could work against each other so strongly. Before I actually fell for him, I never would have been the girl to fall for lies.

I can't help but wonder if all girls think that. If they all think I'm stupid because they don't believe it can happen to them.

It can.

Anyway, the logical part wants to take that glass jar and smash it against a wall. To take a sledgehammer to it over and over until there's nothing left but tiny shards of glass so small, so insignificant, they can no longer hurt me. As fine as sand.

Still, after lying in bed for another hour, sleep not a possibility, I get up and sit at my computer desk. Hating myself more with each letter typed, I do what I've done a million and one times since June. I Google Jason Richter.

Being the girl who was dumb enough to fall for Jason sucks.

Being the one who somehow misses him is unforgivable.

· · ·

When I walk down the hallway at school, it's obvious the novelty hasn't worn off. I'm not sure what I expected. That overnight people would realize I'm not contagious? It doesn't happen, though.

What does happen is I get called into the counselor's office during first period.

I wring my hands as Mrs. Wilson stares at me. I see it in her, too…the questions, accusations. Am I the victim here, or Brynn the man-eater? The girl who tried to get Jason in her trap?

"How are you doing?" She pushes a strand of black hair behind her ear, leaning back in her chair. It's such a psychologist move, something I've seen in a million different movies.

"Awesome." I mean, really? How does she think I'm doing? I hate it when people ask questions they know the answer to.

"You're right. Dumb question." She rolls a pencil between her fingers. "So, I know you skipped school yesterday afternoon. You're not in trouble this time. We're trying to be…sensitive to your situation, but you can't do that, okay? Next time I won't have a choice except to give you detention."

I have to bite my tongue not to reply the way I want to. *Detention? Oh no!* It's strange the things that would have been a punishment before, but now? It might even be a welcome distraction. A way to escape from Dad's silence, while his eyes question. His pain that I don't have to look in a mirror to know reflects in me as well.

So instead of saying that, I nod.

"Did anything happen yesterday? Someone say something? I'm always here if you need to talk." Her eyes crinkle a little, giving me "the look." Pity. I don't know what's better, pity or the emptiness I get from others.

"No." My eyes find the ground, conflicting emotions warring inside me. There's a part of me that actually wants to talk to her. Talk to someone, but I think there's a block inside me. A huge wall, made by unknown hands that won't let me talk about Jason. About the baby or how I feel. About Dad or even Mom. That barrier is still there, holding me back.

"Are you sure?"

"Yep." My eyes find hers, hoping they prove my lie isn't...well, a lie.

"Okay. I know this must be a difficult time for you, Brynn. Please know I'm always, always here if you want to talk, okay?"

Tell me you believe me, and the walls might come down. They might crack or crumble. "Okay."

"I've talked to your dad and we're concerned. We know you're not socializing with your friends anymore. That's not good for you."

"I'm fine."

She sighs. "You have two choices. You can talk to me a couple times a week, or you can go to the community center in town. There are other girls your age and it would help if you talked to them—made some friends. They have many different programs and there's even art classes and pottery supplies you can use. You need to try to get back to how life was before. Make some more friends. And hopefully talk."

What good will talking do? It's not going to bring back Mom. It won't make it so Jason never existed. It won't bring back the baby. It's obvious she's going to push, though. And I'm definitely not talking to her. "I'll go to the community center. It sounds fun." It's amazing how easily the lies come now.

"Good. I'll give them a call so they know to expect you. Have a good day."

Standing, I walk out of the room without bothering to reply.

• • •

The morning crawls by without a glimpse of Christian. I don't know why I notice or why I care, but I do. Not care, but notice. I've been telling myself all morning that I refuse to spend lunch in the bathroom again. I'm not that girl. I don't have to hide out. Jason's taken everything else from me, and I refuse to let him turn me into the girl who hides in the bathroom every day, too.

As I close my locker to head to the cafeteria, I see

them. Diana, Ellie, Todd, Kevin, Ian...and Christian. It's like my feet suddenly refuse to move. I don't know why. I mean, why should it matter? They don't care about me, so I shouldn't care about them. They were friends with Christian before, so it makes sense they would be again now.

Somehow knowing it and seeing it are two different things. If it weren't for Jason, I would be with them. Maybe holding Ian's hand. Maybe not. Maybe reminiscing with Christian or finding out why he disappeared back then. Or maybe I'd be laughing with Ellie. Teasing Diana. Something. Anything, as a part of that group.

The group Christian fell back into so easily. I can't help but wonder how much about me he knows. Wonder if he's told them why he left so suddenly after our dance.

Christian pushes his hair back and laughs at something Ellie says. Playfully shoves Kevin like it hasn't been years and years since they've seen each other. With no thought, they took him back into the group.

It's like a reinforcement of that wall. Like there's now brick built around the wood. My stomach aches and my heart hurts. I don't want to think it, but I do. I want to be with them.

Snapping out of it, I turn toward the lockers, hoping they won't notice. Hoping I can somehow blend in with the stupid puke-colored doors.

"Hey, Bryntastic," Christian says from behind me.

Turn around and face him! Stop staring at the locker! The rest of the group goes silent behind me, like they're wondering why he's talking to me.

Turn around! I tell myself again. *Show them you don't care.* I turn. "Umm, hey." It's a blast back in time to see him. Christian Medina. Even though I looked for him this morning, I think a part of me thought it might have been a dream. Or a nightmare. That it's impossible for Christian to come back now.

I glance over at Ellie and Diana. They're whispering to each other. Todd and Kevin are looking at Christian like he's mental. But Ian's ice-blue eyes are lasers, penetrating me, trying to burn me alive.

"I'm hungry. Let's go eat, man." Todd nudges Christian.

Christian grins at me. It's not a full smile, more like a half one. It makes my stomach tingle but I tamp it down, angry at myself. I'm done with boys. Boys who want sex or pretend they love a girl. I'll never risk that hurt from losing…

My hand rests against my stomach.

"Come on, pottery girl. You're eating with us, right?" My shock must show on my face because Christian then adds, "Did I say something wrong? You're still into pottery, right?"

"Yeah, I'm done here." Ian gives me another icy look before walking away. Everyone else stands there, but you can tell it's for Christian and not for me.

For months all I've wanted is for someone to treat me normally, and now that someone's doing it, I have no idea how to respond. I want to run. I want to hug him. But then Jason's face shoves its way into my head. This is something he would have done. Out of all the girls he could have talked to at the bowling alley that night, he'd picked me. Now, here's Christian trying to pull me in, too.

"No." Shaking my head, I hope I look more confident than I feel. And as stupid and *insane* as it is, a part of me hopes he'll insist. Or say that he'll eat out here with me, but then I don't want him to stay with me, either. Is it wrong to want someone to do something you won't let them do?

Unfortunately, or maybe fortunately, I don't get a chance. Christian shrugs, turns, and they all walk away. They're not five feet from me before they're talking and he's laughing again.

· · ·

Like I do in every class where we get to choose our own seats, I head to the very back of my seventh-period Government and Law class. The seats start to fill up, though the ones by me, of course, people avoid. It's a weird feeling, knowing people are avoiding me. That no one wants to even sit by me. I don't get what they think will happen, but honestly, that doesn't even matter. What matters is, it sucks.

Have I ever treated someone like this? I rack my brain, but I can't think of anyone. We're not like those schools you hear about on TV. I don't ever remember people getting teased or harassed. But did I ever pay attention to anyone being ignored? I wonder if this might be just as bad.

My eyes keep finding the door, wondering who all will be in class with me, which I guess I would know if I didn't skip the second half of yesterday. I've gotten pretty lucky so far. Ellie here, Diana there, but no classes with the two of them together. No classes with— My eyes snap away from the door. Ian, the one who hates me the most.

The fist squeezing my insides loosens when Ian sits on the opposite side of the room from me. And then he shakes his head, rolls his eyes, like I'm a disappointment to him.

I'm paying so much attention to Ian, I don't notice someone step up to the desk beside me. Don't hear the chair pull out. It's not until Ian's stare shifts from me, his eyes widening slightly, that I turn to see who it is.

Christian Medina.

"What's up?" He nods his head once, like boys do sometimes. That confident "hi" thing a girl could never pull off.

He's dressed so differently from most of the other guys, in a pair of cargo pants, T-shirt with a long-sleeved shirt underneath it. I don't know why I'm focusing on his clothes. Probably because it's easier than looking at the rest of him, because Christian is even cuter than he was before.

"Whew!" Mr. Powers slips into the classroom, saving me from replying. "Shh, don't tell. I'm setting a bad example by being late to my own class on the second day. That kind of behavior shouldn't happen until at least the second month."

Everyone in the classroom laughs, except for Christian and me. Almost like the way Ian did a minute ago, Christian shakes his head at me. This time, I feel like I really did disappoint someone.

I didn't even say hello.

Chapter Thirteen

Before

Rolling over in bed, I stretch. The second my arm comes into contact with something that hadn't been there when I went to sleep, I remember what day it is.

Christmas.

My heart dances as I push up in bed and grab the box. My fingers rip at the wrapping paper, which has extra tape holding it down. Mom always does that, trying to make it harder for Dad and me to get into our packages.

Green paper falls to the bed as I keep tearing into the shoebox-size gift. Once I see the box, I don't have to open it to know what it is.

My eyes actually tear a little, which I know is silly. Not many fifteen-year-olds would get so excited about a pair of bunny slippers.

After pulling the lid off the box, I giggle when I see the pink slippers inside. They look just like—

"Ah, so you got them."

Turning my head, I see Mom standing in my bedroom doorway.

"This is an awesome memory gift, Mom."

Every Christmas we give one present called the memory gift. It can't cost more than fifteen dollars and it has to be something that holds a special memory from the past. Mom's parents are super wealthy, which is cool and all, but they're the type who try to buy your love rather than earn it. They didn't help her find "her thing" the way she was determined to help me find pottery. Didn't dance with her or watch her make pottery for hours, like she did with me. Dad said a couple years after I was adopted, Mom made the memory gift rule because she always wanted to make sure gifts were about love and not just materialistic things.

"Well, it is my fault you had to get rid of the first pair." She chuckles. "Let's try not to carry these around with you this time."

I swat her arm when she sits beside me. "I was *four.*"

"When you got them. Not when I finally made you toss them, even though you said you'd never forgive me."

A smile spreads across my lips. "Well, I guess I'll forgive you now."

When I was four, I got my first pair of bunny slippers and I loved them. Some kids carry a blanket or a stuffed animal. Me, I carried my bunnies. I'd been brokenhearted when she finally told me I was too old to carry around slippers I'd outgrown.

"You better." Mom stands. "Now hurry up. I can only

hold off your father for so long. He's going to jump into the rest of the gifts without us."

She gets to the door before I speak. "Thank you. This is my favorite memory gift I've ever gotten."

Mom blows a kiss. "And getting you was the best gift your father and I will ever have."

Me. I'm special to someone as cool as her. It makes me the luckiest girl in the world.

Chapter Fourteen

Now

I flip through the channels, not really paying much attention to what flashes across the screen. I've never been much of a TV person, but now, at least it's something to do. Doesn't seem to make it more interesting, so I just keep going through the stations, over and over like I actually care what pops up on the screen.

Depression sucks. I want it to be over already.

I wiggle my toes in my bunny slippers. This time, I'll never get rid of them. It's so funny how I hadn't thought about my slippers in so many years, until she gave me the memory gift again. She just seemed to know stuff like that. That's how Mom was. Dad called her beautiful, but he always said he loved her for her heart. Because of how beautiful she was inside.

I can't imagine what that feels like. To be loved by a boy with the devotion that he loved her.

"Ugh!" I punch a couch pillow a couple times before throwing it to the floor. I'm driving myself crazy. Mom wouldn't have folded as easily as I am. As easily as Dad is, because though he's still here and hasn't done anything as stupid as I did, I'm pretty sure he's broken now, too.

Glancing at the clock, I see it's about five. I know Dad will be home soon and I also know I'm supposed to be at the stupid community center today. A teen outreach program. When did that ever become me? I was the normal girl, the happy one with the awesome parents. I'm not supposed to need any kind of outreach.

But I do.

I kick off my slippers and push my feet into my shoes. It's a quick drive to the community center. The whole time, my stomach hurts. I wish I was one of those girls who could just say screw it. That I was tough and didn't give a crap about anyone or what they thought. That I could say no without worrying about getting in trouble over it, but I'm not that girl.

I'm not saying I'm perfect, but I'm definitely not used to getting into trouble, either. The only time I did what *I* wanted was with Jason, and look how that turned out.

I bite my fingernails as I walk in the door. It's a huge room with a few people my age in it. There are chairs around the walls and a few long tables. A couch and TV. Even a pool table and air hockey.

I see a couple hallways and rooms. Posters and pictures of kids I assume come here are plastered to the wall.

It's strange, coming to a place like this.

The door pushes open behind me and I have to move out of the way so I don't get hit. It's a boy, and he doesn't pay any attention to me as he walks inside, bumps fists with another guy, and they lean on the pool table talking.

"Hi. I'm Valerie. Can I help you?" an older woman asks. She has thin lips and a pointed nose—features that don't make her look too friendly.

This is who I'm supposed to talk to, so I say, "Umm, yeah. I'm Brynn. I was told to ask for you."

"Oh, yes. We're so glad you could come, Miss De Luca." She launches into a whole story that I only partially listen to. Something about activities and counselors for people who want to talk, classes, yada yada, but she doesn't seem to need my input so I don't give it and hardly listen.

Something catches my eye and I look to the left to see what it is. My heart stutters. Christian Medina is here. It didn't even occur to me that I might run into someone from school.

His hair is half in his face as he walks, not as though he's trying to hide behind it, but just because it's *him* and he doesn't care about anything else.

A little pinch of jealousy squeezes inside me.

Valerie is still talking, but for some reason I'm watching him.

A man steps up to him, and I hear him say something about their appointment before they start to walk away. As soon as he gets to a door, he looks up. Our eyes catch for a second and he gives me a small nod, but he doesn't stop. Christian keeps going, following the guy and closing the door behind him.

Obviously not realizing I'm wondering about
Christian, Valerie points to where he just disappeared.
"Those are the counseling rooms. I'm going to ask you
to meet with me there once a week. We'll pick a time
together."

Any other moment, I'd struggle not to roll my eyes
at what she said—at the fact that she wants me to talk to
her once a week as though that will help. But right now
all I can think about is the fact that Christian is going into
those rooms. Someone thinks he needs counseling, too.
My mind won't stop wondering why.

• • •

"Excuse me." A girl with short black hair steps up next
to me, reaching for a plastic cup and the water dispenser.
With how close I'm sitting to it, I suddenly feel like I look
as though I'm trying to guard the thing. Music fills the
room, but it's not too loud. Valerie finished showing me
around and told me she wants me to just relax and make
myself at home today. I guess the talking comes later.

Scooting out of the girl's way, I lean against the wall.
She has piercings up and down her ears. Her hair is
almost cut like a boy's and it's messy, but not unkempt if
that makes sense. It looks like she wants it like that. Her
eyes are colored with a bright-purple eye shadow that I'm
not sure I could ever pull off.

Her clothes are huge, but again, I think she wants the
look. She's wearing a big jacket and baggy pants.

"I'm Emery, by the way." She waves at me before filling her plastic cup with water. "This your first time here?"

She's the only person besides Valerie to actually approach me since I arrived. "Yeah. I don't go here." As soon as the words leave my mouth, I feel like a jerk. Like I think coming here is bad or something. It's not. It's just not somewhere I ever saw myself needing to be.

Emery holds out her hand. "What's your name?"

"Brynn." I shake her hand.

"Hi, Brynn. Nice to meet you."

Chairs line the wall beside me and she sits in one. When she does, her jacket pulls a little tighter and I see a bump in her belly. Not a huge one, but still, it's obviously a baby bump. My hand finds my stomach. I don't feel like I'm controlling the movement as it rubs the flatness there.

I could look like her right now. I had a life inside me. It hits me at the most random times—that emptiness. What really happened—what could have been. The depth of my loss and the track my life was on at sixteen years old. A track that would have been scary as hell, but one that I would have taken, even if I didn't keep the baby at the end. After everything Mom and Dad went through to try to have a baby of their own, I couldn't have had an abortion. But I didn't have to. It's gone nonetheless.

"I'm only five months, but I swear I think I look eight." She touches her stomach, too, like it's the most natural thing in the world.

I had a baby inside me like that, but now it's gone.

My chest feels a little tight. "You... You don't look eight months." And she doesn't. I can definitely see something's there, but it's not that bad.

Emery playfully rolls her eyes. "Okay, I *feel* eight months."

I can't stop staring at her. She can't be any older than me. But she's having a baby. Questions slam into my skull and I want to ask. It's so hard to know what's okay or not. It's hard to make myself say anything because I don't want to talk. Talking makes you closer to people and I've already lost Mom, Dad, Jason, *my baby,* my friends.

"You can ask, you know? I can practically see the questions in your eyes." She shrugs.

Heat surges in my cheeks as anger and pain slam into me. I can't stop thinking of all the things I lost and will never find again and she's here and she has it and she's okay. Normal, even though she's pregnant and a teenager, just like I was. Why did I lose it all?

"I…I have to go." Pushing to my feet, I walk out of the room. I'm always running away from people.

• • •

When I get home, Dad isn't here. I kick off my shoes, step into my slippers, and go straight out back. My pottery room sits right across from the back porch like always, and everything inside pulls and tugs me to it. I want to go there so badly — to lose myself in something until I forget about everything else — but I can't make myself do it.

I can't make anything in that room ever again.

That's when I hear music playing and I look over the

fence and into the neighbor's yard. Christian is sitting on his back porch, a guitar propped on his leg, his head down in concentration. His brown hair falls forward, creating that wall between us that I wanted earlier, blocking his eyes from me. I don't know if I should be thankful his house is set a little higher than ours or not, because if it wasn't, the fence would be another barrier blocking him from me.

My first thought is I want him blocked from me — need it. Just like everyone else, I don't want to get close to him. Not when it risks losing some of those good memories.

My second thought is the most ridiculous thing: *I didn't know Christian played the guitar.* Maybe he hadn't when I knew him.

I turn to walk into the house when he says, "Hey to you, too."

I almost keep going. God knows I want to, but for some reason, I stop. "I don't feel like talking."

"Huh…interesting," is all he says before his fingers start gliding over the strings again.

My feet itch to walk away but instead I open my mouth and say, "What is that supposed to mean? 'Huh, interesting'?"

He looks over at me, pushes his hair behind his ear, stands, and sets his guitar on one of the chairs. Then, he grabs the other one, walks over, puts it against the fence, and then stands on it, looking over at me. "Well, I guess it's supposed to mean I find it interesting you told me you don't feel like talking. Not too many ways to spin it, Bryntastic."

Another random thought pops into my head—he's different. I can't pinpoint exactly what it is, but he's not the same boy I knew five years ago. Then I remember I'm not the same girl, either, and that urge to go hide out hits me again. "Why is that interesting?" Crinkling my nose, I realize I'm surprised I asked him a question.

"Because you don't want to talk, but you took the time to tell me instead of just walking away. That's what I would have done if I didn't feel like speaking. Just walked away. My counselor would probably say that means you really *do* wanna talk. If not him, my mom would. She's always saying stuff like that to me."

My cheeks flush in annoyance. "What? Maybe I just don't want to be rude? Don't pretend to know me." But we both know I don't have a problem being rude lately. I've done it before by running away from him when he tried to speak to me.

Christian looks completely serious when he says, "I think it's pretty safe to say I don't really know you anymore, Bryntastic."

His words slice into me, stinging when I know they shouldn't. Or is it that they shouldn't or I don't want them to? "Why do you go to the community center?" It occurs to me that he can tell me to go to hell. That I just told him I don't want to talk. And I probably deserve that.

Instead, Christian shrugs. "I used to have some anger management problems. Mom makes me go. She volunteers a lot and she's always analyzing everything."

I cock my head, looking for any sign of embarrassment from him at the way he just spit that out. Not as though it's a huge deal, but he just says it likes it's nothing. Anger management problems definitely don't sound good, but there's no shyness or *anger* when he admits it. It just *is*.

Then I stand there and wait for it. Wait for him to ask me the same thing. Why was *I* there? Why don't I hang out with my friends anymore? Or he probably doesn't need to ask, because he already knows.

"Cute slippers," he says, surprising me because it's completely out of the blue. "Do your PJs have a bushy tail, too?" He's got that same half smile on his face from earlier. That flirty, I'm-a-hot-boy-who-can-have-any-girl-I-want look, and I'm suddenly annoyed again. I hate that cocky-guy look and that cocky-guy grin and I will not be pulled into that trap again.

"Cute way to try to look at my ass." I let one of my brows raise, a little swell of pride in my chest that I'm calling this how I see it.

"Hey, it's a good line, and I don't remember you being such a grump."

A grump? *A grump?* His words make me stifle a laugh. A sarcastic one, sure, but a chuckle all the same. "Bad job at your analysis. This is *not* me being grumpy. That's a whole lot worse."

Christian shifts on the chair a little, then pulls his sleeves down to cover his hands. "Observation, not an analysis."

My porch light flickers a little but stays on. *Think, think, think!* The urge to get the best of him simmers inside me. I used to be pretty good at getting in the last word. "I... Whatever." Awesome. I rocked at that. *Not.*

"I would say I know you are but what am I, but then, that doesn't make much sense, I guess. It would be right along the same lines as *whatever*."

I search my brain for more silly sayings, not letting myself overthink what I'm doing. "I'm rubber, you're glue." A grin pulls at my lips.

"Gummy bear?" he asks.

I wait for the punch line before I realize he's really asking me if I want some candy.

Christian pops a few into his mouth.

Gummy bear? Talk about a subject change. I'm at a loss for words. First, I've never known a guy who carries gummy bears in his pocket and second, weren't we just having this strange, immature sort of witty-banter thing going on? But then…this little flash of a memory spouts in my head. That sugary smell when we danced. The box of… "You used to eat Jujubes, didn't you? I remember you always had a box of them with you."

He shakes his head. "Nope. It was Dots."

"Oh yeah!" I laugh. "Dots. I remember now. I…" I bought a box of them. I put them on my desk so he'd see them, think we had something in common, and fall madly in love with me. My cheeks burn. Wow, I can't believe I did that. Mark that on my ever-growing list of things I will never again do for a boy.

"You what?"

So not going there. "Nothing. So what's up with the candy?"

After shrugging, he pops a couple more into his mouth and then says, "Sweet tooth, I guess. What's your vice?"

His question comes out of nowhere. Most people I know wouldn't ask something like that. "Umm, I don't know. I guess I don't have one."

Christian snickers. "Not possible. You can borrow mine till you figure yours out, if you want. Gummy bears make the world go round and all that."

"Oh my God." His words are so ridiculous I can't stop myself from laughing. Hard. Like real, loud belly laughs. I'm almost not sure it's me at first. "Gummy bears make the world go round? I think you're pushing it a little. Or a lot."

"No way. Have you had these things lately? They're pretty good. The world would be a much better place if everyone chilled out and indulged in a gummy bear every now and again."

"Yeah, might be the answer to ending world hunger."

"Screw that. It's the answer to world hunger and peace."

Another spontaneous laugh jumps out of my mouth. A second later, Christian is doing the same.

"Brynn!" My head turns toward the house as Dad steps outside, frowning. "What are you doing? Who are you talking to?" His voice is firm, holding a sound of... something, I don't even know what it is, but I've never heard it directed at me before.

"Nothing... No one." Which is stupid because it's obviously someone and he's hanging over my fence with a mouth full of gummy bears. Dad's head is so red it looks like it might explode.

"I brought dinner. Time to come in for the night."

Time to come inside? It's seven o'clock and I'm in my backyard. "Umm, okay?"

Dad's eyes cut toward Christian, who just pops a few more gummy bears like nothing is going on.

"It'll get cold, Brynn," Dad reminds me. His eyes dart toward Christian, glaring. Then they find me again and he's looking at me the same way.

"Yeah…okay."

"Catch ya later, Bryntastic." Christian jumps down from the chair, heads back to his porch, and picks up his guitar again.

Dad stands there, waiting for me to go inside, which I do. He follows me. "Who is that?" he asks, his voice still tight. I turn to see him lean against the kitchen counter, still not looking like the easygoing dad I know.

"Christian, a guy from school."

"Well, I don't know if I want you out there talking at night. I've never even met the kid."

"Huh?" I don't have to finish my thought when it all comes slamming back into me. Jason. What Dad thinks. "Oh my God. Do you think I'm out to have sex with our neighbor now? I screwed up once and now you think I'm trying to get with every boy in sight?" My eyes sting, but it's nothing compared to the pinch in my chest.

"What?" Dad has the nerve to sound surprised. "No, it's not… I trust… It's them."

"Yeah, obviously." It's then I know I was right. He doesn't believe me. He thinks I lied, that I knew about Jason all along. That's probably why he let the case go so easily, why he's even quieter with me. Why he struggles to look at me, and…and probably wishes he and Mom hadn't chosen me. "I'm not hungry."

"Brynn, wait." Dad's voice cracks, but it's too late.

Without another word, I walk out of the kitchen, up the stairs, and straight for my room.

And to think, ten minutes ago, I'd actually been laughing. I'd actually felt normal. Somehow, I'd forgotten how bad everything is.

But now, I remember.

Chapter Fifteen

Before

"You and your mom are going shopping today, right?" Diana asks when we pull up in front of my house.

"Yep. Sorry I couldn't go with you guys, but you know how Mom is with dances. She wants to go with just her and me." Which honestly, I don't mind. I mean, it would have been cool to go with Ellie and Diana, but I like spending time with her, too.

"It's okay. You're lucky she wants to go with you. My mom couldn't care less." Ellie frowns.

"That's not true. She's just busy right now. You're way too cool for anyone to not want to hang out with you all the time." I hug her, knowing how hard dealing with her parents is for her. They don't spend time with her, or eat dinner with her every night like Mom and Dad do with me, or even Diana's parents do with her. It's like they have their own life and Ellie is just baggage.

Ellie squeeze me back. "Thanks, Brynn. You're the best. I don't know what I would do without you and D."

"Friends for life." D holds out her hand. I link a pinkie with her, and then Ellie does the same.

She's always been super sentimental, though she only shows it with us. She's also really tough, too. She makes herself hard so she doesn't feel hung out to dry because of the way her parents pretty much ignore her, but Diana and I both know how important the people in her life are to her. She needs to know we'll always be there.

"Always," I say first.

"Always," Diana adds.

Suddenly, Ellie looks toward the ground. "I have to tell you guys something, but you can't say anything. Not that I don't trust you, but I don't want Kevin or Ian to know and tell Todd."

I put a hand on her shoulder. "I'd never tell Ian something you didn't want me to. You know you can trust us."

Diana agrees with me.

After a few deep breaths, Ellie says, "I think I'm going to…you know, go all the way with Todd after the dance. I'm going to surprise him. It *is* a dance, after all. That's what you're supposed to do, right?" Ellie giggles.

"What?" My grip on her loosens and my eyes go wide.

"Oh my God! Maybe Kev and I will do it, too. I've been trying to hold him off. But I love him, and if you guys are going to… It'll make the night perfect." Diana bounces excitedly.

I don't think I want to have sex with Ian. Not the way

we break up and get back together. He's never even told me he loves me.

They continue talking about it and I nod and agree, even though their words are fuzz. It would be kind of cool, though. The three of us losing our virginity the same night. Maybe it'll even bring Ian and me closer together, so we can be more like Diana and Ellie are with their boyfriends.

"Now hurry up and go shopping, Brynn. You need to get a dress before all the good ones are gone."

We all jump out of the car and hug good-bye before Ellie and Diana take off and I head inside. My body feels all electric. I can't wait to go shopping with Mom. To find the perfect dress for the perfect dance and to maybe even take that next step with Ian.

"Hey. I'm home." Walking into the living room, I see Mom sitting on the couch. "Are you ready to go?"

Looking over at me, she gives me a sad smile. "I'm not sure if today is the best day, kiddo."

The buzzed feeling starts to dim. "What? You promised. There's only a week left until the dance and you and Dad are going to be gone tomorrow."

"We can go after. I'll make sure I tell Dad we have to leave early for our mother/daughter shopping trip."

"But I was going to stay at Diana's tomorrow night, remember? Let's just go now. It won't take long."

She knows how much I love dances. Diana, Ellie, and I have been making plans for this one for two months.

"I have a headache, and I'm feeling a little nauseous." Mom shifts on the couch.

"I'll grab you some Tylenol."

I move toward the stairs but Mom stops me when she says, "We're just going to have to wait, Brynn, okay? You're being ridiculous."

I flinch slightly. "Dude, you're the one who wouldn't let me go with Diana and Ellie. You don't have to snap at me and make this my fault."

She sighs before standing. "I'm not." Mom grabs hold of the couch and leans on it. "I'm not trying to snap at you but I also don't appreciate you getting so upset. It's not a big deal. You know I would never let you end up without a dress for the dance."

"I can call Diana and Ellie and go with them."

"I want this to be something we do together. It's not—"

"Don't say it's not a big deal again because it is to me. You know it. I don't get why you won't just let me go without you!"

This is a big night for me. Ian is driving us for the first time. We're eating at a restaurant with all our friends, the first time we're able to do things like this without our parents. *And Ellie and Diana might have sex, and maybe I'll decide I want to as well.*

"Brynn…"

"Fine. Whatever. Make me wait." I drop my backpack by the door. "Thanks for ruining my day."

Without another word, I run past her, into the kitchen, and out to my pottery room.

It's the last time I see Mom alive.

Chapter Sixteen

Now

Dad's never been one to really tiptoe around anyone. He's quiet, yes, but tiptoe, no. But the morning after our little incident with Christian, he's definitely walking on eggshells around me. While I'm eating my bacon, I notice him watching me, a strange look on his face. He opens his mouth, closes it. Opens it, closes it, and then gives me that *poor Brynn* smile. The one that says, even though he thinks I lied about Jason, he feels sorry for me.

Mom definitely never would have done something like have sex with an older guy and then been stupid enough to get pregnant. But she did lose babies. A couple of them, both before and after they adopted me. The adoption almost didn't go through, either. They fought so hard for me. It used to mean I was special, but I have no idea if it still does.

My head knows that's stupid. Regardless, I know my

dad and I know he loves me, but our heads and hearts don't always travel the same wavelength. Sometimes they're not even on the same frequency…like they're a whole galaxy away from each other.

The rest of the morning, I can't stop myself from wondering what he was going to say. *When you speak, make it count.* He's told me that a million times. Make it count. Is that why he can't speak? Maybe he's still trying to figure out how to make it count.

When I get to school, there's some crazy part of me that kind of expected—or hoped? No, not hoped because after last night, I'm done pretending. That few minutes with Christian didn't make anything go away. Actually, it made it worse. But yeah…a part of me did kind of wonder if he'd be at my locker. Walk up to me sometime in the morning and offer me a gummy bear, but it doesn't happen. I don't even see him until after third period and of course, he's with the crew, laughing and talking like nothing has changed.

Which is right, I guess. Nothing has changed, so why should he pretend it has? Still, it stings. Until the whole group of them walks by me, and he waves and *winks* at me. Then, it just pisses me off. Ian gives me one of his dirty looks. Todd and Kevin don't notice the wink or anything else, but Ellie and Diana do, and I can see the questions in their eyes.

The second I walk into health class, I hear it. That tiny baby cry that has no business here. My eyes dart around the room, trying to see if anyone else looks as surprised by the sound as I do. To see if anyone else looks like they even hear it. For all I know, I'm going crazy.

But I'm not. At least, not yet.

Mrs. Mulligan stands in the back of the room with an electronic baby. She's fiddling around with it, pushing all sorts of buttons while two girls from my class stand there giggling and trying to help her. They all think it's funny that they can't turn off this electronic baby, flipping it around while they try to shut it up, and all I can think about again is: *I could have been a mom.*

"Excuse me." There's a slight shove to my back as someone squeezes by, reminding me I'm trapped in the doorway like there's some sort of invisible force field.

I suddenly feel like crying, but I can't. Not here.

The bell rings, making me jump a little. Mrs. Mulligan finally gets the baby to be quiet and then looks up at me. "Come in, Brynn. Take your seat please." She has this clueless, happy expression on her face and I want to yell at her. Tell her I had a baby inside me for seven weeks and lost it! Scream it at the top of my lungs, but then remember I'm still in high school. Too young to be a mom anyway, so do I even have a right to be mad about it? A right to feel cheated out of something I'm not ready for anyway?

One foot in front of the other, I make my feet keep moving. Make them carry me to my desk, because I have no other choices. I can't run out of this room. Can't give them something else to stare at, to whisper about me.

You can do it. You've made it this far. Keep going, keep going, keep going.

I never used to talk to myself before. Never used to

have to chant to myself just to make it through, but now…
now it's all I have.

For forty-five minutes, my heart races, my stomach
churns. Mrs. Mulligan is nothing but a muffled voice in
the background, speaking in some foreign language that I
don't understand.

I'm pretty sure she's talking about babies. Pretty
sure we're going to have to take turns carrying that doll
around.

Pretty sure I'm going to lose it.

When the bell rings, it's all I can do to grab my stuff
before I run out of the room. Run down the hall, pushing
my way through people like I haven't since that first day I
ran from Christian.

I hardly make it to the toilet before I heave. Before
my breakfast and coffee and everything else in my
stomach empties. The whole time I'm wondering what
I'm doing. Why I'm losing it like this, but I can't stop.

When I retch again and nothing else comes up, I flush
and fall against the stall. It's then I realize I didn't even
close the door. That it's lunch and a miracle no one came
in—unless they did and I didn't notice.

Scrambling up, I push the door closed and lock it
before putting down the toilet seat and falling onto it. It
stinks in here, like it hasn't been cleaned or something,
but I still can't make myself move. I don't know if my legs
will work. It's obvious the rest of me is broken, so they
probably are, too.

I just lost it over a doll. A freaking *doll*. I can't stop
thinking about it. I also can't stop seeing it. Can't stop

wondering. Can't stop remembering when I took the test. Remembering Jason telling me to get rid of our baby. The look on Dad's face when the doctor told him what was happening. When the nurse asked about the pregnancy and I made him leave the room.

"Did you see Brynn De Luca's face in class?" My eyes dart to the closed stall door. I hadn't even heard anyone come in.

"It was like a freak-out. I thought she was going to blow at any second," a girl says.

"It's probably guilt. I'd feel guilty, too, if I got knocked up and then had an abortion."

"She had an abortion? I heard she lost it."

I did! I want to tell them. I'm not the type of person who's going to look down on someone else if abortion is the right choice for them, but I didn't do it and I don't want people thinking I did. I can't say anything, partly because I'm too weak to talk about it and partly because I'm ashamed. Everyone knows about Jason and the baby, but God, it still sucks to be the girl who got pregnant.

"Of course she's going to tell people she lost it," the first girl says. "Why would she go around announcing she had an abortion?"

Their voices are getting farther and farther away until I hear the door creak and know I'm alone.

The urge to vomit threatens me again, but I can't. There's nothing there, so before I have the chance to start crying again, I push to my feet and slam open the door.

They think I did it. People think I got rid of my baby.

I stare into the mirror. I look like crap. Wetting a

couple paper towels, I try to clean up.

How many people think that? Is it going around the whole school? Is that why people don't know how to talk to me?

I toss the paper towels into the trash. Heat sizzles and scalds its way through my veins, burning me alive. I'm mad. I'm sad. I'm... I don't even know what I am.

When I get to the hall, the bathroom door slams closed, startling me. I look to the left and suddenly the heat inside me scorches even hotter.

Christian is leaning against the lockers, Annie Jacobs, the most popular girl in school, with her perfect long blond hair, standing in front of him. She keeps moving closer and closer to him. Christian's popping gummy bears like they're going out of style. Is it me or did he just move away? No, why would he? And why do I care?

Just then, he looks up, his bright-blue eyes snaring me. When I start to turn away, he calls out, "Brynn! About time you got here. You're late." Then he says something to a pissed-off-looking Annie before coming my way.

I keep walking and he files in beside me.

"Thanks for the save, pottery girl. That chick's a few cards short, if you know what I'm sayin'."

It's never stopped the other guys from caring. That's what guys like, right? I mean, almost every boy in this school has gone after Annie at some point or another, even Ian on one of our breaks. "Pfft. Like that matters."

"You go for girls who aren't playing with a full deck?"

I look at him and roll my eyes. "I'm so not in the mood for lesbian jokes today."

"Huh. I thought it was pretty funny." He eats another gummy bear. "I thought you were finally loosening up with me last night, but looks like I need to work my magic a little harder."

I stop, cross my arms, and look at him. The halls aren't very busy, everyone off eating their lunch wherever it is they eat. He's wearing another T-shirt with a long-sleeved shirt underneath. It's like some kind of retro nineties look, if my memory of old teen shows is correct.

"I know you must have heard what happened with me." It was a stupid thing to say.

"I don't listen to rumors and shit like that."

"Yeah, right. Everyone listens to rumors. Even if you heard otherwise, I don't put out."

Christian stops mid-chew and shakes his head. Then he closes his eyes, like he's taking a time-out or something. It feels like forever until he opens them again and mutters, "Wow..."

Wow? *Wow?* "Wow what?"

"You're pretty damn conceited, aren't you? First I want to look at your ass. Now I want to sleep with you. Did it ever cross that pretty little head of yours that I don't want you? I mean, you're hot, I'll give you that, but you kind of ruin it when you open your mouth."

I'm so shocked, I can't move. Can't speak. I just stand there, frozen and probably looking like the biggest idiot in the world. He's right. I'm being a bitch. What's wrong with me?

Still, I don't move. Can't, even when Christian steps closer to me. Closer still. And closer until he's leaning forward, his lips right next to my ear.

"Did you ever think, Bryntastic, that I might want to be friends?" he whispers close, so close to me I feel his breath on my neck. My body begs to jerk away. My hand burns with the urge to punch him. And a part of me wants to pull him closer.

"That I remember the girl who used to love laughing? Who used to blush all the time? The first girl I ever danced with?"

I gasp.

I was the first girl Christian danced with?

Suddenly, he jerks away. "But, nope, you didn't think about that. Sucks, but I'm not the kind of guy who's going to beg a girl to be friends with me. Life's too short to spend it trying to make everyone else happy. Have a good day, pottery girl." After popping a couple more gummy bears in his mouth, this time, it's Christian Medina who walks away from me.

And it's my own damn fault.

Chapter Seventeen

Now

The rest of the day, I force myself not to make eye contact with Christian. It's not too hard to do, considering he doesn't look at me, either. I don't blame him and wish it were easier for me to tell him, but that fear is still engraved inside me. Fear that he'll disappoint me. Maybe that's not the word, but I'm afraid he isn't who I thought he would be. It'll hurt too much to go through that again. Christian is tied to happy memories of my childhood that I want to hold on to.

If I keep things cut off now, I don't have to worry about them ending the way they did with Jason. Or even Ian.

After turning off the car, I get out at the community center, really wishing I didn't have to come today.

When I walk inside, it's full of people like it always is. Automatically my eyes scan the room for Christian, but I don't see him.

"Hello, Brynn. How are you today?" Valerie stands in the doorway to one of the counseling rooms.

"Good." I walk toward the room. She waits until she closes the door behind me before she speaks.

"You look a little sad today. Did anything happen?"

Yes. The boy I used to think I loved was nice to me. He was nice when most people aren't and I was horrible to him because as it turns out, it's scarier to deal with someone treating me normally than being ignored.

"No. Nothing happened. I'm just a little tired, I guess."

The way she's looking at me, you'd think my nose was growing to prove my lie.

"Have a seat." I do and she continues. "I know it seems silly that talking can help, but it really does. It's important to get your feelings out, and sometimes it enables you to see things from another side."

Yeah, talking to a strange woman definitely doesn't sound like something I want to do. Maybe if I had Diana and Ellie, things would be easier. But then, I didn't talk to them when I had the chance.

"Your dad said you make pottery. Have you spent any time in our art room? Art is a fantastic way to center yourself and clear your mind."

A flash of the last fight with Mom plays in my mind. How I ran to my pottery room to clear my head while she died. No, thank you. "Pottery is easier for me to do alone. I have my own room for it at home."

Valerie nods and I wonder exactly when it was I became such a good liar.

We spend the next forty-five minutes talking about nothing, really. She avoids most of the topics I don't want to talk about, except she does ask about my friendships at school. I tell her Ellie, Diana, and I have drifted apart, which is true.

"Okay, Brynn. We're good until next week, but I want you to work on trying to participate more—here and in other aspects of your life. I'd love to see you get involved a little more, or to try and find a way to open up, okay? This will only help if you're involved one hundred percent."

I stand, my fight with Christian today playing on my tongue, but I can't make the words jump out. I've never had to *really* talk to someone I don't know—someone I didn't choose. I always had my friends or my parents there. I can't just force myself to say or do what she wants from me.

"Okay. Thanks."

I had just closed the door when I hear a commotion on the other side of the room.

"Not in the mood today, man." There's an angry edge to Christian's voice that I've never heard from him before. He crosses his arms and leans against the wall.

"It's not really an option, Christian. You know that." The counselor I saw him with that first day stands straight, crossing his arms, too, as if to tell Christian he's not screwing around.

"It's just a day. One fucking day. It's not going to kill me to miss our meeting."

My heart speeds up and I know I should turn away.

This isn't my business. I wouldn't want people watching me, either, but it's like I'm nailed in place. He's being so different from the boy with the smile and the gummy bears.

"In my office, Christian."

"Nope." He turns and pushes the front door open so hard, it slams against the wall.

Before he steps out, a woman says, "Christian!" from across the room. I see him freeze as a Hispanic woman who looks an awful lot like him approaches.

She gets close enough to him that I can't hear her when they speak. I see him shake his head but then she says something else. Christian closes his eyes and even from where I'm standing, I see his chest rise and fall in deep breaths. The room is silent—the only noise a loud beat in my ear.

Without another word, Christian turns my way. My body sets in stone, still unable to move even though I know he's coming my way. That he's heading into the room right next to the one I left.

Christian's eyes briefly run over me—no, it's more like they cut through me—but then he faces forward, walks over and into the office.

I open my mouth, wanting to ask him if he's okay, but he closes the door before I get a chance. When the woman slips in the door behind him, I turn, ready to get the heck out of here, but run straight into Emery.

"Jeez. What'd I ever do to you?"

"Oh my God. I'm sorry. Are you okay?"

She wrinkles her forehead. "Yes. I'm pregnant, not

made of glass."

Oh. Duh. But my mind is still with Christian, so my eyes dart to the door, wondering if he's doing a better job at talking than I did and wondering if it helps.

"What's wrong?" Emery asks.

"Nothing." I shake my head but then stop, wanting to say something but not sure exactly what.

"Come on. Let's go. I can tell I'm needed." Emery shocks me by grabbing my arm and practically pulling me through the center. She stops, peeking in different rooms—the game room, art room—until finally pulling me into the movie room.

When I step inside, I realize it's empty. "Emery, really, I'm fine."

"So? That doesn't mean you don't have something on your mind."

And she's right. The big surprise is I want to share it with her. I need to talk to someone, and Emery makes me feel way more comfortable than Valerie does.

"It's not really that big a deal." And in reality it isn't. Not when you compare it to other things people deal with.

"Again, so? Can you imagine how boring life would be if the only things people talked about were *really big deals*? Or maybe not boring but depressing, at least."

She's right. I walk through the room and plop down in one of the chairs, Emery right behind me. My stomach is a little uneasy. It's crazy how quickly someone can get used to not really opening up to people.

"Moving your mouth helps."

I don't expect the chuckle that jumps out. Then I continue to keep opening my mouth and speaking so she can't tease me anymore. "There's just this guy."

"Sigh…isn't there always a guy?" Emery asks.

I roll my eyes. "Not that kind of guy." Though he used to be. Or I wanted him to be. "But he's nice to me when most people aren't anymore. Or I guess they don't take the time to pay attention is a better way to word it. Anyway, he does. Did. And I was a bitch to him on more than one occasion. Today was worse than the others and when I saw him later, he was really upset. He kind of lost it and he's usually so level."

I don't know when Emery came into the room earlier, but I still don't tell her who I'm talking about. Still, she probably knows. It sort of feels like giving away something that's his. Or at least his business to tell. He told me earlier that he doesn't listen to gossip. Who knows if it's true, but I figure if it is, I at least owe him this.

Emery puts a hand on her stomach and my eyes are briefly drawn there. "So he likes you or what? And you hurt him and he's upset, so now you feel guilty?"

"No…he doesn't like me. And I don't think I hurt him, I was just a bitch to him. I don't know if that's why he had a bad day but—"

"Brynn," she interrupts me. "I mean this in the best possible way, but not everything is about you. You might not be the reason he lost it, as you say."

My cheeks heat when I realize she's right. Christian sort of said the same thing to me earlier—that I make everything about me. "When you put it like that…"

"I'm not saying it is or isn't the reason, but don't beat yourself up too much unless you know it is, ya know? I'm pretty sure you're a lot like me. And we have enough to worry about that we don't need to create new reasons if we don't have to."

Again, she's right. It makes so much sense when she says it that I wonder why I didn't think of it on my own. "Still." I look away from her. "That doesn't mean it was right to treat him like crap."

"True. I hear apologies go a long way." She raises a brow.

"You're being sarcastic," I tell her.

"No, I'm being funny."

So many more admissions beg to come out, but they're locked in a lot tighter than this one was. Talking to Emery was a step, though.

No matter how small it is, it makes me smile.

Chapter Eighteen

Now

I decide to take Emery's advice. I mean, for months I've been wishing I had friends to talk to, right? And now I kind of have Emery. If she had been Ellie or Diana, I would consider what they had to say, so I should do the same with her. Apologize to Christian. It shouldn't be that hard.

Ha. Yeah, right.

On my way home, I stop by the store to grab some chocolate. I'm not a huge candy person but there are times in a girl's life when we all need a little sugary energy.

I scan the candy aisle for a good three minutes before deciding on a king-size Twix. I'm going all-out today. Or stalling. There's a possibility I'm doing that as well.

I'm almost to the end of the row when I spot the bag of gummy bears hanging from a peg. My hand lingers for a second before a voice in my head reminds me it's a silly thing to stress over. If I'm going to apologize for being bitchy, there's nothing wrong with getting him some gummy bears, too.

I'm able to go through the express line, so it takes no time at all to get through checkout. As I walk out the door, my eyes are glued onto my Twix wrapper as I try to open it. When a hand comes down on my shoulder, I jerk my head up.

"You should watch where you're going, Red. You'll run someone over."

My fingers fumble with the package in my hand, my stomach going sour as though I ate too much chocolate when I haven't had any yet. "Don't call me that, Jason."

I wait for him to try to stop me when I step around him, but he doesn't.

"Sorry. Old habits die hard."

For some reason, his statement makes me stop.

"Go to the side of the building with me. I just want to talk."

Before the words leave his mouth, I'm already shaking my head. "No."

He steps toward the edge of the store, brushing my arm with his as he does. "I just wanna talk with you, real quick. No one has to know. You're not scared to talk to me, are you?"

"No," I snap.

Jason sighs. "I'm going over there. I hope you come, but I won't wait long." And then he shrugs before walking down the sidewalk.

People move past me, in and out the door, as I watch Jason until he gets to the edge of the building. Watch him as he walks around the corner and out of sight. My hands tremble, but still I take a step forward, then another one.

I'm not stupid. In my head I know what's going on here. A person can be smart enough to know when someone is playing her, but if your heart wants to believe it enough, that's all that matters. Emotions are a powerful thing. Way stronger than knowledge or experience, because there's always that hope. Hope that he'll apologize and admit he lied. Hope that the warning in your head is wrong.

Hope is probably the most dangerous emotion we have.

Jason's leaning against the wall toward the back of the building. I count my steps, forty-eight of them, until I stop in front of him.

"I miss you." He reaches out to touch my hair, but I jerk my head back.

"No, you don't." Anger burns through me, singeing the palm of my hand, making me wish I had the courage to slap him. He's a liar. Nothing out of his mouth is ever the truth. "You just called me—you were an asshole. And now you miss me?"

Jason's arm falls to his side. He ignores my question. "Is your dad still freaking out about me? Does he still talk about me and stuff?"

"No. He's over it. We're both over it. We never even think about you."

Jason frowns at that. "Well, I think about you."

"Oh, God." I shake my head. "I can't believe you just said that." How did I fall for him so easily before? I think it was hope again. Hope that what he said could be real and that he could love me. "You can't trick my anymore."

He studies me for a second, chewing on his bottom lip. "That sounds like a challenge."

My heart speeds up. "It's not. Like I said, I'm over you. You'd better leave me alone or I'll tell someone. You'll get in trouble for talking to me."

Jason rolls his eyes. "No, you won't. If you wanted to tell someone, you would have done it when I called. If you didn't want to see me, you wouldn't have come over here."

The shell I tried to build around myself starts to crumble.

"You've always been like that. You pretend you don't want something when you do so you can play nice little Brynn. I see you, though, Red. I always have. You miss me. Even if you hate yourself for it, you miss me." There's a calm, almost angry edge to his voice.

My eyes squeeze shut when Jason reaches out, pushing my hair behind my ear. By the time I open them again, he's rounding the corner.

My stomach cramps and I lean against the wall. There's something wrong with me. There has to be, because some of what he said was true. And the fact that I have no idea who the man is who just walked away from me. I have no idea who I am, for that matter. Maybe I don't know anyone.

I pause at the trash can on the way back to my car. A second later I throw the gummy bears inside.

Chapter Nineteen

Glancing at the speedometer, I see the needle edge closer and closer to 105 miles per hour. When something scary or exciting happens, people always say their hearts raced. I've said my heart has raced, but it's not been anything *compared to the rapid-fire rounds it's shooting off right now. So fast I can't even count the beats. So fast I can't catch my breath. Jason's always liked to drive fast. His car is his prized possession, but this is beyond fast. This is a death wish.*

"Jason..." I manage to squeak out, but nothing else emerges.

Obviously he knows what I want because he says, "Relax, Red. I know what I'm doing. Let loose a little, huh?"

I nod, trying to do what he says, but I can't help clutching the armrest. That's one of the things I love most about Jason. He knows how to have fun. He likes to have fun with me, and if I can just make myself chill out and enjoy the way his car speeds around each turn, I'll have fun, too.

Closing my eyes, I try to concentrate on my heart rate, willing it to slow down. Willing myself not to have a stupid heart attack. Jason's dad taught him to drive and according to him, his dad's a great driver. It's the one thing they've always had in common...fast cars.

When a scream breaks through the car, I twist, a gasp caught in my throat when I see a baby in the backseat. Never, ever mention your heart can't beat faster, because it can.

"Jason! Stop, slow down! There's a baby in the backseat!" My hands beg to grab him, to jerk him until he listens to me, but I know I can't. That will just make us wreck.

"Chill out. We're fine. I told you, I know what I'm doing. The little guy likes it, don't you?" He looks into the backseat, at who I know is our baby.

"Watch where you're going!" I yell. Please make him stop. Please don't let us crash. Please, please, please. *It's all I can think. I'm a mom; I'm supposed to protect my child. That's what Mom always did with me. I don't want to let her or my baby down.*

Jason laughs. "You're so funny, Red. Always freaking out. I got it under control." His eyes rest on me and still not on the road.

Our baby cries again, and my frantic stare shifts to the perfect little boy strapped in the car seat. We shouldn't be here. I should be taking care of him better than this.

"Look, Brynn. No hands." Jason laughs again, lifting his palms from the steering wheel.

Nausea assaults me. "Stop. It's not funny!"

"Oh, shit!" Jason shouts, grabbing the wheel and wrenching it to the left. I look up. It's too late. We're too late.

I scream as our car slams into a tree.

My eyes pop open. I gasp, then do it again, still not able to catch my breath. Part of me knows I'm in bed, but I can't stop my eyes from darting around the room. From looking behind me to make sure there's not a baby here. A little boy. I don't know why, but I'd always thought it would be a girl.

I wobble as I get out of bed. I don't feel like walking, but there's no way I can lie back down. After that dream, I'm not sure I'll ever be able to sleep again.

Trying to find my legs, I pace around the room, the dream playing on repeat in my head. I used to hate it when Jason drove fast, but he'd never gone *that* fast in the car with me. It was one of his many stupid hobbies. Guys, their fast cars and all that, but what if he *had* tried to go that fast with me? Would I have been strong enough to tell him no? Would he have laughed at me like Dream Jason did? I want to think no…that I wouldn't have been with a guy capable of that kind of cruelty, but he showed me just how cruel he could be, didn't he?

In this moment, I somehow hate him more than I ever have.

And I want to find a way to evict him from my life… from my head.

"Ugh!" I kick my bed. Mature, I know, but it's all I can think to do. Hoping it's not raining outside, I slip on my bunny slippers, put my coat on over my pajamas, and sneak out my bedroom door.

I didn't take the time to look at the clock, but I know it's late…or early, I should say. Maybe three or four in the morning. I can't help but wonder if Dad will be pissed if he finds out I'm going outside at this time of night.

I can't stay, though, can't find a way to breathe inside, and I miss my haven. I miss my pottery and clay. Miss making something out of nothing. Having something that's *mine*. Mom might have worked to give it to me, but still, pottery has always been *mine*.

Almost more than I want to forget about Jason, I want that back.

Quietly, I slip out our back door. I'm just at the door to my pottery room when I freeze.

A shuffle sounds from over the fence. Do I want it to be Christian or not? We haven't talked since that day in the hall a few weeks ago. I should have apologized a long time ago, but I'm not sure how to go about it.

It's easier not to talk to him at school because he's always with my old friends, but it's harder at the center. There all I do is visit with Emery or have my lame weekly sessions with Valerie. Emery and I never really talk about anything important, which is nice. Valerie is always poking and prodding.

My instincts scream at me to keep walking. To open this door, walk in, and close it behind me. I don't need him or anyone else. I don't trust him or anyone else.

A little flash of that stupid speedometer zips into my head.

My hand twists the knob, but then I stop, for some reason, just needing to know. A nightmare brought me out at this time of night and I wonder what would bring Christian out.

Trying to be all inconspicuous, I glance over my shoulder, toward the house on the other side of the fence, but it's not Christian. It's the Hispanic woman from the center. She's taking a drag of a cigarette when she sees me.

"Busted," she says, her shoulders going up and down. Her voice sounds more ethnic than Christian's. He has that Hispanic lilt to his voice, but hers is thicker. "Is there any chance we can keep this a secret?" She holds up the cigarette.

When she smiles, I notice it's the same as Christian's... light, happy, like they don't have a care in the world. For some reason, it makes me want to do the same. "Umm... sure? I don't know who I would tell anyway." Talk about an odd request coming from someone's *mom*.

"Shh. Christian is a light sleeper and he's got the back room. My son doesn't like smoking."

Go, Christian! Still, it's strange that she's hiding it from him. "Sorry," I whisper, sort of wanting to laugh at how she looks over her shoulder to make sure Christian isn't coming.

"It's okay, *mija*. It's not your fault. I'm too old to be out here sneaking cigarettes, but I'm down to one a day. Not too bad if you ask me. My boy is a tough critic, though."

Yeah, no kidding, I want to tell her, when I think about that day in the hall.

"What are you doing outside this early in the morning? I can't keep closet-smoking secrets for you. At least I'm of age." Christian's mom winks at me.

"No, no. I don't smoke. This is my…" *My pottery room. I was coming out here to try and claim something of mine back.* "Couldn't sleep," I finish lamely.

"Story of my life. There's nothing in the world worse than being tired and not being able to find sleep. Probably not as tough on you young ones as it is on us old ladies, though." She takes another puff of her cigarette before putting it into a soda can and then slipping that into her robe pocket. "I have a secret hiding place." She laughs, this time a little more loudly. I guess she doesn't mind the risk of waking him after she's finished.

"Ignore me. What's that saying? Do as I say, not as I do. Smoking is bad for you." She shakes her finger at me. Just as it happened with Christian that night, a laugh sneaks up on me.

"No worries. Zero chance of me ever touching one of those things."

"Good girl." She smiles and I realize I'm smiling, too. She reminds me of my mom.

Christian's mom cocks her head at me, studying me. "You're much too pretty to look so sad, *mija.*"

My first instinct is to blush, but then, I feel like crying. I want to tell her I'm broken. I want to tell her about

Mom, about Jason…even about Dad. I want to tell her… someone…everything. That little taste of talking with Emery the other day makes me crave more, but my fear always steps in the way. "I'm fine."

She shakes her head. "I have a daughter." Her voice suddenly sounds as alone as I feel. "I've started to know what it sounds like when someone says she's fine but she's really not." Just like Christian did all those weeks ago, she grabs the chair from the porch, walks over, puts it by the fence, and stands on it.

It's such a strange thing to see a mom do. I can imagine my mom doing it, but I've never met another parent like her.

"I'm Brenda." Another kind smile. Big blue eyes that match her son's.

"Brynn." For some reason, I whisper.

"Well, Brynn. It's nice to meet you. We don't know each other, but you ever want to talk, I owe you a secret. As long as it can't hurt you, I'll repay you that secret, okay, *mija*?"

There's something so comforting about her. The way it feels to slide into my favorite slippers or curl up on the couch with hot chocolate on a rainy day. There's no judgment in her eyes, or even too much curiosity. Just genuine kindness.

"Okay." I nod.

"Okay," she confirms before stepping down from the chair and walking back over to the porch. "I'm holding you to that. We all need friends. I might be old, but I make a pretty good one. I see you at the center. You sit with Emery but you still look alone. It won't do you any good if you don't talk. We can go together sometime, if you want."

She waits as though she wants me to reply, but I don't.

"Now, if you'll excuse me, I have to go brush my teeth and wash my hands before my partner or that boy of mine wakes up." With another wink, Brenda is gone.

• • •

Emery falls into the seat beside me and lets out a deep breath. "My feet are swollen and they're killing me."

I frown. "Is that normal? I mean…is everything okay?"

"Yeah, they said I'm fine. They're keeping an eye on everything. I'm not supposed to be on my feet a whole lot, though."

"Oh." There's so much about pregnancy I didn't know. My feet might have swelled and they could have told me to stay off them. It's a small thing, but something I probably should have known.

Emery grabs another chair and sets it in front of her before putting her feet up on it. Then, she leans back. "You've never told my why you come here. Are they forcing you or something?"

"Pretty much. They gave me an option of the school counselor, but I chose this."

She lets out a small laugh. "Ohhhh-kay. You're like a thousand-piece puzzle or something. Tough to figure out and a total mystery when I'm staring at the pieces."

And she's not? Before I can say so, she continues. "It's not that bad. Max used to give me shit about coming, but I kind of like it. Gives me something to do, ya know? Now that we're splits, it helps even more."

My eyes dart to her stomach again. Max must be her ex. Did he treat her the same way Jason did me?

"You're not very smooth. I'll tell you all the details— you don't have to ask. Sixteen, Max dumped me, parents kicked me out, and I'm giving my baby up for adoption. I think that about covers it."

She cocks a brow at me and I'm sure my mouth is hanging open. It's crazy to me that she can be so nonchalant about such a big deal. Dad may not be able to look me in the eyes, but I know he never would have kicked me out. Even if I didn't lose the baby, he would have helped me.

"I'm sorry."

"Eh. What can you do? That's life, right?"

How do you do it? I want to ask her. She's friendly and talkative and looks happy when everything in her life is so screwed up. I want to be able to hold it together like that. I want to be strong, but I don't know how. Just when I think I might open my mouth and ask her, Valerie comes into the room. "There you are, Emery. Are you ready to talk?"

Emery sighs, but somehow I can tell it's more because she doesn't feel like getting up than because she's afraid to talk. "Sure thing." She pushes to her feet and gives me a small wave before walking away. As she does, I notice a piece of paper falling to the floor.

"You dropped something," I call to her.

"Oh, it's just a doodle. You can have it."

When she's gone I open the piece of paper. It's incredible. Way more than a doodle. It's a drawing of a tree in perfect detail. It looks like an old one with knobs and holes in it.

Emery is an artist.

"I used to make pottery," I say. No one's close enough to me to hear.

Chapter Twenty

Before

Standing up, I stick my hand deep into the open top on the piece of pottery I'm making. I let the wheel circle, my hands smoothing out the inside.

It's almost done. And it's going to be gorgeous.

"Brynn De Luca! Get your butt out here. It's almost time to get ready."

I roll my eyes at the sound of Mom's voice. Just as I turn around, she and Dad walk into my pottery room. Dad's standing behind her, and he puts his finger up to the side of his head and makes a circle, as if to say she's crazy.

I chuckle.

"Do I want to know what your father is doing behind my back?" She smiles.

"What? Me? I'm not doing anything at all, am I, *dolcezza*?"

"Nope. Nothing at all."

Mom crosses her arms and pretends to pout. "I don't believe either of you. Stop ganging up on me on my favorite holiday."

"Whose favorite holiday is Halloween?" I say at the same time Dad says, "I thought that was Christmas. Every holiday can't be your favorite. That's cheating."

Mom turns to him. "I do not cheat, Anthony, and don't you accuse me of it again. Halloween and Christmas are tied for number one and all the other holidays are number two."

Dad and I both laugh at her. She always makes us laugh.

"I'm too old to dress up," I tell her.

"There's no such thing. Your father and I are dressing up and I'm pretty sure we're older than you."

"You don't act like it," I tease.

"Only on Halloween. I deserve one day a year to be a kid. Now, scoot. You have about fifteen minutes to finish up in here before you need to get on your costume. We have a haunted house to run."

"Brynn, help me!" Dad laughs, a smile on his face as Mom drags him from the room. I finish my piece and then go get dressed.

My stomach hurts from laughing so hard as I watch Dad chase kids around the haunted house. Mom makes all sorts of corny noises that I'm pretty sure she thinks are scary but sound like a Disney princess trying to act tough.

After about an hour, my friends call to ask if I want to do something with them.

"You can go," Mom says, but *yes* isn't even an answer I'd consider.

"That's okay. We're having fun here. I'll catch up with you guys tomorrow," I say into the phone.

After I hang up, Mom clips me with her hip. "Did I hear you say this was fun? I thought you were too old."

"AHHHH!" a group of kids yells as Dad starts chasing again.

My eyes catch Mom's. "There's no such thing as being too old for Halloween."

Chapter Twenty-One

Now

Is it ridiculous that I've spent the past couple weeks leading up to Halloween watching Christian's house? I'm sure it is, but in the grand scheme of things, it's one of the smaller reasons I have to feel ridiculous.

I can't stop wondering what he's doing in there, and wishing I hadn't thrown away those gummy bears, and my apology along with them. I can't stop thinking about Brenda and remembering how she smiled at me and how she almost, for one second, made me feel like I had a mom. Or maybe not a mom, because I don't know her, and there's no one in this whole universe who could take Mom's place. Mom was beautiful and vibrant. Loving and perfect. But Brenda gave me a couple minutes where I felt like there was another adult I could trust. Someone who I could maybe talk with, and also be quiet with, the way I could with Mom.

She was awesome at that. I used to think she had some kind of magic feeling detector. Like she could read me. She knew when I needed to talk, when I needed to be held, or when I just needed quiet. When I would want her to sit and watch me make a piece of pottery just because it felt good to have someone there.

But it wasn't just with me. She and Dad were like that, too. She always knew what he needed. She finished his sentences. When he had a bad day at work, she somehow knew and made his favorite meal.

I wish she were here to make things better. Not just for me, but for Dad, too. I think every day he misses her more.

Every day, I miss them *both* more.

"Are you sure you're going to be okay, Brynn?" Dad seems sad as he stands in the living room, looking at me. He has those little wrinkles by his eyes and I try to remember if he's always had them or if they only popped up since Jason. "Maybe I shouldn't go... I'm not sure I should leave you..."

It's Saturday. Halloween, to be exact.

Dad conveniently has some conference or something to go to and I can't help but wonder if he just needs to get away. I imagine him spending the night, driving the streets and looking for all the haunted houses he can find and wondering if Mom would like them. Knowing Mom's would have been better.

"I'll be fine, Dad."

He shakes his head, clearly at a loss. My arms suddenly tingle, and I wish I had the power to hug him and take the pain away. "I don't know, Brynn... It's the first time I've left you since...everything. And it's Halloween. I'm sure you'll be going out with your friends, and I should be home."

Anger eclipses my sadness. Be out with my friends? He knows damn well I don't have friends anymore. That I haven't gone anywhere besides the stupid center in months. "When's the last time you saw my friends, Dad? You know I'm not going anywhere."

Dad pops his knuckles. When did he start doing that? Mom would be appalled. The sound used to drive her crazy when I did it. If at all possible, his eyes look even more pained as he walks over and sits by me on the couch.

"Do you...do you want to talk about it, *dolcezza?*"

I can't help but wonder if it's strange that I can't speak to my own dad. I mean, how would I even do it? Explain to him that I thought I was in love. That I had sex and got pregnant and now, even though I wasn't ready to have a baby, I feel a little empty knowing it's suddenly gone. Just poof! Like magic. No, not magic because Mom was magic, but like some sort of dark force that swooped in and hollowed me out.

But I sort of want to talk to him. Or at least, I want him to wonder. Want him to ask, and hold me, and call me *dolcezza* because even if he can't have his *bella signora*, I hope he can have his sweetheart. That I hope I can be enough. Most of all, I want to take away his sadness. I dream at night for a huge eraser that I can use to delete the parts of our past when everything started to change.

"Is it because of Ja— That boy?" His voice gets tight all of a sudden, and even though I hate the shame I hear when he speaks, my eyes sting because he's asking. Even though half the time he can hardly look at me, there are still moments he wishes he could make it better. I wonder where he would use his eraser—if he would mark this out for me.

But telling him the truth, spelling it all out for him and telling him I've seen Jason, talked to Jason, makes me wonder if he would be even more disappointed in me. "Dad…I can't."

He sighs, and I think it's a mixture of relief and fear. "What about another counselor? We could get you someone else to talk to if you don't like Valerie. I know I'm not good at this stuff. Maybe someone else would be better."

Mom would be better at this. I know that's what he means.

"No." I pick at my pajama bottoms. "I'm okay."

"What about a teacher at school? Anyone?"

"Okay," I tell him. It has to be hard on him, too, having a daughter who always had a full house, who he never had to worry about, who now only leaves to go to school. "I will. Actually, maybe I can call my friend Brenda. She's new. I just met her a few weeks ago. There's also another girl named Emery I met at the center."

The half smile that tugs at his mouth tells me using a name helps.

Trying to continue to play the part, I swat his leg. "Now get out of here. You don't want to get to your hotel too late. I'm going to watch scary movies, call Brenda, and eat way too much ice cream."

Again, his mouth starts to tilt downward. "Brynn…"

"It's okay. I'm okay."

After another sigh, he's gone.

• • •

I stare at the screen and my finger freezes on the remote control. I know I should turn it, but it's like the villain from the scary movie has jumped from the screen into my life and severed the connection from my brain to my hand.

No, even a movie villain has nothing on the face covering the screen right now.

Jason. He's doing a local commercial?

The urge to throw the remote makes my arm tingle, but I still can't move. What gives him the right to act so happy?

Really, I can't blame it all on him. I should have been strong enough to see who he was. Even if I didn't, I shouldn't have given him the pleasure of knowing he still gets to me. I feel like one of the girls from the scary movies who goes off on her own or falls every time the monster chases her.

Jason is my monster, and I'm tired of falling.

Finally I make my finger work and push the power button. I'm done with TV, but the silence in the house is just as difficult. Even though I managed to turn off the commercial, he still won. He still stabbed me to death, and if I had my friends, they'd be finding my body by now while some creepy music played in the background.

No. Before I can change my mind, I push off the couch. This is another ridiculous thing that I will probably regret later, but for tonight, I don't want to be the girl from the movies who separates from the group. I want someone—anyone—to talk to, and there is only one person I can think of.

I grab my cell and keys and head for the door, wondering when I became the person who had no one else to hang out with on Halloween besides someone else's *mom.*

When I climb the porch stairs to Christian's house, my steps falter. It will be awkward if he's here, since I haven't managed to apologize yet. But it's Halloween. There's no way my friends would stay in tonight, which means he's out with them.

I make myself knock, little sparks of electricity going off inside me when I do. It's the first thing I've done for myself in so, so long. You know your life has gone downhill when knocking on a door suddenly makes you feel liberated.

"Just a sec!" Christian's voice comes through the door.

Holy crap.

Christian's home.

I don't feel so liberated anymore. What am I supposed to say? *Hi, is your mom home?*

Automatically I turn, hoping to get out of there before he answers. Maybe he'll think I'm an impatient trick-

or-treater or something. As soon as I take a step toward saving face, though, the door creaks behind me.

"Had to grab some more— Brynn? Aren't you a little old for ding dong ditch?"

Okay, I totally need an excuse. First, I don't have a reason for being here and second, I have even less of a reason for running.

Don't be the first one killed in the scary movie, don't be the first one killed in the scary movie. I reach for some of that liberation I felt a few minutes ago and turn around. Christian's standing there in a white T-shirt and a pair of flannel pajama bottoms with a huge bowl of candy in his arms.

I fight the urge to think how adorable he is. Thoughts like that can only lead to more pain.

"Is your mom here?" I blurt out and immediately regret the words.

Christian doesn't even look at me funny when he answers. "Nope. She's out. I get to be the one giving candy tonight."

I'm distinctly aware of him. That he's in pajamas and I'm in pajamas and that we haven't spoken to each other since I made a fool of myself in front of him. Since I let Jason take one more thing away from me. Not that Christian is mine, or that I want him, but in some ways he represents a normal I no longer possess. He's my past. When I knew him, I didn't know any of the pain of the world. "Okay. Thanks."

Still, I stall, trying to piece together the words in my head. Trying to figure how to apologize for how I've treated him. Can we be friends? I'm not sure, but I also don't want to be that girl. I hate the anger festering inside me like an infection—gangrene taking me over and rotting me from the inside out.

It's crazy, but Emery pops into my head. She's strong. She's having her baby. She still smiles and laughs even though her own parents kicked her out. Internally, I search for my inner Emery.

Before I can find her, Christian says, "Watch a movie with me, Bryntastic."

It's not a question, and I somehow wonder if he knows that if he had asked me, I would have said no. But this way I can pretend I don't have the option of turning him down. Because I want to stay. I want to just *be* with someone. "Okay." I shrug.

Without another word, he turns and walks inside. My heart beats once, twice, three times before I suck in a deep breath and follow him.

The TV is off in the living room and a sudden burst of panic explodes inside me. Does he want me to go into his room with him? Maybe that was a line like the ones Jason used. If it came down to it, maybe Christian would use me for sex, too.

Somehow, I make myself push those thoughts aside. For one night, I'm going to try to forget the perfect, smiling face I just saw on TV. Try to be the Brynn De Luca from before.

"So…how ya been?" Christian sets down the bowl, picks his guitar off the couch, and leans it on a stand in the corner. He hadn't been watching a movie at all, and I suddenly feel like I'm intruding.

"If you're busy…"

"I would have said so." He sits down, his legs out in front of him, comfortable in who he is. I used to be like that. Or at least, I think I was. If I were really that confident, I'm not sure I would have fallen for Jason.

"I'm sorry," I blurt out before I lose my nerve.

Christian sighs. "Took you long enough to apologize." He stalls and I wonder if he's going to ask me to leave when he adds, "We all deal with shit. I've seen too much and I don't play games, so we're cool or we're not. You choose."

"What have you dealt with?" I ask.

"Just stuff. My mom works at a teen center, remember? I've seen a lot. She's taught me and told me tons."

Which makes sense, but there's something off about it, too. Something that makes me think there's more to the story than Christian wants to share. I never would have expected that from him. He seems like such an open book.

"I haven't heard you in your backyard much. That's your studio out there, right?"

No, I haven't been out there. There's not really a point. It's not like I'm making anything.

"Haven't been in the mood." For something to do, I sit on the opposite side of the couch from him. It's brown leather and makes a little sound when I sit. Across from us, the TV is mounted to the wall, with shelves beneath it filled with all sorts of boy TV stuff. And then, I turn my head and look at him. I didn't want to because I hate the way he looks at me. Hate it and love it at the same time. Not because I like him, because I don't—I won't—but I love it because it's normal and hate it because it makes me feel naked. Like he's seeing inside me in a way Jason never did.

I'm pretty sure we both know I'm lying. Know I don't go into my room because it makes me feel even more lost. That I don't go out there because I can't make anything ever again. I send tiny little wishes into the universe that he doesn't call me on it. That he doesn't ask me why I'm not in the mood, or why I'm here to see his mom, or why I watch him and then treat him badly.

Christian gives a slight shrug before he leans forward, past the candy bowl and toward his bag of gummy bears. He pours some into his lap and hands me the bag, which I take. I pop one into my mouth, briefly getting a whiff of that sugary smell that reminds me of him.

"I only do old-school horror flicks. *Nightmare on Elm Street* is in. That cool with you?" he asks around a gummy. For some reason, I wonder if we're eating the same color.

"Perfect."

For the next two hours, there's nothing but scary dreams, knife fingers, and Freddy's messed-up face. No questions, no small talk, and it's just what I need.

Right as the credits start to roll, the front door opens, propelling me off the couch. *Calm down, Brynn. You weren't doing anything wrong.*

Brenda walks in, dressed like a Mexican dancer. "Whew, I'm tired— Oh, hey! How are you?" She smiles at me.

"Fine. We were just watching a movie, but it's over, so I'm heading home now."

Christian walks forward, scratching his head. "Where's Sally?" he asks his mom. For a second, I wonder who that is, but I remember he has a sister. I've never seen her, but there's another woman I see come and go. Could be her, too.

"She'll be home soon. She's on an ice cream run." Brenda turns toward me. "You don't have to go." I get one of those "Mom" looks from her.

"No, I should get home. It's pretty late. My dad's gone until tomorrow afternoon and he might call the home phone to check on me." Which is true.

"She came to see you." Christian crosses his arms and stands next to me. He's not close enough to touch me but somehow I feel him. My skin warms and pebbles with goose bumps at the same time.

"I just wanted to say hi. I was bored over there by myself. I'm getting a little bit tired now, but I appreciate the offer to stay."

"Breakfast!" Brenda claps her hands, confusing me. Breakfast?

"I know you have to go, but come eat with us in the morning. Do you like chorizo?"

Christian talks before I get a chance. "Mom, are you trying to show off? Pulling out the big guns on her?"

Huh?

"I am not! I'm being nice, *mijo*. Her dad is gone, I missed her tonight, and yeah, I can cook a mean breakfast."

Christian shakes his head, a smile tilting his lips. "Whatever." Next he turns to me. "I'll walk you home."

"You don't have to do that," I rush out.

"I know."

All I can do is nod and wonder what just happened. I'm obviously coming to breakfast tomorrow.

"See you at nine," Brenda calls as I follow Christian to the door.

"Okay, thank you."

When we get on my porch, Christian stops. "You'll be okay?"

I nod and walk in. "Yeah, I'm good. Luckily we don't live on Elm Street. Then I might make you stay awake with me all night."

He smiles at my lame joke. "You wouldn't have to make me. I'd protect you from Freddy. Or make my mom protect both of us."

"Oh, big strong boy needs his mom. I see how brave you are." There's a flutter in my stomach that I struggle to ignore.

"She's tough. You'll see when you get to know her better."

"I have no doubt about your mom's toughness."

"Smart girl." He tilts his head toward his house. "I'd better go. Catch ya later, Bryntastic," Christian turns and jogs back to his house. I watch until he slips inside.

After a quick trip upstairs to brush my teeth and grab my blanket and pillow, I curl up on the couch. Mom and I always had living room sleepovers any time we were alone. It's kind of nice to do it again.

Thinking of her makes me remember the movie with Christian. How tonight, I wasn't alone. How it felt good to have someone to be quiet with.

Chapter Twenty-Two

Now

Even though it feels strange to be going to Christian's house for breakfast, I don't even have to talk myself into it. I *want* to go. To laugh at his mom who sneaks cigarettes. To meet Sally or his elusive dad—if he's even around. I suddenly feel a little guilty for not knowing. And I also hope I might find out why he left.

After changing into a black-and-white-striped sweater and a pair of jeans, I tie my red hair back in a ponytail.

After pushing my feet into my pink-and-black Nikes, I head over to Christian's—no, *Brenda's*. She invited me to breakfast. She's the one I went to see last night. Not him.

Inside me, there's a little kernel of thankfulness that he was there, though, because I'd needed someone, *something*, and just by letting me watch Freddy slash people in their nightmares, he gave it to me.

A few seconds after I knock, Brenda opens the front door. She looks almost like she did that first morning, a robe wrapped around her, but this time, she looks much more awake.

She hugs me tightly, her arms around me squeezing the heart in my chest. My body melts into the comfort of her embrace.

"Thanks for coming, *mija*. I cooked all sorts of food and Christian is still in bed. He's lucky I don't throw water on him to get him up!"

I can't help but laugh, part of me wanting to witness Christian being awakened by a flood. "That's okay. Did he go out or something, after I left last night?" I want to snatch the question out of the air, take it back. I want to dissect the reason it came out of my mouth in the first place. "I mean, I'm just curious."

Leading me to the kitchen, she shakes her head. "No, but he probably stayed up half the night playing his guitar. He's a night owl. It helps him relax. Guitar is his form of meditation." When we step into the kitchen, there's another woman standing at the stove. I assume it's Sally. She's definitely not Brenda's daughter, because they're close to the same age, and even though she has dark hair, it's obvious she isn't Hispanic like Brenda and Christian.

"Brynn, this is my partner, Sally. Sally, this is Christian's friend and our neighbor, Brynn."

Partner? The wheels in my brain start to spin, all the little gadgets clicking into place. Oh, *partner*. I've never known a lesbian before. I don't have a problem with it—people should be able to love who they want—but it's just not something I've been so close to personally.

"Hi." Sally holds out her hand to me. "It's nice to meet you." As we shake, she turns to Brenda and says, "Check the food. I don't want to mess it up."

They both laugh. Brenda grabs Sally's free hand and gives it a brief squeeze before she flips the food in a skillet. The gesture does something to me. Makes my eyes fight not to cloud over because it's so easy...so *natural* that it reminds me of Mom and Dad.

Brenda finishes cooking while Sally and I sit at the table. I find out she runs a little coffee shop one town over and Brenda works part-time in an office. She's also been going back to school for psychology and somehow finds the time to volunteer at the center five days a week.

They joke about Christian's morning grumpiness and his obsession with teaching himself guitar. Apparently, he's pretty independent and doesn't like to need things from other people. I can definitely see that about him.

"Part of it is just because he likes to learn. He reads my books from school for fun, and teaching himself the guitar started out as the same thing. Now he loves it."

"That's cool."

A few minutes later, Brenda sits a huge plate of food in front of me, another for Sally, and then one for her. "Should we wake him up or brag later that he missed breakfast?"

I say, "Brag later," at the same time as Sally, and the three of us laugh.

Looking down at the plate, I'm not sure where to start. There are tortillas and beans and meat that I assume is the chorizo she mentioned. She also piled scrambled eggs and fruit onto my plate. Honestly, I'm a little out of my element. We do sauce and pasta (though not for breakfast). Since she mentioned the chorizo, I start there, putting a bit in my mouth. Two chews later I feel like my mouth is erupting into flames. "Oh my God!"

Sally and Brenda both look at me with wide eyes. I'm fanning my mouth and my eyes are actually watering.

"You don't do hot, *mija*?" Brenda asks, obviously shocked, while Sally jumps up and grabs me a drink, which I immediately suck down.

Now, it's only my cheeks that are burning. "No, no. It's good. I just wasn't expecting it."

Brenda reaches across the table and grabs my hand. "Just like my Christian. He can't handle the hot, either."

. . .

The rest of breakfast goes by without any incidents. I don't eat the chorizo. Brenda smirks every time she looks at me, and Sally harasses her for not warning me she likes to eat food hotter than an inferno. Christian never makes an appearance.

But I have *fun*.

I love listening to their banter. They don't ask me many questions. A little bit about Dad, his job, and making sure he won't mind that I'm here. They both apologize when I tell them about Mom, but it's the kind of apology that feels like it's healing some of the emptiness inside me, not the pitying, uncomfortable kind.

"I have an idea!" Brenda claps her hands. "Do you want to go to the center with me? They're having a girls' day, no boys allowed. We'll listen to music and have lunch. Play games."

"Umm, sure. Yeah, I'd like that." The cool part is, it's true. I'm not ready for this day to end.

Brenda gets another one of those grins on her face that reminds me of Christian. Sally kisses her cheek and says, "I'll clean up while you girls get ready to go."

I run next door to grab a couple things while Brenda finishes up at home. I'm a weird mix of excitement and nerves, but I decide not to focus on it and just enjoy myself.

A few minutes later, I actually twiddle my thumbs in the car. I'm not sure what to do or what to say and that seems to work better than anything else.

Brenda sits next to me in her flowy skirt, happiness radiating off of her, and I wish there was a way to siphon some of her positive energy. To not dread something as simple as what we're going to do.

But it's not really simple, is it?

I pull my hands apart and rub them on my jeans. All I want is to push those thoughts of before and now out of my head. I just want to live in the moment—find a way to, anyway, and my only chance is to stop myself from dwelling.

"So...have you done this long? The volunteering?" I

ask.

Brenda turns and nods. I sit back in the seat.

"I haven't been at this center very long. Just since we moved here." Her accent tints every word. "I've done it before, though. It's hard being a teenager. I didn't realize that until after Angelica. I want to be there for kids who might not have anyone else there for them."

Her voice is soft, almost sad, making questions spring to life inside my head. I try to decide if I should ask about it or not. It's hard, reading someone else's pain. Knowing the right thing to do. I've drowned in my own so much, had so many people add to it—on purpose or not—that I want to tread the surface carefully. Little ripples dancing across the water instead of jumping in and causing a huge wave.

Ellie and Diana caused me waves. Even Dad, though not in the same way. The last thing I want to do is make the water flood over someone else's head, too.

"Can I ask who Angelica is?"

The corners of Brenda's eyes tilt down a little. "My daughter. I think I told you Christian has a sister. She's a few years older than he is."

The word *is* makes my heart jump slightly. I feared a *was*. *Was* is so hard when you're using it in regard to someone you love. "Oh. Where is she?" Is it bad that Brenda's pain makes me feel another tie to her? I don't want her to hurt. Don't want anyone I know to hurt, but in a way it makes me feel less lonely.

It takes Brenda a few seconds before she replies. "I'm not sure. I think she's with her father. She doesn't want anything to do with me."

My chest cracks open for her. How can anyone not want something to do with Brenda? Does Angelica talk to Christian? I think about Dad. Things are strained between us, but I know he would never cast me out.

"When I left her father for Sally...well, you can imagine things were hard on her. It was hard on Christian, too, at first. I mean, he had to leave here, and all his friends behind."

Oh. So now I know why Christian disappeared all those years ago.

"I'll always regret how I did that. I should have been smarter about it—my children deserved that. Angelica took it the hardest. I should have realized how hard, but I didn't. I let her be angry and let her tell me everything was okay. It's one of the biggest mistakes of my life, *mija*. I will always feel like I failed her. I don't want any other kids to feel like they don't have someone there for them."

"I'm sorry." All I can think is how incredible she is. Just like Christian, they're both still going. Sure, there are little bumps in the road. Maybe Christian's outburst at the center was one of them. But they're not folding in on themselves like I am. They're living...and I'm just being.

I'd like to try to live again.

Before I get the chance to say anything else, she announces, "We're here! This is going to be so much fun!"

• • •

The first thing I notice when I see Emery is the red tinting her eyes. The frown on her face. She's never sad, and seeing her like this immediately makes my gut sink. All I can think about is the baby, and I'm hoping and praying that nothing is wrong with her.

"Are you okay?" I ask as I approach her in the corner. Another sign something is wrong. Emery is in a corner alone.

"Peachy." There is a roughness in her voice I'm not used to.

But I remember crying and how I felt when I lost my baby and it's all I can think about—the bump under her shirt. *Please let everything be okay with her baby.*

Emery turns and pushes her way through the crowd. I find myself following her. She stomps down a hall and I'm right behind her when she goes into another room.

"Is the baby okay?" My voice squeaks, and I can't even finish the sentence.

"Yes! *God.* Why is it always about the baby? Either it's all people care about when they talk to me, or they're so mad about the baby they won't talk at all. Baby, baby, baby!" Emery falls to a chair and starts to cry.

My eyes are watering, too. I don't know what's wrong with her or what to do, but I find myself walking to the chair next to her and sitting down. I put my arm around her the way no one did to me—the way Dad tried but couldn't bring himself to—and I let her cry.

And she does. So many tears that I wonder how she has any left.

I just sit there with my arm around her, hoping that

I'm doing the right thing. That this somehow helps, because if I can't help myself, it feels good to do it for someone else.

When the tears finally stop, she wipes her eyes with her sleeve, and then her demeanor completely changes. "Wow. I totally freaked out on you there. I'm sorry about that." She smiles at me. I can't believe she's smiling after she just cried so much.

"I'm being stupid," she continues. "I just got in a fight with my boyfriend and I lost it for a minute. I'm fine now."

"I thought you didn't have a boyfriend?"

Her mouth widens as though she just made a mistake. "I don't. I didn't mean that. He's my ex; I just said the wrong word. I'm having a bad day. It's hormones and stuff."

"Oh." Her reply doesn't sit right with me. There's something off about it, but it's not like I'm going to call her a liar. I know how it feels to have people doubt you.

"Thanks, though…for talking to me. I needed to get that out." Emery reaches over and gives me a hug. "Thank you," she whispers again and I hug her back. The way she says it, combined with the way she hugs me, makes me wonder if she could possibly be as lonely as I am. You'd never know it by looking at her, but as she clings to me, it seems truer and truer.

"It's okay. I didn't really do anything."

Emery shakes her head. "Yeah you did. I know how hard talking without being prompted is for you, and I appreciate it."

I roll my eyes. She might not have known me long, but she seems to know me well.

With that, she heads for the door. With her hand on the knob, she turns and says, "Can I ask you a favor?"

"Sure." I shrug, still trying to figure out what I did to help. But also feeling good that I did it.

"Can you not tell anyone I saw Max? It's just…it's embarrassing."

I get it. I know what it's like to be embarrassed, for everyone to know your business. And it's not like I don't have my own secrets, too. I shudder with the memory of seeing Jason at the store. Of following and talking to him, proving how weak I am. I don't even hesitate to say, "Your secret is safe with me."

Chapter Twenty-Three

Now

I stand at the door to my pottery room, willing it to be different this time. I've had an awesome day. I spent an hour and a half at Brenda's, laughing, smiling, and being Brynn. I was there for Emery when she needed me. It wasn't a lot, but it was hard for me and I did it, and somehow, it seemed to help. Again...old Brynn. She isn't so bad, is she? I want to be her again, not this person I've become. I want to try to get back some of the things I've lost.

You can do it, you can do it, you can do it.

The door creaks as I open it. I don't remember it always doing that, or maybe I just never paid attention before. Maybe I'm stalling by standing here wondering about this.

But do I have a right to go in here? The right to sit down to do the thing I did while she was dying?

I step backward.

I can do this. I can do this.

I can't do it. Why can't I go inside? Mom would want me to go inside, I think...

And I do. I step inside and go straight to the CD player and turn it on. It's one of Mom's favorite songs— Jermaine Jackson and Whitney Houston. It was her and Dad's song and I'd been listening to it that day because I always listened to music out here.

It's all too much.

"Ahhhhhhhh!" I let loose a scary-movie scream and slam the palms of my hands into the door. It flies backward and hits the wall. The scream that's probably been trapped inside me since before Jason. Since the day Mom said she had a headache and I got annoyed with her and went to my pottery room. Everything blurs together now and it's hard to know what is and was fact or fiction in my life.

"Ahhhhhh!"

I'm out the door now.

A loud crash sounds behind me and I stumble backward again, clutching my chest.

"Holy shit, you scared me. Are you okay?" Christian stands behind me, breathing hard, his guitar in his hand.

"Yeah...yeah, I'm fine." Maybe a little crazy, but fine.

He looks around like he expects someone to jump out at any second. "Do you always scream like that when you're okay? I was sitting on my porch and it sounded like someone was murdering you over here."

"Umm, you thought someone was trying to kill me

yet you brought your guitar with you?"

"Jumped the fence with it and everything," he says, semi-smugly.

"What were you going to do? Hit him with it?"

Christian actually blanches. I swear the boy pales. "Are you kidding me? This is my prized possession."

I shake my head at him. And here I was thinking myself crazy. "Again, then why did you bring it?"

"Well, that's obvious. What if the scream was a distraction to get me over the fence so someone else could steal my guitar?" He stands there looking absolutely serious.

"Oh my God!" I playfully push him. "You're nuts."

We both laugh for a few minutes before he quiets and then looks at me, *really* looks at me like he wants to figure me out. Like I'm a puzzle and he wants to fit all my pieces together to see what I make. I'm curious what it would be, too.

"Seriously, you cool?" he asks, all humor gone from his voice.

I don't know if it's because I'm caught off guard or what, but I say, "I can't do it. I've always been able to lose myself in my pottery and now I can't even go in the room."

Christian stares at me, and then the right side of his lips tilts up. God, he is so cute. I wish he wasn't.

"Maybe it's the music. That shit would kill my creativity, too."

Without an invitation, he goes inside and turns off the power on my CD player. Then, he heads right over to one of the extra chairs, sits down, and starts to play a song that sounds a lot like the Plain White T's.

"Hey there, Bryntastic, sit your ass down in that chair."

Something twitches in my chest. "I think I like, 'Hey there Delilah, what's it like in New York City' better," I tease him.

"What?" His fingers are still moving on the strings. "How can you say that? My words are original *and* fit the situation, so quit stalling and sit down." When I cross my arms at him, he adds a "Please."

This is completely stupid. I know there is no way that listening to Christian play his silly song is going to make me find my muse again. It's not going to make me feel okay about doing what she gave me when I let her die. "I can't." My voice cracks.

"You can. Just come inside. You don't even have to make anything."

Shaking my head, I say, "This isn't going to work."

"Damn, you're negative."

"No. I'm honest." I wonder if it's his mom's psychology books—the ones she said he reads—that make him seem so much smarter than me, or if it's just because he's already been through so much and he found his way out of it.

"Doesn't hurt to try. Plus, you can't tell me you don't want to hear me play, *chica.*" I give him the evil eye and he winks at me. "Can't hurt, right? Just come in and listen. If it helps, cool. If not, you're no worse off than you are now."

"Why?" I creak out. "Why do you care? I haven't been

very nice to you." I hate myself for it. I've been horrible.

"Maybe I remember who you used to be. Maybe it sucks to see people lose themselves. Or to lose yourself."

My heart starts to thunder. He's talking about his sister. He saw her lose herself. And maybe he did a little, too.

Then, another grin. "Or maybe I just like to show off. You know, my mad guitar-playing skills." Christian nods toward the chair. "Come in. Sit down and listen to me play."

His eyes leave me, his head facing down as he concentrates on what he's doing. Christian's dark hair falls forward, but it doesn't seem to bother him. Nothing does. He's so deep in concentration, I wonder if he remembers I'm here.

I take one step in. Then another and another until finally I'm sitting in the chair at my pottery wheel for the first time since Mom died.

• • •

I lie in bed, remembering what it felt like to sit in my pottery room tonight. I didn't touch the wheel once, but still, I was there. That has to count for something. I'm trying to fight and claw my way back to normal little by little.

I think Mom would be proud about that.

I let Christian pop into my head. His hair in his face and his fingers dancing on the strings the way mine used to do in clay. How even though it felt awesome to just sit and *be* with someone, I know to the marrow of my bones that it wasn't just him that got me in that room. Yes, he was a part of it because something about him is calming and normal, in my world that feels both ever-changing and also completely stagnant. But I'm not sure Christian's hand lit the match.

It was his, and maybe Emery's, Brenda's, and…

In a way, I think it was mine. Mine because I took the step to let him in. Or maybe I'm being crazy, trying to look for something that isn't there. Some part of me I never realized still needed someone the way I obviously thought I needed Jason.

Rolling over, I let my eyes find the red numbers of my clock. I stare at them until they start to blur. It's a little after 4:00 a.m.

Riding my new burst of courage, I sneak out of bed, downstairs, and out back. My heart drops when the porch on Christian's side of the fence is empty. It only takes a few seconds of my standing there and wondering what I'm doing before I hear a door opening quietly. Brenda steps on the porch, pulling out her secret cigarette.

A heavy breath finds its way from my lungs. I don't know why I need to talk to her so badly, but I do.

She walks toward the fence, and I do the same.

"Couldn't sleep. I felt like a little fresh air." Which isn't the truth at all. I came out here looking for her because I want her to tell me what to do. To help me figure out all the mishmashed thoughts in my head. The most important being, am I ready to try to move forward?

To try to come out of the shell I've built around myself? To light not only my love of pottery, but also the flame of my whole life?

It's a scary, scary thought, and honestly, I'm not even sure what that would entail, or if it's possible, or where all these thoughts are suddenly coming from, but for once I don't feel like screaming, and I want to hold on to that.

"And I'm ruining it with my smoke."

"You should quit," tumbles out of my mouth. The light from my porch makes it so I can see her expression, and there's no annoyance at my statement.

She doesn't reply, though. "So, my son says he was over with you this evening? I hope he made up for sleeping through breakfast."

"Umm, yeah. I saw a mouse and screamed and he came over to check on me. Then he just played his guitar while I worked on my pottery."

Brenda laughs softly. "I'm glad to see you guys are spending time together."

"We're not! Spending time together, I mean." We're not. I'm not spending time with any guys that way. Never again. "We're just friends. I mean, we're not even friends." Her frown makes me reword. "I mean, we're kind of *friends*, but…" I really, really need to shut up.

"Relax. I didn't mean anything by my comment. Whether you're friends or not, that's okay, but if I can be honest with you for a second, *mija*…and I don't say this to hurt you, but I think you could use a friend. Christian, too."

"Why?" I blurt out. "What's wrong with Christian?"

She sighs and then takes a pull on her cigarette. "Nothing, really. Let's just say he can be stubborn."

And then my thoughts of Christian are eclipsed by what she said about me, about my needing a friend, too, and it's true. So true, but still I find myself asking, "What's wrong with me?"

She shakes her head. It's such a Mom thing to do. It says she's hurting for me, that she knows more than I realize.

"Nothing is wrong with you." Her voice cracks slightly. "You know, and I might be fully off base with anything I say, so if I am— Actually, no, I'm not. I'm a mama and we know everything." For a second, clouds cover her eyes. "I know it can be scary to move forward sometimes, *mija*. Leaving my husband? That was the scariest thing I'd ever done, but I knew I didn't belong with him. And I knew a lot of people weren't going to understand. Hell, I didn't even understand everything I was feeling, but I did it. Whatever it is you're working through, you can do it too, okay?"

For the first time, I think I really want to try.

Brenda pushes her cigarette into her soda can, and then back in her robe pocket it goes. "One last thing, *mija*. It was worth all the pain and anger. I'm not saying I don't have regrets, but I'm also saying it was worth it." She gives me a confident nod. "Now, I need to go hide my can and sneak back inside before Sally or Christian catches me." She walks back to the porch, climbs the stairs, and disappears.

I can't stop thinking about what Brenda said. Her

words float around in my head like little thought bubbles all through my shower, getting dressed, eating breakfast. What she did was huge. And if she could do it, maybe I can, too. I'm tired of not fighting for anything.

Of not living…

I'm not sure how much I can do, but I miss friends. I miss having someone to talk to, and if Christian is willing to look at me without those same condemning glasses everyone else wears, I'm going to hold on to that.

Brenda was right. I need a friend.

As I drive to school, I can't believe I'm going this crazy over something as simple as talking to Christian. But then, this is different. It isn't just talking to someone. It's me trying to move forward—whatever that really means.

. . .

I don't pay attention to anyone while I weave and dodge people in the hallways. Our school really needs an upgrade. We're still small, but the number of students continues to grow and the walls and classroom sizes don't.

While at my locker, I look around for my old friends, for Christian so I can try to talk to him. Of course, since I'm ready to actually do something, there's no one in sight.

By the time lunch rolls around, Brenda's words have been traveling the maze in my mind all day, pushing their way to the front. I'm doing this. I'm taking my life back.

I make a quick stop by my locker and grab my lunch, then head in the direction I know Christian and my old group will be. Nerves tickle my insides, but it's not just nerves. It's excitement, too. Eagerness because I set myself on a path, and I'm going to see my way through it.

Just then, they round the corner. Christian is in the middle of them, the two couples on either side and Ian on the very end, by Diana. My feet move quicker as I walk toward them. If I talk to Christian and start being friendlier—if they think I'm turning back into the old Brynn—will Diana and Ellie want to be friends again?

Ellie's eyes catch mine, and I swear I see something in them. Something that mirrors how I imagine I look at her, with sadness and nostalgia, but then she glances over at her boyfriend, like I'm not here.

I don't let it bother me because I'm trying to be friends with *Christian* right now. Trying to show him I appreciate him and that I'm sorry I can't get my crap together.

My eyes land on him.

His land back on me.

The group is almost right next to me by now, walking in the opposite direction. Once they're right across from me, I open my mouth to say hello. Christian nods at me as if to say hi but just keeps walking, still talking with my friends, passing me, like I don't matter at all.

. . .

I'm sitting on my porch swing when I hear a car pull in the driveway next door. I keep my back to the house, hoping if I do, they'll just disappear.

"*Hola*, Brynn!" Brenda calls from next door. It's not her fault her son is a jerk, so I figure I don't have an excuse not to reply to her.

"Hey." I glance over my shoulder and give her a quick wave. Christian is next to her, with what looks like a bag of groceries in his hand. I hear them talking but can't make out the words. I'm about to stand up and go inside when I hear someone jogging toward me.

"Mom wanted me to invite you to dinner. I'm pretty sure you're her new best friend." Crossing his arms, Christian leans against my house, like this is any other day. Maybe to him it is any day and maybe it should be to me, too, but I can't help it—I'm hurt. And I'm so tired of hurting, so tired of pain fighting to pull me under.

"No, thanks." I push to my feet and try to walk by him, but Christian reaches out and grabs my hand, stopping me.

"What's the problem?" He lets go and my hand drops back to my side, tingling and warm.

"Nothing. I thought… You know what? Never mind."

He reaches for me again, but I pull away this time. Christian is faster than me, though, and moves over so he's standing in my front door.

"Move," I tell him.

"No."

"Yes."

"Make me." His lips quirk up in a smile.

"Ugh! How are you like this? How do you let everything just roll off your shoulders? Why are you always happy?"

"Please, I'm not always happy. I think you got a little taste of that at the center a while back."

"Yeah, but it was one time. Once isn't a big deal. I had to work up the courage all day to try to talk to you. I know it's stupid. It's not like we haven't talked before, but this was *me* initiating it. Me risking myself, but you just kept walking."

Slowly, his lips move. He's not smiling any longer, the sides of his mouth tilted down. "What are you talking about?"

I throw up my arms. "Today! At lunch. I tried to say hi and you just kept walking like I wasn't even there. I mean, I know everyone else ignores me ever since Jason, but you..." And now I'm fighting myself not to turn away. I want nothing more than to lock myself in my house and never go out again.

"Jason, that's him, huh? I've heard stories about him."

"Yeah, it's him. He hurt me and I haven't been the same since, but I was trying. I tried today and you ignored me." I know I'm overreacting, but it's how I feel. I'm tired of holding my feelings in. If I wasn't, I know I never would have said any of this to Christian.

He sighs. "I might be good, but I'm not a mind reader. How in the hell was I supposed to know you were going to talk to me? Every time I try to talk to you in public, you run away. Last time we talked at school, you made it pretty damn obvious you wanted nothing to do with me there. I was just following your lead, Brynn."

And he's right. "I know, but today. I wanted to talk to you today."

"So that means I should automatically fall in line with what you want? I'm not trying to be a jerk here, but you're the one who's been hot and cold with me. I wasn't planning on chasing around after you, waiting for you to decide I'm worthy. I don't work that way. And I'm not perfect. I never could have known what you wanted today unless you told me."

Again, he's right. Why does this all have to be so hard? It should be better by now, shouldn't it? *I* should be better.

"I know…" I walk over and plop down on the porch swing. "I know," I say again, like they're the only words I can speak. "It's just…I'm all mixed up right now."

Christian mumbles, "Shit," under his breath before walking over and sitting beside me. We swing for a minute, no noise besides the creak of the chains and the occasional car purring by. I try to work through my thoughts so they make sense. I just swing, and sit, and be with him until I decide to just speak whatever comes out.

"I'm sorry. This isn't me. The bitchiness. I'm just—"

"All mixed up," he continues for me. My head whips to the side and he's smiling that Christian smile, and I return it.

"I'm not always happy, Bryntastic. I've dealt with shit, too. I just got to the point where I was over it. Tired of letting anger and pain run my life. I've seen what it can do, caring so much what other people think."

Because of what he went through with his sister.

Another eternity passes before I find the courage to speak again. I've already admitted a few things to Christian this afternoon that I never would have before. I decide here and now to keep going. Even if it's baby steps. "I need a friend. I think I want that to be you. Can we start over?" It makes sense, when I think about it. Trying to start over by regaining a piece of my past—my friendship with Christian.

More quiet. His breathing. My breathing. My heart slam-dancing in my chest. He's quiet for too long.

Finally he leans back, reaching into his pocket and pulling out a bag. "Gummy bear?" He holds it out to me and I take one. "There's the Brynn I remember."

I nudge him with my arm. For the first time in forever, I realize I have a friend. Maybe even three friends if I count Brenda and Emery.

"Thank you," I tell him.

"No problem," he says. "Jason—do you want to talk about him? Shit, I'm like one of the counselors. Pretend I sounded way cooler when I said that."

Christian is good at making me laugh, and this is no different. "Not yet. I'm trying, but I don't think I'm there yet."

Christian nods. "Gimme your phone."

I reach into my pocket and pull out my cell. He takes it from me and says, "I'll put my number in there so you'll have it if you ever want to use it."

He does, and I nudge him again, hoping he knows that's a thanks.

After he hands me back the cell, we keep swinging. Swinging and eating gummy bears.

Chapter Twenty-Four

Before

"Hey, Bryntastic." Christian smiles at me. We're all at the park after school. Christian showed up not long after Ellie and Diana disappeared somewhere. I'd stayed at the swings. I love the swings. The wind rushing by me is like freedom. The swings make me feel like I can fly.

"Hey," I reply.

"I like your hair. How it flies around when you're swinging." Christian looks down, and I see a smile making his cheeks move. I'm about two billion degrees. I probably look redder than my hair. Christian is so freaking cute, and he just told me he likes my hair.

"Red hair is lame," I say.

"Nah, it's unique." He sits on the swing next to me and starts pumping his legs. "Kind of like pottery. I don't know anyone else who does that."

"My mom helped me find it. It's my favorite thing in

the world to do. What's yours?"

Christian keeps swinging. A hundred years pass before he speaks again. "I haven't found it yet."

"You will." I pump my legs as hard as my eleven-year-old legs can.

"Yeah?"

"Absolutely. Everyone has one. My mom says."

Together we keep flying through the air. I see Christian pop a piece of candy into his mouth. I grin, thinking I suddenly like Dots a whole lot. "For now I'll say eating candy."

"That's not the same."

He ignores that. "You want one?"

"Sure." Butterflies suddenly start racing in my belly. Christian doesn't stop swinging, just holds out his hand. I almost stop because there's no way we can pass a piece of candy to each other while we're going like this. But then...I decide to just try.

I hold out my hand, too, and when we're both all the way forward, all the way to the sky, our hands touch, Christian passing the red Dot to me.

It's almost like we're holding hands, but of course it's only about one second, and then he's gone. Suddenly I'm flying higher than I ever have. I put the candy into my mouth. "Thanks."

"Any time, Bryntastic. What are friends for?"

Chapter Twenty-Five

Now

After I roll over in bed, I grab my cell phone from the table. Without letting myself think about it, I dial Christian.

"Hello?" His voice is scratchy from sleep.

"Bet you didn't know when you gave me your number that I'd use it in the middle of the night." My chest swells at the sound of my relaxed voice.

"Eh, I'm not worried about it. I'm learning you like to keep me on my toes."

I decide to pretend that's what's really going on here. "I used to love the swings," I blurt out.

Christian doesn't laugh or ask me where that came from. He just says, "I remember."

My mind wanders back to that day, with the Dots on the swings, and I wonder if Christian is thinking about the same thing. "I remember swinging with you. You gave me a Dot."

Christian chuckles. "I think I just wanted to hold your hand."

My heart jumps into my throat, but then Christian adds, "It was a big deal to hold a girl's hand back then."

"So all the girls had to watch out for you? Christian Medina, holding hands and breaking hearts?"

"Yeah, something like that."

From there we talk about a show he saw on TV and a class Brenda and Sally are taking. He doesn't ask why I called so late, even when I apologize for waking him up. Soon, I hear his guitar through the phone, and I ask him what songs he's playing. From there, our conversation switches to music.

There's not a moment I feel stupid for calling him in the middle night—only glad that I did.

. . .

I'm brushing my hair the next morning when there's a knock on my bedroom door. "Come in." I don't bother to turn, since I can see the door in the mirror. Dad comes inside with a frown on his face.

"The boy from next door is here. Christian? He wants to see if you need a ride to school." The tone of his voice, confusion mixed with something I don't understand, tells me he doesn't think this is a good idea. Dad never would have cared before if I got a ride to school with a boy. It puts a small dent in my new armor.

"Okay." I shrug. "He's just being nice."

Dad sighs, looking older than he should. "Brynn...I'm not sure." He shakes his head. "I just don't know."

Each of his words is like a little hammer, chipping away at me. This is a dad. *My* dad. He's not supposed to sound so unsure. He's supposed to know everything. He's supposed to trust me.

"You have your own car," he adds.

"I know." Which means I don't really need a ride, but something inside me wants one. Wants to sit in the car and talk with him the way I did last night.

I turn to face him. "He's just being nice. We're only friends." The words don't sound as foreign on my tongue as I imagined they would.

He shakes his head in a way that says, *I give up.* I wish he wouldn't give up on me so easily. Not like I don't want to ride to school with Christian, but I don't want it to be a big deal. Or maybe I want Dad to fight me on it, like it is one. For him to fight *for* me.

"Yeah, I guess," he says. "Just be careful, okay?"

"We're just friends, Dad," I reiterate.

"Okay. I'll see you after school." With that, he turns and walks away. Setting my brush down, I look in the mirror one more time. Take a couple deep breaths and then head for the living room. Dad is walking out the door, leaving Christian standing right beside it.

"Don't tell me you're one of those girls who takes three hours to get ready every day? If so, I might have to rethink this whole *carpool to save the universe* thing."

His words break the tension I didn't even know I felt.

"We're saving the universe?"

"Carpooling. You know, decrease the amount of smog and all that."

"What I meant is this is news to me." I walk farther into the room. This friendship thing is easier than I thought it would be. I wish I'd tried it earlier.

He actually rolls his eyes at me. "I'm ashamed of you, Bryntastic. Here I thought you cared about the environment."

"Whatever. You hardly seem like an environmentalist, but I'll play along. You know, for the universe and all."

"For the universe," he says and tosses a gummy bear at me. "We'll eat on it." I catch it and plop it into my mouth. "Oh, and you drive tomorrow."

I think I can handle that. I might even like it.

• • •

I feel like I'm in *Twilight*. Yes, the movie, the sparkling vampire. When Christian and I pull up at school together and get out of the car, people watch us. I admit it's not everyone. Christian isn't putting his arm around me and telling me we're going to hell, but it's still too similar for comfort. What was just an easy ride to school is now a million eyes on me. Looking...wondering.

Or maybe I'm just being paranoid.

"People are—" I cut myself off because I almost just became Bella. "Are we interesting or something?"

"What are you talking about?" Christian swings his

backpack on his shoulder.

"People are looking at us."

"Maybe it's because we're hot." I whip my head toward him. "What?" he asks all innocently. "We are. But I think you're trippin' out. No one gives a shit what we're doing, which is just walking into the school, by the way."

It sounds so simple when he says it. Everything is so easy for him. He doesn't get it, but then I remember what he said—what his mom said—and I remind myself things aren't always easier for him. He just deals with it differently.

We separate when we get inside the building. The morning goes by just the same as every morning does.

I'm at my locker at lunchtime when something pushes into the back of my knees, making them buckle slightly. "Wha'cha doing, Bryntastic?" Christian asks.

Butterflies dance in my belly, making me wonder how and when I can get him back. "Since it's lunchtime, I'm thinking about eating. I don't know, it's a tough call."

"Wow. She has a sense of humor? I never would have known." He winks. "Where are you eating?"

I shrug. "I don't know."

The halls are starting to clear out by now, people either flooding the cafeteria or the quad for the forty-five minutes of freedom. Christian slides down the lockers and sits on the floor by my feet. For the first time, I notice he has his guitar with him. "I feel like playing. Let's eat here."

He crosses his legs, his fingers lost on the strings in no time, leaving me feeling silly just standing there, so I grab my lunch bag, close my locker, and sit next to him.

He plays more.

And I eat.

Another song.

I grab my chips.

He sticks his hand in my bag and then pops a chip into his mouth.

"Help yourself."

Christian smirks. "I did. Plus, I share my gummy bears, you can share your chips."

Then he's lost in another song.

I down my soda. For some reason, my heart is beating a little too fast.

But it's easy and natural, almost like being by myself, but not lonely. It's amazing how much more alone you can feel without someone sitting beside you. Just feeling the heat of another person's body and hearing his breathing and knowing he's completely comfortable with you. That he's not questioning you, or looking inside you to try to find answers you're afraid to give.

In a way, it's freeing.

"You're thinking hard over there," Christian says.

"Just listening to you play." I glance over at him.

"Well, it's because of you I even play the guitar."

My heart jumps. "What? How is that?"

"When we moved, things weren't easy for a while." I realize he doesn't know what his mom told me. Christian continues before I decide if I should bring it up or not. "That's when I started getting pissed about stuff. When Mom made me talk to a counselor about it, it helped, but not completely. I don't know what made me think about it, but I remembered you with your pottery. I decided I needed to find something that was mine. So yeah, when I'm famous one day, you'll be able to say Christian Medina plays the guitar because of me." He grabs another one of my chips and pops it into his mouth.

Words get trapped in my throat. My body feels all jittery. "Really? Because of me?"

"Yep."

He didn't have to tell me that. It makes me want to give him a truth, too. I feel like I owe him one. "I know you've heard rumors about what happened to me... About what I did."

"I told you I don't listen to that stuff. I don't know the story until I hear it from you. My mom taught me that."

"Still, you've heard it and I know what everyone thinks... And I didn't... Lie, I mean. I know people wonder if I knew about Jason or if I lied about my age, and I didn't. I usually don't bother denying it, since I know people won't believe it anyway." A weight lifts off my chest with the admission. I didn't know who Jason was. I never would have lied about my age. It's something I should have admitted sooner. Should have made sure everyone knew, instead of hoping it would just go away.

I consider telling him about Jason talking to me at the store, about the phone call, but decide against it. Baby steps.

"I believe you. They taught me that in counseling. To trust people unless they give you a reason not to."

My arms itch to reach out and hug him. "Thanks."

Before he can reply, the bell rings. Lunch is over, plumes of students filling the halls again. Christian stands and holds out his hand to help me up. I take it and he smiles. "Thanks for eating with me today. See ya last period."

And then he's gone.

• • •

After school, I grab what I need from my locker and head toward Christian's car. My old friends are out there, talking, their cars parked next to one another—next to Christian's. Another one of my inner demons sprouts up. Like that game kids play where you hit the mole with the mallet, there's always more cropping up.

They're talking to Christian through his window and he's laughing at something. A week ago I probably would have waited to go out. I'm tired of being afraid, though, so I put one foot in front of the other and keep going.

"Hey, slow ass," Christian teases when I get in the car.

"Hey." I pull my backpack to my lap. Ellie wraps her arms around her boyfriend's waist and looks over at me. For a second, I think I see the flash of a smile, but it's gone too quickly for me to know for sure.

"I gotta go. Robin's waiting for me," Ian says.

"We're out of here, too," Kevin adds. "Later, Christian. Later, Brynn." Ian looks at him, his jaw tight, and Kevin just shrugs.

"You ready to get out of here, Bryntastic?" Christian

asks while everyone is still at the window. I give him a nod, he starts his car, and we pull away. "Want to tell me why things are so weird with you guys?"

Without thinking, I reach over and grab a few gummy bears from the bag in between us. "No." I feel bad for my reply, but it's true. I don't want to tell him. I don't want to talk about any of it with anyone.

"I'm crushed. I thought we were friends? I give you my gummy bears. Drive you to school, and this is the thanks I get?" I look over at him, surprised, and then his eyes find mine. "Relax—I'm giving you shit. Kind of…"

Something about the way he says it—not probing, not questioning, just curious—makes me open my mouth and speak. "It has to do with what I told you at lunch. They think I lied to them. That's what Diana and Ellie say. We were close. I didn't lie, but I…I guess I wasn't completely honest, either. Plus, I sort of pushed them away when Mom died." Still, I wish for the benefit of the doubt. Wish that they would believe me, or at least forgive me. *Have I asked?*

"Girls are seriously screwed up."

"What?"

"I'm not trying to be a jerk, but it's true. So you lied—"

"I didn't!"

He shrugs and grabs a bear. "Who cares? Even if you did, why do they drag it on forever? Why does everything have to be such a big deal? Seriously, get over it already. No offense, but girls are your own worst enemies. You don't even have to worry about guys screwing you over because you do it to each other."

It's not something I haven't thought before, but it also annoys me, too. It's one thing for a girl to think that, but different when it's a guy. "That's totally sexist."

"No it's not. I'm serious. I can't tell you how much I hear in the hallways at school. Someone's always talking shit about someone else. 'Don't tell so and so I said this, but...' Talking about what their best friend is wearing or whatever, and then they're all smiling and hugging two minutes later. That's the kind of stuff my sister used to deal with, except they said a lot to her face. I don't get it. If Todd lied to me about something, I'd tell him he's a douche and get over it, punch him in the nose and get over it, or I wouldn't care and I'd get over it. I can promise you I wouldn't be whispering in the hallway and shooting daggers out of my eyes and making other people's lives hell."

Words won't find their way into my mouth. This is the most worked up I've seen Christian except for when he got angry at the center. There's something in his eyes, something a little harder—more serious than I usually see from him.

I wait for him to continue but he doesn't. Christian keeps his eyes on the road, his jaw locked.

"You okay?" I ask.

"Not right now, Brynn."

I turn my eyes to face forward, quiet for the rest of the ride. Questions simmer inside me but never boil over. The air in the car is thick the rest of the way home. Christian doesn't say a word and I don't either. It's not until we pull into his driveway that he looks my way. "I didn't mean to go all postal."

My shoulders lift in a shrug. "All you did was pout. You're forgiven for that."

"What? I didn't *pout.*"

Smiling at him, I reply, "Yeah, you kind of did. But I've pouted before, too, so we'll forget it ever happened."

"It just pisses me off." Christian sighs. "My family went through a lot. Especially my sister. I don't get why people are such assholes."

"At least you said *people* this time and not *girls*."

"No, not just girls, but you have to admit, *chica,* girls are *loco.*"

I open my mouth, and laugh so hard I can't get any words out. So I nod my head, hoping he knows I agree.

"What are you gonna do today?" Christian asks when we finally stop laughing.

"Ugh. I have so much homework."

"Yeah, me too, so I'll just pretend I don't have any."

"What? Oh my God. You can't do that."

Christian grins and I wonder if anyone in the world does it as much as he does. Just a few minutes ago he was angry, but he managed to work himself through it so quickly. "Actually, I can. It's pretty easy. You can try it, too, if you want. Hell, even leave your backpack in my car. Out of sight, out of mind."

I look at him, trying to figure out if he's joking or not, but I can't tell. I realize I kind of want him to be leaning toward not. The thought of going inside and opening my books and working alone puts a weight in my gut. Today I've felt almost like the old me, and I don't want to let that go.

"What are you going to do?" I ask, trying to sound much more relaxed than I feel. It's such a simple question, but it's also putting myself out there.

"I have to grab some food to bring down to the center for Mom."

"Do you like going?"

He shrugs. "Sometimes. I used to hate it when I first started talking to a counselor in our old town. Now it's okay most of the time. It helped. There are days I don't feel like it, though. I know you saw me there."

My eyes dart to my lap. "I was a bitch to you that day."

He huffs. "It wasn't your best day. That wasn't all it was, though. Sometimes we just have bad days, Bryntastic. It goes with the territory of living." He raises his eyebrows. "I read that in a book, too."

I swat his arm. "You are so crazy." Pause and then go with my gut. "Are you sure you don't mind if I go with you?"

"I don't know… Not sure if I want to be seen with ya."

"You suck." I cross my arms and pretend to pout before I realize what I'm doing. That I'm teasing him the way I would have before.

"Plus, my mom would kick my ass if I told you no."

"That's because she's smart."

"And you're smiling," he says before he gets out of the car, without giving me a chance to reply. I'm happy for it. Glad I don't have to make excuses or feel bad or stress about having fun. For the first time in a long time, I just want to try to do it.

Chapter Twenty-Six

Now

It doesn't take long for Christian and me to grab the food and drive to the center. We go through the back and I help him carry everything inside. People hurry around, shouting orders and laughing and talking. It feels good to be a part of it. To help with whatever random reason they're using to throw another party.

It's cool that they plan so many get-togethers. It must help the people who have nowhere else to go. People like me, I guess.

Christian looks over at me and gives me a little head nod. My legs go weak. Catching my foot on something—I don't even know, my other foot, I guess—I almost trip.

"I don't remember you being this clumsy. You almost ran me over the first day I came back and now you're tripping all over the place," Christian teases.

I roll my eyes at him. "I'm not clumsy." And I'm

not, but it's pretty impossible not to trip when Christian Medina looks at you the way he just looked at me.

When he leans toward me, I freeze, unable to move. Warning bells go off inside me. He's getting close. Too close. I haven't had a boy close to me since Jason.

"Maybe I just have that effect on you," he whispers close to my ear.

I jerk back.

Christian's eyes crinkle. "I was just playin' around. I didn't mean anything."

Oh God, I freaked out and hadn't even realized it. I'm so tired of this. "I'm sorry. It's not you." I playfully return the nod he gave me. "Should we go to the main room?"

He shrugs, and I wonder if I've offended him. We walk through the kitchen and into the main hall. At the end of it is the front room where they hold all the major events. It's packed with a lot of the usual kids I see here and some new faces, too.

"Brynn! Christian!" Brenda's voice rises above the noise. She happily jogs over to us before pulling me into a hug. "Good to see you here, *mija.*"

"What about me? Is it good to see me here, too?" Christian asks.

"Of course it is. You know that."

With that, someone calls her name again and she's running away. "She loves this." Christian looks at her. "I think it's a little crazy, but different strokes, I guess."

We both watch his mother help one of the teen guys hang something, and then she's laughing with him. Her joy radiates all the way across the room. "It makes her feel good to help. Maybe like she can fix the past by making the present a better place."

Watching her, I think I might want that, too.

When Christian doesn't speak, I risk a glance at him. His jaw is set tight, his eyes still plastered on his mom. Ugh. I shouldn't have brought up their past.

"It's bullshit. It wasn't her fault."

I'm suddenly hoping Christian says more. Maybe if he talks, then I will. We can both unload our baggage together.

"What?" he asks. "You're staring at me."

He's right. I'm totally staring at him.

"Brynn!" Emery walks up to us. "Wow. Look at you, socializing and stuff. With someone other than me, that is. You brought your very own hottie." She looks at Christian, who seems to pull out of his trance. He looks at her like he thinks she might be a little crazy. Maybe he's right.

"What? He's not *my* hottie."

"But you admit I'm hot?" Christian asks.

My eyes go wide as I look back and forth between them. "What? That's not... I..." What the heck do I even say? Christian's hot. A girl would have to be blind not to see it, but I can't tell him that. Can't take that step that almost feels like...flirting. I also can't say no, either.

"I think she's going to self-combust," Emery says.

Christian takes me in with his too-blue eyes. "It's cool, Bryntastic. I think you're hot, too."

He turns and walks away, leaving me battling the war going on inside between the parts of me that should tell him never to say something like that again...and the part that likes it.

...

"So what's with you and the guy?" Emery asks as we take a seat in two of the chairs spread throughout the room. I'm not sure where Christian went, but I keep glancing around the room for him.

"Nothing. He's my neighbor." He's also the first boy I ever danced with. The first boy I ever thought I loved. Of course I know now that I didn't but at the time it had felt real.

"I wish my neighbor was that hot."

I whip my head toward her. "Don't you have a boyfriend?"

Her eyes dart around the room. "Shh! And no. I told you Max is my ex. You promised you wouldn't mention him."

"I'm sorry." I have no right to care if she thinks Christian is hot, anyway.

"It's okay." She's quiet for a minute, but I can feel her eyes on me. Feel them probing me for answers, and I'm not sure if I like it or if it makes me want to run again.

"Something happened, didn't it? With you and a guy."

Yes. Something did happen. My mom died and Dad got lost and I thought Jason loved me. I just wanted someone to love me again. "I don't want to talk about it."

"Whatevs. It's no big deal."

Earlier, I'd been looking for an opening with Christian, but here Emery is giving me one. As hard as it is, I know I need to take it. "I was pregnant, too... I lost my baby the day I found out everything my boyfriend ever told me was a lie."

Her eyes go wide. "Oh no. I'm so sorry." Absently she puts a hand on her stomach, as if to make sure her own baby is fine.

"I'm sorry about it all, too," I whisper. There's so much more I can say, but I don't try to make the words come. Not today.

"Thanks for telling me. You're actually pretty cool."

I wrinkle my nose. "Umm, thanks? I think."

We both giggle. She pulls up another chair and puts her feet on it like she did last time. Then, thankfully, she changes the subject. "I know. I'm probably milking it a little, but I swear, my feet do kill me."

"That's okay. You have a good excuse." All her clothes look new. She's wearing long sleeves and stretch pants under a skirt. "Where do you live?" I ask.

"A foster couple took me in. Can't have kids of their own. I don't get why that makes them want to deal with a pregnant teenager, but since I have nowhere else to go, it works. They eye me like a friggin' hawk, though. I guess they don't get that I can take care of myself."

She shouldn't want to take care of herself. I used to think the same thing. Not that my parents weren't there for me or anything, but I just sort of thought I had all the answers. If that were true, Jason wouldn't have gotten to me. "Will they get your baby?"

"What? No. That would just be creepy. I couldn't live with the person who'd soon be a mother to my daughter. It would be too hard."

My heart jumps at that. "It's a girl?"

"Yeah…" She almost sounds a little sad about that. "We just found out not too long ago."

The urge to take away some of her unexplained sadness rolls through me. "I was adopted. I got picked by the best mom in the world. My dad, too." Then it's like some of her sadness kind of leaks through to me. This ache fills the pit of my stomach for how much I miss my dad.

We live in the same house, but I miss him so much.

"Really?"

"Yeah."

"Good." She looks down at her stomach. "I want her to be happy, ya know? I know who she's going to and they seem like good people, but you just never know."

Without even thinking about it, I reach over and touch Emery's hand. "She'll be happy. I know it."

The words pulse through me. Ride on my heartbeats and swim through my veins. I want to be happy again, too.

"Thanks. I don't know what's wrong with me. I'm so much more emotional than I used to be," Emery replies.

Just then, Christian steps up beside us. "You ready to go, Bryntastic?"

I glance at Emery.

"See ya later," she says and then mouths, *So hot!*

Shaking my head, I say, "It's not like that." I stand up and again don't let myself hesitate before saying, "Maybe we can hang out sometime? Like…do something. I don't know what, but—"

"That'd be cool."

"Okay, what's your number?"

I gasp when Emery shoots out of her chair and hugs me. Her arms wrap around me so tightly, it's hard to breathe. It takes me a second, but then I hug her back. As we stand there, I realize she's not as strong as I thought. She needs people, craves love the same way I do. The way she hugs me shows that.

Once we unravel from each other, we exchange phone numbers. It's not until we get out the door that Christian says anything. "I see her now."

I stop and look at him. "Um, see who?"

"You. The girl I used to know."

Chapter Twenty -Seven

Now

For the next week, Christian and I rotate who drives to school each day. We eat lunch in the hallway together. I wonder if he'd rather be with everyone else, but he seems okay, sitting on the ground, eating gummy bears and playing his guitar.

In my car on Friday after school, Christian's in his own world in the passenger seat with his hood pulled over his head. I watch him pluck his jeans like they're the strings on his guitar. His eyes are closed as he leans his head against the seat. His lips move like he's singing a song. Little whispers come out of his mouth, but I can't understand what he's saying, so instead I watch his brown hair and see how it hangs around his face. I wonder what it would feel like between my fingers. What his little whispers would be like against my skin.

Emery was right. It's not like I haven't always known

it, but Christian is gorgeous.

Beeeep!

"Crap!" I jerk the wheel to the left, embarrassed that I swerved into the other lane while watching him. I have no business looking at Christian like that.

"Spacing out, huh?" He chuckles and I know he knows what I was doing.

"Whatever."

"We're back to that word again? I thought you could talk to me now, Bryntastic."

"I *am* talking. You're just trying to embarrass me, and I won't let you."

"You're hot when you're feisty." His voice is playful when he says it, but the words make me freeze again. *Don't do it, don't do it, don't do it.* I used to love to joke around. I can't let myself lose that part of me. So I make myself roll my eyes.

"Whatever," I say again with a smile.

He doesn't reply. In some ways, he's so wide open. Like he doesn't have a secret in the world and he will say anything. But in other ways, I'm not sure I ever really know what's going on inside him. He's good at staying quiet and losing himself in his head. He wasn't like that when we were younger. He was loud, always talking and screwing around.

I wonder if that changed because of everything with his parents. Because of things with his sister.

It's only a minute later that I pull into my driveway. Dad's car is in there, which surprises me. He's not usually back this early.

"We're home," I say before realizing it's stupid. Of course we're home. Christian lives here. I'm pretty sure he recognizes the place.

"That we are." He winks at me before getting out of the car. I take a deep breath and then do the same. My eyes dart to Dad's car next to mine in the driveway before I look at Christian. He's leaning with his arms on the top of my little Toyota.

"What are you doing tonight?" he asks.

I can't help but wonder why he wants to know. He hasn't asked me anything like this before. Does he want to take me on a date? The thought makes nausea and excitement strum through me at the same time. But then, one date will lead to two. That's when guys start wanting more.

But I have *plans*. I can't believe I almost forgot I'm going out with Emery. It's been so long since I had something to do.

"I thought maybe we could hang out. I could work on my music and you might be able to do your clay stuff, or something."

Oh. This has nothing to do with a date. Just the fact that he knows I'm all screwed up and can't do my pottery. "Pottery," I tell him.

Instead of replying, he says, "Hang out with me." There's a huskiness in his words that sends me back to my previous thoughts. Could Christian, the boy I crushed on all those years ago, like me now? I don't want it to happen. Can't let it. The only boys I've ever even kissed besides a stupid game of spin the bottle were Ian and Jason. Ian never really cared about me, and Jason just wanted to use me. He saw a girl he could take advantage of.

I will never be that girl again.

"I can't…"

"Brynn."

"I'm hanging out with Emery." It was the first day we could plan after talking at the center last week.

"Cool. That's good. She's cool, but I think she's a little *loco*, too. Not like Ellie and Diana, but really crazy in the head."

"Hey!" I wish for something to throw at him. "She is not. She's nice. She's my friend!"

The words just come out and I want to say them again. Because she is, I think. Emery is my friend. And I'm glad for it. Glad to have someone again whom I can call a friend.

Christian grins. "Would you defend me so strongly if someone called me crazy?"

Looking at him, I realize I would.

He's joking. I know it, but I can't stop myself from looking at him seriously and saying, "I would." The nod he gives me says he knows what I mean. That he's my friend, too.

"That's what I like to hear."

I freeze when Christian's hand reaches up and he cups my cheek. Briefly, I close my eyes, just savoring the feel of his skin against mine. He's gentle. So, so gentle. I want to believe it's not an act.

"I should go."

Christian nods and drops his hand, and I walk away.

. . .

When I get inside, Dad's asleep on the couch. It's not something I've seen a lot. Dad's not the kind of guy for that. If he needs a nap, he goes to his room, and besides, he's almost never home on a workday like this.

Glancing at my phone, I see that I don't have much time before I need to meet Emery, so I head to my room to get ready. I change clothes before standing in front of my mirror to do my hair. As I brush through the red, I flash back to Dad on the couch. Wonder what he's doing there. Maybe he's sick? Has a headache… "Oh my God."

My brush hits the counter as I run down the stairs and into the living room. My heart beats like crazy as I go. My vision blurs with tears when I fall to the floor by him. "Daddy! Wake up. Please wake up!" My hands grab his shoulders and shake him. His eyes pop open, fear reflecting in them, and I bury my face in my hands and cry.

I'd fought with Mom. Didn't worry about her headache, and then she died. She looked so normal when I found her. Like she was sleeping. Like Dad.

"Brynn? Honey, what's wrong?" Dad jerks up into a sitting position.

"I thought you were dead." Nothing could have held back the words, even though I wish I could have. "I thought I was ignoring you while you were dying."

"Oh, *dolcezza*. No, baby girl. I'm okay. Just a little headache. It's not the same thing as Mom. I promise." He climbs to the floor and pulls me to him. I let him pet my hair the way Mom would have. Listen to him shush me and call me his sweetheart.

I don't know how long we sit like this. All I can think is I could have lost him. I could have stood in another room while he died just like Mom. "Are you sure you're okay?" he asks a few minutes later.

"Yeah." My tears are drying and I feel stupid for them and want to cling to him, too, but instead I pull away.

"My sinuses were bothering me, so I came home early from work. I didn't mean to scare you. Everything's okay, though. You know that, right? I won't leave you, Brynn."

I look down at him. See him as he still sits on the floor, and it's so unlike my dad, but somehow like him, too. When he wants to, he can say the right thing. It's just that he loved her so much, sometimes the right thing isn't as important as she was.

"Thank you. I feel stupid." I close my eyes, wishing I could take back the last few minutes.

"How about we order a pizza tonight?" Dad stands. "Maybe rent a movie or something?"

"I can't. I have plans." I look at him. *If you ask me to, I'll stay. I miss you.*

"You've been hanging out with that neighbor boy quite a lot, Brynn. I don't even know him. I'm not sure I like you hanging out with a boy I don't know." He crosses his arms. Not angrily, but contemplatively.

"What are you talking about? We ride back and forth to school together and that's all. We went to the center once, but *you're* the one who makes me go there, so that's not my fault."

Dad sighs. "I don't want to fight with you. I'm trying here. I just think after everything, I'd like to get to know the people you're hanging out with, that's all. I don't think there's anything wrong with that."

My face feels hot; a mixture of embarrassment and anger. "After everything? You mean after I seduced Jason, right?"

"I didn't say that. Stop putting words into my mouth, Brynn, or you won't be going anywhere with him tonight. I have a right to know who you're spending time with."

Maybe. But he also has the obligation to believe in me. It makes my chest ache that he doesn't. "Mom would have trusted me." The way his face pales, I know I just hurt him. But I'm hurt, too. "I'm not even going anywhere with Christian. I'm hanging out with Emery. She's a *girl* from the center *you* make me go to. I'll be back in a couple hours." On the way out the door, I grab my purse.

Dad doesn't try to stop me.

. . .

"The movie doesn't start for an hour. Do you mind if we get some food? Eating for two, remember?" Emery points down at her stomach and smiles as I approach her. We decided to meet here to visit first, but hadn't made specific plans on what we'd do. There are a few restaurants around us, so it makes sense to grab a bite.

Her smile does something to break through the wall

Dad built around me today. I almost texted her to cancel, but the second I saw her, I'm glad I came.

"Sure, we can eat. I'm hungry, too."

"Thank God. I get grumpy when I don't eat. You don't want to see me grumpy."

I laugh and we walk over to the little strip of restaurants. I expected today to be awkward, but it isn't. As we walk into the little pizza place, I realize it's the normality that makes it so perfect. It's just any other day. I'm a regular girl, eating with a friend.

"Glad we're eating, then. I can't imagine you grumpy."

We go to the counter and I order a Coke and a mini pepperoni pizza. Emery gets a root beer and just about everything in the diner on her pizza. We sit down in a booth and she says, "Excuse me," as her feet push up onto the bench seat next to me.

"Sorry. I have to put them up as much as possible."

"No worries," I tell her.

Emery takes a drink. "Ugh. I hate root beer."

"Why do you drink it?"

"Caffeine. It's not good for the baby and this is caffeine-free. And I hate water even more than root beer."

"Oh." I look at my drink. I hate root beer, too. I never even considered having to change what I drank just because I was pregnant.

"How do you hate water? I thought everyone liked it."

Emery rolls her eyes, but with a smile on her face. "No, silly girl. People drink water because you have to.

Even I do sometimes, but no one really *likes* it."

This time it's me rolling my eyes. "That's the most ridiculous thing I've ever heard. It doesn't even have a real flavor."

"Exactly," she retorts. "How can you really like something if it doesn't have a distinct taste that you enjoy?"

Okay, so maybe she has a small point there, but still. "I promise you, there are people who love water."

"Are not." Her voice is playful, and I can tell she's doing this just to have fun with me.

"Are, too." I play along with her game of pretending we're eight.

"Name one."

"My mother" shoots right out of my mouth, but then I add, "Well, she did. Obviously she can't love it anymore."

I wait to see if she's going to ask me what happened, but when she doesn't, I tell her anyway. "She died. She had an aneurysm."

"I'm sorry. That sucks."

"Yeah, it does." That about explains it perfectly.

"Oh, I forgot. I was bored the other day and drew this for you." Emery reaches into her pocket and pulls out a folded piece of paper.

My palms are sweaty as I grab it from her and open it.

"It's nothing," she says. "Just a doodle."

My eyes scan the page, taking it all in. It's a vase, with hands touching it, arms ending on the edge of the paper so you can't see who is touching it. My fingers yearn for pottery in my hand. My thumb brushes that paper as though I'm molding clay.

"It's lame," Emery whispers.

"No, it's not. It's awesome. Thank you." It's the nicest thing someone has done for me in forever.

"So what's up with you and the hottie?"

I manage to pull my eyes from the drawing. "Emery—"

"It's not a big deal, Brynn. Let's talk boys. Tell me about you and the hottie."

I sigh, knowing she won't change her mind on this. There's no question in my mind on who the hottie is. "Nothing. There's nothing going on with Christian and me. We're just friends."

"He looks at you like he wants to be more than a friends. Friendship with a guy like that almost feels like a waste."

I want to laugh at that thought because it is pretty funny, but I'm too distracted by what she said first. "Christian doesn't look at me like anything. He knows I don't want a boyfriend. Not that I think he would want to be mine, because I don't, but it wouldn't matter…boys suck."

The waiter sets each of our pizzas in front of us. Emery picks up a piece and immediately takes a bite. Then she taps my leg with her foot. Her eyes soften and not in the way that tells me she's feeling sorry for me, but one that makes me feel like she understands. "That's what girlfriends are for. To make you feel better."

"This is the first time I've gone out with a friend in a really long time."

"I guess that means we really should have fun, then," she says.

"Which is kind of a shame; I was really looking forward to being miserable." My words are meant as a joke, but they strike a chord of familiarity inside me. I've spent so much time being miserable lately. I'm determined not to let myself do that today. "Now the pressure is on. I've changed my mind and I'm expecting to have a good time."

She raises her glass and I clank it with mine.

"Most definitely," she says.

Even more so than before, I know it was the right decision to come.

Chapter Twenty-Eight

Now

We stay in the restaurant until about five minutes before our movie starts. And I laugh. A lot. Emery is funny and has an attitude and she's very open about her life. I don't ask her about Max, and she doesn't offer, but she tells me about her parents and how she never got along with them. How she never felt close to them and she thinks the pregnancy was just the excuse they were looking for to kick her out.

When I tell her I'm sorry, she shakes it off and moves straight into talking about her foster family. How they remind her of a perfect family and sometimes she thinks they might be cyborgs, but I think she likes them more than she wants to admit.

Before we know it, we're laughing again and talking as we make our way back to the movie theater. Emery orders popcorn and we go inside. The movie's a comedy and I find myself thinking a few times how much Mom would have liked it. Romantic comedies were her favorite, but basically anything that could make her laugh. She liked to laugh more than anyone I know. I try to remember what she sounded like, but it's almost as if it's further and further away. Soon, I wonder if the sound will be gone from my memory, leaving an open space from where it used to be.

When I hear a buzz from beside me, I look over to see Emery pull her cell out of her pocket. It's facing away from me as she looks at it, and then she turns it over in her hand again. When she glances at me, I try to look away, but I know it's ridiculous. She had to have seen me looking at her. "Rochelle, my foster parent," she whispers and I nod. It's not like it should be any of my business who texts her.

Her phone goes off two more times in the last twenty minutes of the movie. I feel the vibration each time and I know it's a silly thing to say, but it almost feels wrong. I'm about to tell her we can leave early if she needs to. I don't want to keep her from something important, but then the credits are rolling.

"You ready?" Emery stands.

"Sure."

Emery's quiet as we walk out to the parking lot. Her eyes dance around it.

"Where'd you park?" I ask her.

"I don't have a car. Rochelle is picking me up."

"Oh. I can drive you home!" I feel like an idiot for not even thinking to ask her if she had a car.

"That's okay. She's on her way already."

"I'll wait with you, then."

"It's cool. You can go."

"Okay. Thanks for hanging out. Maybe we can do it again sometime." I definitely want to.

"Absolutely. I would love that." Emery pulls me into a tight hug. "Thanks for coming. And for treating me normal. Most people just see the belly, ya know?"

"No problem." My car is parked at the far end of the lot. I'm all the way there before I realize I don't have my purse.

When I was young, I forgot my Minnie Mouse purse in the theater. Mom told me I should always keep it on my lap because it was too easy to forget it on the floor. I always kept my purse with me after that. Fear climbs through me. First, the sound of her laugh, and now, the purse. I'm forgetting her, forgetting the lessons she taught me.

As I race back toward the theater, it's Emery who pulls me out of my thoughts. I see her get into an old, beat-up car that's painted as many different colors as her fingernails. The person behind the wheel definitely isn't her foster mom. It's a guy with a shaved head who can't be much older than us. Ice slithers down my spine. She lied. The guy is Max, I know it.

But then, who am I to talk? I saw Jason and didn't tell anyone. When he called, I pretended it didn't happen. Emery has a right to see who she wants.

As I watch them pull away, I feel like I'm doing something wrong. That I'm somehow letting her down.

Chapter Twenty-Nine

Before

"Sorry, Sam's home today. I thought about rescheduling but I missed you. I figured we could hang out here for a few hours to have some time to ourselves." Jason kisses my forehead as we stand at the door to our hotel room.

"It's okay. This is kind of cool anyway."

"Wait till you see the room. I wanted something special for you." He swipes the card. When the green light flashes, Jason opens the door and steps out of the way so I can go in.

And it's gorgeous. There's a plush king-size bed in the middle of the room. On the other side, there's a hot tub by a huge window. The TV is mounted on the wall, smooth black accessories making the room look way more posh than anywhere I've ever stayed. "It's incredible."

"Thanks, Red."

I kick out of my shoes and Jason does the same. We sit in the middle of the bed and talk about our favorite movies and about pottery. He listens when I talk about Mom, and asks about school and says how he misses it, now that he's homeschooled.

After a while, Jason orders food and we continue to sit right there in the bed eating it. "How did you afford this, Jason? I feel bad. It had to have cost a lot."

"I have enough money. And hey, it's not like I have a whole bunch of other things to spend it on."

Which I get. Ian was the same way when he got his job. His parents paid for his car and gas so he always had cash.

Once we're done eating, Jason asks, "Do you wanna get in the hot tub?"

"I don't have a suit," I say but then add, "Though I guess I could go in my bra and panties. It's just like a bikini." Nerves tickle my insides but I ignore them. Girls do stuff like this all the time. Ellie, Diana, and I went in our bras and panties when we sneaked out to the lake with Ian, Todd, and Kevin one night. We just made the boys turn around and not look until we were in the water.

But then we're not at the lake, we're in a hotel room. It makes things more intimate. I love Jason and I definitely want to lose my virginity to him. Today might be the day, but then it might not, too. I'm just not totally sure.

"Absolutely. Hell, I've seen bra and panties that cover more than a swimsuit does. It's not a big deal."

Standing, I keep my eyes on Jason as he does the

same. He pulls off his shirt and drops it on the floor. My instinct is to turn away but again, he's my boyfriend. I shouldn't be embarrassed to see him with his shirt off. But then... I'm not embarrassed anymore. My eyes take in each of his muscles, before landing on his collarbone. I have no idea why I focus there but I do, before my vision travels up to his messy hair that looks like he's run his hands through it a million times.

My heart is beating a million miles an hour thinking of taking mine off in front of him, though. After taking a few deep breaths, I make myself do it. My cheeks are burning, but Jason's words help wipe it away when he says, "You're so beautiful, Red."

Ian never called me beautiful. "Thanks."

Jason takes off his pants and then walks over to the Jacuzzi in his boxers. Ignoring my threatening heart attack, I take mine off with shaky fingers. After laying them on the chair, I walk over to him.

"Go ahead and get in. I'll grab some towels and stuff."

I scramble into the water, hoping it somehow hides me and takes away some of the embarrassment. A minute later, Jason returns. He sets two towels beside us but climbs in with something in his hand.

"I wanna show you something." He scoots over beside me and shows me an iPod. On the screen it says, "Brynn's Playlist."

"I know it sounds cheesy, but these are the songs that remind me of you. I want to add them to your iPod, too."

The gesture makes my chest swell so much, I think it could burst. "It *is* cheesy...but sweet too." It's so funny how different situations are when you're in them. I would tease Ellie or Diana if they got all mushy over a playlist, but when it's the boy you love, the heart doesn't always dislike a little cheese. "Thank you. I love it."

Jason turns it on and sets it on the edge of the hot tub. We listen to my playlist, most of the songs about love, but some about sex. They play for at least an hour as we sit in the water and talk. This day has been perfect and Jason is perfect and I want to show him just how much he means to me. How much I love him.

"I'm ready," I whisper.

"What?" He rubs his thumb on my cheek.

"I know I've been scared but I love you and I'm ready… I wanna…you know…be with you."

This is the day I lose my virginity to Jason Richter.

Chapter Thirty

Now

Christian looks tired as he walks to my locker at lunch. He slides to the ground and when I sit next to him, he immediately picks up my lunch bag and starts to look inside.

I kind of love it. It's so…intimate in a way. Something you'd do with a person you feel completely comfortable with, and I like being that person to him. I think back to that dance in seventh grade. How much I thought I loved the boy who is now pulling Cool Ranch Doritos out of my bag, and I remember crying in the bathroom because of him. Because he made me so happy just by asking me to dance. I wonder if that's a good thing. That a boy could make me shed those kind of tears with something as small as a dance. I think it could be okay, as long as I didn't lose myself in him.

"What?" Christian asks as he eats one of my Doritos

before handing them to me.

I try not to blush. It's not like I'm going to remind him of that dance. Tell him he's the first boy I danced with, too, and that I thought I'd been in love with him. "Nothing. You look tired."

"I'm tired as hell." He leans back against the locker. His guitar case is next to him, but he doesn't pull it out. "Mom and Angelica were on the phone last night and they got in a fight. It's the first time she's heard from her in a while. She always gets all freaked out when they talk, like it's her fault Angelica couldn't deal with shit. "

"It's not always that easy—to just get over something, I mean."

"Maybe it should be," he tosses back at me. "I'm not trying to say I'm perfect, but when I needed to talk to someone, I did it. I found a way to get over it without pretending it's the end of the world."

His words, even though they aren't meant for me, are like a slap in the face. "So because you can do something, everyone should be able to? Are we all supposed to follow the Christian Medina handbook to 'getting over it'?" I turn away from him.

"Couldn't hurt."

"Whatever."

I try to stand but Christian grabs my wrist and mumbles "Shit" under his breath. "Let's just ignore that part of the conversation. It's been a bad day."

I sit back down but Christian doesn't let go of my wrist. His hand is gentle and warm, making shivers dance through me. This would really be easier if Christian

Medina wasn't so hot, so sweet and fun to be around.

I can't seem to turn my eyes away from him and he's not looking away from me, either. And then he's leaning forward and I don't know what to do. We definitely shouldn't be kissing, especially after we just got into an argument. Still, I don't turn away.

Closer…closer he gets and those shivers multiply and add some tingling, too. His lips are right there and if I don't turn away now—*bam!*

Christian and I both jerk back at the sound of someone slamming a locker. My heart is going a million miles an hour. *Talk about something! Change the subject!* "So…your mom?"

He clears his throat. "Yeah…my mom. I was up late because of her. Then Sally tried to cheer her up and that's definitely not something you want to hear through the walls—"

"Christian! Oh my God! Don't even talk about that!"

"Not like I want to." He grins at me, the tension between us already disappearing.

"Then *don't.*"

"Holy shit, you're blushing. *Dios,* I didn't even say anything."

"*Dios,*" I repeat, knowing it's "God." "You said enough."

He shakes his head and rolls his eyes. I don't know what I find so funny about that, but it makes me laugh. The more I do it, the more I want to keep it going until Christian joins me, too.

"*Loco.*" He points a finger at the side of his head and

moves it around in a circle, which only makes me laugh harder. It's so amazing, how wonderful it feels to let loose. I took it for granted before, and now I want to remember each and every laugh that ever comes out of my mouth.

"Looks like we missed a joke." Kevin's voice comes from next to us. My eyes dart up to see him, Todd, Ellie, Diana, and Ian standing there.

"Brynn's funny." Christian looks completely serious. Completely comfortable, like always. "What's up?"

"We gotta figure out that project, man. It's due next week and we haven't done shit on it," Kevin says.

"Sit down, then, we'll figure it out now." He looks over at me and I hate that he's checking to make sure I'm okay. I've known these people my whole life. I shouldn't let myself be freaked out because of them and I won't. Not anymore. I've actually started to be happy lately and I'm not going to let them change that.

Kevin sits down and Diana follows right behind him. Then Todd and Ellie and Ian last, just like I thought he would be.

Ellie and Diana start to talk to each other while Kevin and Christian discuss their English project. I listen to Kevin and Christian as they try to figure out what they want to write their discussion paper on.

"What about great literary loves?" It jumps out of my mouth. All the eyes in the circle shoot to me like they're shocked I spoke. It fuels me, makes me eager to prove I'm not that girl. The girl who can't just relax and be herself. Who can't really talk.

"That sounds more like a chick thing to me," Kevin

says and I roll my eyes at him.

"Then go at it from a different direction," I tell him. "Compare those characters who everyone thinks have the best love story and tear it apart. Romeo and Juliet? They fell in love just with one look? I'm sure you guys disagree with that."

I'm not sure if I do. I used to believe in love at first sight. That's what Mom had with Dad. It hadn't been one look that made me fall for Jason, but by the end of that one night, I thought he was special. Thought because he called me beautiful, it meant something.

"I like where you're going with that, Bryntastic."

"Why do you call her that?" Ian cuts in.

Christian doesn't miss a beat. "Why do you give a shit?"

Ian shakes his head but doesn't push it. Christian and Kevin both turn their attention back to me. Todd is kind of just hanging out not really paying attention to any of the rest of us. When I look at Ellie and Diana, both of them turn quickly, as though they weren't looking at me. Not as though they're angry, though…maybe curious?

"You going to tell us more, or what?" Christian asks.

Letting out a deep breath, I say, "Yeah, yeah, I am."

We spend the rest of lunch talking about Christian and Kevin's project. When the bell rings, Christian pushes to his feet and holds out his hand to help me stand up. It's so simple, but not something any boy besides Christian has done for me. That says something about the kind of guys I used to like. *No, not me*, I think. *Them.*

"Thanks for the help, Brynn," Kevin says before

grabbing Diana's hand and walking away. Before I know it, people are moving all around us, but Christian is the only one left from the circle of people who were just sitting on the floor.

"You gonna help us write it, too?" Christian winks. I shake my head but don't answer. All I can do is smile. Ellie and Diana might not have talked to me, but that's okay. I didn't let it stop me from joining in, and I want to bask in that for a little longer.

Chapter Thirty-One

Now

"How have things been going, Brynn?" Valerie asks as we sit in her office.

I'm picking at my jeans and not really looking at her, but I do answer truthfully. "Better."

"That's good. Before you would have told me everything's fine when we both knew it wasn't. Admitting things are better is not just being honest about them being bad before but it also shows your growth in moving away from keeping everything to yourself. I'm proud of you."

I look up at her, surprised she got all of that. I didn't mean for it to be a big thing. It was just how I felt. "You got all of that out of the word 'better'?"

She laughs. I'm pretty sure it's the first time I've seen her do it. "Yes, I did. We counselors are funny that way. We're always looking for hidden meanings. Do you think you can tell me how things are better?"

I stall for a minute, trying to decide what to say. Then I realize thinking about it just makes things worse. I'm always overthinking everything, and maybe I just need to open my mouth and speak. "Emery and I went to the movies. We've been texting, too."

"That's good. I see you guys hang out here a lot."

"I missed having a friend."

"I think she's a good one to have. Emery's a special girl. You two can be there for each other. Everyone needs someone to lean on. Anything else?" she asks.

"I don't know." I shrug. "I just feel more like me. Not perfect, but different than I did a few weeks ago. Christian and I are friends, too. I've also been talking to Brenda. And trying...just trying to be me."

Valerie leans forward. "No matter what happened, you've always been you. I'm glad you're finding comfort in your new friends, though. What about your dad? How are things at home?"

A pain pierces me at that. I miss my dad so much. He's there but...out of reach. Fear burns through me, making me scared I pushed him too far. That he really does wish they hadn't adopted me. "It's fine."

"Ah, there's that word again. Most of the time when people say they're fine, they're really not. I see your dad is off topic for now but it can't stay that way. You've made progress this week, so I'll let it slide."

We talk a little bit about pottery after that. I don't tell her I haven't made anything, but I do share how much I love it. Valerie seems honestly interested in it, which is kind of cool.

Our session is over before I know it, so I go find Emery. We sit in our favorite corner at the center, people doing their thing all around us; chatting, playing video games, pool, and other games. Brenda has fluttered through a few times. She's like this huge ball of energy, with a smile on her face.

My session with Valerie sticks in my mind. Her words about Emery specifically—about how we can be there for each other the way Diana, Ellie, and I used to be.

"You're quiet. What's up?" Emery asks.

I shrug, thinking about seeing her with Max and not sure if I should bring it up or not. But then, how many times had I wished someone would take the choice away from me and open the lines of communication? Maybe I need to do that here. "I saw Max at the movies...I know you said not to mention him, so I wasn't sure what was going on with you guys. Or why you lied about him picking you up."

Emery groans. "I know what I'm doing. I'm not stupid." The anger in her voice pricks at me.

"I didn't say you were. I don't even know what happened," I snap back.

She shakes her head before burying her face in her hands. It doesn't seem like something Emery would do. "Ugh. I'm sorry," she says into her hands.

"What's the deal with him, Emery? Why did you tell me not to say anything about him?" *I have no right to harass her like this. I didn't tell about Jason.*

Instead of replying, she says, "He's the baby's dad.

He's eighteen and of course wants nothing to do with us. I thought maybe… Does it make me sound horrible that I thought maybe if I was having a boy it would change his mind?"

"I don't know," I tell her and it's true. Maybe that's why my mom got rid of me. Maybe it was because her boyfriend wanted a boy, so she gave me up.

"That's why I was kind of bummed when I found out she's a girl. That probably makes me the worst mom ever. Not that I'm going to be her mom."

My lies about Jason shove their way in. How I told my friends I was the one who didn't want them to meet him when it was really his choice. "It doesn't make you a bad anything. Sometimes we all do or think crazy things. Maybe it just makes us human."

She nods and mumbles a thank-you before continuing. "Anyway, we got into a fight one time and… he hurt me, but it wasn't really that big a deal. I egged him on. I was yelling at him and calling him names and he just snapped. That's why I'm not supposed to be around him—"

"Emery—"

"He won't *hurt* me again. And I wouldn't let him. I don't even really spend time with him. I just wanted to tell him about the baby. That's the only reason I got in touch with him the other day. He deserves to know that, right? I'm not sure why he showed up at the movies. It's not like I invited him."

I can tell I've pissed her off, but still, I say, "You were texting him."

"Wow. Thanks for keeping such close tabs on me, *Mom*."

Her words almost feel like a slap. "I just don't want anything to happen to you." *Because something happened to me. Jason didn't hit me, but he hurt my spirit. He didn't want me or our baby and he lied to me.*

Emery sighs and looks at me. "I know, and I'm sorry I freaked, okay? I promise I'm not doing anything stupid. I even told him at the movies that I don't want to see him again. I haven't texted him since. I'm not going to do something that will hurt the baby."

"Or you," I tell her.

"Or me." This makes her smile. "Now what about you? I just told you something huge, Brynn. Now it's your turn. This is a give-and-take friendship." She smiles. It's almost impossible to be in a bad mood around Emery.

This is my chance to get out the fact that I've seen Jason and for me to make a vow that I won't see him again. "The guy who was the father of my baby... I'm not supposed to see him, either. But I have. Only once and it was an accident, but I also talked to him. And he called me once, too. If my dad found out, he'd freak." He'd more than freak. He'd want to go to the police or something.

Her eyes stretch to the size of quarters and then turn accusatory. "So you're doing the same thing I did?"

"No." I shake my head. "Jason never hurt me like that and I would never leave with him. I don't even *want* to see him again. If my dad found out, he'd lose it."

"He never hurt you?" The way her eyes dart to the ground makes it seem like she's almost wishing he had.

Not that I believe Emery wants me hurt, but maybe she doesn't want to be alone.

"Not physically, but he did in every other way." The urge to give her something else hits me. To show her she's not the only one who can make a mistake. "And I let him get away with it. Let him manipulate me—and I guess I still am."

She doesn't ask me anything after that. I jump a little when she reaches over and grabs my hand. We sit like that for what seems like hours, but I know it can't be. It just feels good to have her support. To know she's there. When it's time to leave, Emery looks over at me. "About Max...I promise I'm not going to see him again. You really won't say anything, will you?"

"Let's make a pact," I say. "We both promise not to see our exes again, and if they try to see us, we'll tell someone else. We need to prove to them they can't take advantage of us anymore." The words fill me up like nothing has in a long time. I'm going to do this, and I will do it with my friend Emery.

She nods. "Let's do it."

"Promise?"

"Trust me."

And I do. I wanted people to automatically believe in me when it came to Jason, so I'm going to do the same for Emery.

• • •

"I'm thinking we should make a trip into your pottery room today," Christian tells me as he drives us home from school the next day.

"I don't feel like it." The words come out of my mouth before I think about them.

"Liar."

"I'm sorry. I didn't realize you were me." I cross my arms.

Christian laughs. *Laughs.* "I'm not. I've just learned that when you hold shit back, things always end up more screwed than they were before. You want it, Brynn. If you didn't, I wouldn't have seen you sneaking out to your room so much. What's the deal?" He turns into his driveway.

"Why do you care?" I snap and then feel like a jerk. "I'm sorry. It's just…hard."

"Welcome to the real world. We all have problems."

His candor always shocks me. My feelings about it are a mixture of love and hate—there's a part of me who likes that he pushes me. That he doesn't tiptoe around or ignore me. But the other—well, the other hates it because like everything else, it's *hard.* Like oil and water trying to blend together, I never know how to feel when Christian says things like that.

"I was doing it. Making something. In my pottery room. When she died." My sentences are clipped, but they still come out. That's what matters: that I opened my mouth and pushed the words out. That I want Christian to know.

"Shit. I'm sorry. But I think…" He pauses and reaches

over to grab my hand. "You still need to get it back. It's still yours. Don't you want it? That thing that no one can take away from you?"

I do. I just don't know if I can reach out and grab it. And as I look at him, in those blue, blue eyes that seem to go on forever, I wonder what someone took from him.

"What did you lose?" I ask.

Christian shakes his head. "It's not really a big deal. We'll talk about it later. Right now I just want to play my guitar and see you make something."

I sigh and look down to realize we're still holding hands. To see his darker skin contrast against my pale white. It makes me sound ridiculous, but I've only held hands with three boys in my life: Ian, Jason, and now Christian. I know it's different with Christian and me, because with him, I feel his support. The way he squeezes and the texture of his skin feels different. The warmth in his body. It's not about hooking up or walking down the hall with a girl in your arms. It's about comfort. And it feels good to have someone comfort you. To not always have to do it for yourself.

"Come on, *chica*. You want this. I know you do. Let me play for you. Let me watch you create something."

Those words pump me up. They give me a voice when I want to keep quiet. "I'll try," I tell him.

His smile skates over me. I feel it warm me even though my eyes are still on our hands.

. . .

"I can't believe my music isn't inspiring you. Guys who play guitar are supposed to be hot, right? I know I find hotness inspiring."

I shoot Christian an annoyed look, although it's hard to hold back my grin. He has the ability to make the corners of my mouth turn up when I least expect it. Whether I want them to or not. Though why would anyone not want to smile? That's what Mom would say. "No talking about hotness."

"Because you think I'm hot?"

Obviously. "Because I said so."

"Whatever. We always have to play by your rules," he says teasingly. And then he looks down again. His hair falls and I find myself wanting to touch it. Fight to hold back the thought that I shouldn't want to because it feels good to want something normal. To try to pretend I'm like every other girl I know.

I watch as Christian's fingers pluck the chords. As they move along each string, making a melody I've never heard before. It's not someone else's song. It's Christian's.

My eyes don't leave him as I see his lips start to move. No sound comes out, but after a few seconds, I hear his voice. His words as he sings about overcoming obstacles in your life.

Slowly, his head tilts up. He doesn't stop playing, but the words change and instead of his song, he sings to me, to stop watching him and start working. Shaking my head, I can't help but chuckle as Christian continues with his song and I let my hands move through the clay. I wet them and again savor the feel of clay sliding through my fingers. Know that all I have to do is shape it. Move my fingers and create something, to claim that lost part of myself.

I close my eyes and just let myself feel. Feel and listen. Mom would have loved Christian's music. I try to move my hands, begging myself, *Make her happy, create something. I know her and know she would want me to still have this. Show Jason he didn't win. That you're worth more than he thought you were.*

But who am I really? Even though I want to go back to who I was because it was so much easier, I don't want to be that girl because that girl let Jason take advantage of her. She wasn't strong.

"I can't." I push away from my pottery wheel.

I expect Christian to argue with me. To look at me like he's disappointed because I know he is. He doesn't get it. He's able to just *move on,* but all my roadblocks keep stopping me.

"Come here." He nods toward the spot next to him on the small couch. It makes my heart speed up, but I try not to concentrate on that.

"I have to wash my hands." Walking over to the sink, I do just that. Dry them and then sit next to him. It's not a big deal. And I am determined not to make it into one.

"You ever play the guitar?" he asks, and I shake my head. Christian sets the guitar in my hands. "I'm trusting you with my baby."

"I have no idea what I'm doing."

"Then I guess it's good that I'm here."

"It is," I say. "I'm glad you're here. I appreciate

everything you do." It's important to me that he knows it. I don't think I've ever told him.

"It's the least I can do for the girl who taught me how to dance." His voice is soft, sweet.

"I didn't *teach* you how to dance."

"Maybe I practiced so I could dance with you."

My heart stops. Then jump-starts and speeds up. His words are exciting and scary and a million other things I can't express. Christian doesn't give me time to freak out, though. He doesn't give me time to reply, either.

"Here. Put your hands like this." He rearranges my fingers on the guitar.

He gets on the floor in front of me. "This is C." Christian moves my fingers to put the right pressure where it's needed and so they're in the right spots. "Strum here," he tells me, touching a finger. And I do. Christian teaches me a few notes. I almost drop the guitar once and he gasps, but it's playful. We fool around, the sounds I'm making nothing compared to the beautiful music that dances off his fingers, but it still feels good to try.

"If you can't get your pottery back, maybe you can have this," he says. The words are like little knives, stabbing into my soul. Not because I don't appreciate them, not because I wouldn't like to play the guitar. But I don't want to lose pottery. Not forever. I want it to be a part of me. It's a part of Mom and me, and my eyes sting when I think about never getting that back.

"I won't lose it forever. Pottery will always be mine."

Christian looks at me. I wait for a smart-aleck reply or a smile, but get neither. Just his blue eyes sucking me in like a whirlpool. "That's what I thought you would say. So you just have to keep fighting for it. Keep fighting to get it back. It's what *all* the books say." He grins, but I'm too entranced to do the same.

My eyes won't leave his and his mine. And he's hot. God, he's so hot, I just want to focus on his cuteness. I want that to be all that matters. When his hand comes up and cups my cheek, I gasp. He brushes his thumb under my eye and licks his lips and I'm frozen and on fire and close to having a heart attack and anxious, too.

There's a different air around us than there had been when he almost kissed me at school. Intimate and emotional and...*more.*

Slowly, he leans forward, and I know he's giving me time, and my heart is leaping and I want to feel his lips. This is Christian. The boy who asked me to dance. The boy I used to tell Mom I loved. The first person who has made me feel normal since everything happened.

But I'm so scared. Scared of messing it up. Scared he'll decide he doesn't want me. Scared of losing him. Of getting hurt.

He gets closer and I smell his sweet, sugary scent. See his mouth and wet lips and that hair I want to touch.

See the one person besides Emery I have. The one person I can't lose. "Wait," I say, and Christian stops moving. He's still close. So very, very close that his lips are only an inch away from mine. "I'm scared," I admit.

"I won't hurt you."

And I swear a part of me believes him. Maybe all of me. But how do I know if that's the right decision or not?

And kissing always leads to touching and I don't know if I can do more with a boy ever again.

He runs his hand down my face and touches my hair. I love that he's not nervous to do it the way I am with him, and I watch his fingers, brown against my red hair.

"Go out with me, Bryntastic. Let's go do something this weekend. Don't keep running. I won't even try to kiss you again unless you tell me to. Or I'll wait for you to do it. Just let go. Live."

His words are what I want. I want them so badly and they sound so perfect that it's hard not to just scream *Yes!* right now. "Why?" I ask him. "Why are you so nice to me?"

I love his strength. Love that he doesn't even hesitate before saying, "Because you were my first crush. Because I used to watch you follow your dreams with your pottery and listen to you laugh with your friends. You were happy, and I loved your smile. Because I had to work up the courage to ask you to dance and I did. Then we had to move and the one thing I missed was that smile. I watched my sister lose hers and watched my family fall apart and when I came back here? I wanted to see your smile again. Because you're beautiful when you smile and you've lost it, too. I want you to conquer this because what the hell is the purpose in it all, if the first girl I ever danced with loses her smile?"

I don't realize I'm crying until Christian wipes my tears. "You think I'm beautiful?" Mom called me beautiful. Dad called me beautiful. Jason did, too, but it had been a lie.

"Yeah, but it doesn't matter unless *you* think you are."

"Hey, Brynn. I was thinking—" Dad pushes open the door to my pottery room, and Christian jumps away from me. I see Dad's face twist. See the wheels running in his head, but all I can think of is what Christian said. Do I think I'm beautiful? Hell, what *is* beautiful? Not just looks, but love is beautiful, right? What Mom and Dad had. Pottery. Christian playing the guitar. Sally and Brenda. Smiles.

"What are you doing?" Dad asks.

Christian pushes to his feet and holds out his hand. Before he can introduce himself, I jump up and say, "Dad, this is Christian Medina. He's going to stay for dinner."

Chapter Thirty-Two

Now

We order pizza. I'm a little embarrassed about this because it feels so cliché. Girl and Dad living alone after Mom dies and no one cooks. They order pizza.

Christian rolls with the whole dinner thing the way he rolls with everything. He doesn't know why I asked him over. Dad does. I can see that he's glad to officially meet Christian so he can size him up, but he's also not happy about it. If I'm letting them get to know each other, it means I want to spend more time with him, and I don't think Dad wants me to spend time with a boy ever again.

For my sake or the guy's, I'm not sure.

We're sitting at the kitchen table. The pizza just arrived, and it feels so different from when I sat at the table with Brenda and Sally. It's much more strained, but Dad doesn't seem to notice. He doesn't notice much of anything because all he's doing is eating and staring at

Christian.

Me, I notice that and more. It's the first time we've had someone else at our dinner table in a long time. It's three again, only the other person isn't Mom, and it feels okay and horrible at the same time.

"You lived here when you were younger?" Dad asks Christian.

"Yeah, Dad. I told you that, remember?"

"It's cool, Bryntastic. I can talk," Christian says.

"I know you can talk. That's not what I meant."

He doesn't reply to that. Only looks at my dad. "Yeah. I was born here. I went to elementary school and part of middle school with Brynn. We moved during seventh grade."

Dad clears his throat. "That's nice. Where did you move?" They go on and on about things that don't matter. Things that don't really tell him anything about Christian and are just for looks.

No one is eating pizza anymore, but Dad's asking Christian about school and his favorite classes and about his mom.

"I live with her and her partner, Sally. You'll have to meet them sometime." The way Christian says it, I can tell it's a test. That's how he is. He wants to see how Dad will react to knowing his mom is a lesbian. In a way, I think Christian looks for injustice so he can try to set it right. Part of me knows that's what he's doing with me, and that makes my heart hurt. I don't want to be about fixing something for him or anyone else. *Then I need to learn to fix myself.*

At Christian's words, Dad looks up. I get it. It's a little

shocking, which it really shouldn't be. I just think it's not something someone expects to hear, but I'm proud of him when he smiles and says, "That would be great. I'd love to meet them. I feel bad that I haven't gone next door and introduced myself yet. I've seen them come and go."

That's the Dad I remember. The one who was strong and who always did what was right. But he doesn't seem as strong now, and I hate that. I need my old dad back.

"They'd like that. I'll tell them."

"Were you watching Brynn work? She's really amazing." Dad's face lights up. It's pride. I've wanted to see that look from him for so long, but it rips me apart. Because it's a lie. He has no idea I haven't made anything in months.

My eyes dart to Christian, silently begging him not to say anything. To keep my secret even though I know to him, it makes me weak. If he couldn't do something, he'd admit it.

"Yeah. Brynn is pretty awesome," is his reply. He doesn't say my pottery. He says me. My heart gives a little extra jump.

Christian pushes to his feet. "Thanks for having me for dinner, but I'd better go. My mom will be home in a little while and I have a few things I'm supposed to do for her."

Dad stands, so I follow after the two of them. "I'm sorry. I didn't mean to keep you," Dad tells him.

"It's no problem."

I feel Christian's eyes on me. Feel him telling me to say something about us going out sometime. I have no idea how he knows. Maybe it's just a dating thing, something girls should automatically do when a boy meets their parents.

You and Christian aren't going out. You're only friends.

"Dad?" I say.

"Yeah, *dolcezza*?"

"Christian asked me to hang out this weekend... just as friends. It's not like a *date* date or anything." *Obviously, since I almost lost it when he tried to kiss me.*

"Oh," is Dad's reply.

"There's a coffeehouse in Brighton. It's about an hour away, but it's pretty cool. They have open mic and some really good musicians play there." Christian smirks at me. "Since you like the guitar so much, I thought you might want to go."

I roll my eyes. "*I* like the guitar so much?"

"Yeah. You planned a fake attack so you could steal it, and today you tried to play it."

"What? A fake what?" Dad jumps in and Christian and I both laugh. Dad looks upset at first, but then he joins in, too. It's crazy because he has no idea why we're laughing, but he's right along with us. I think it might be the first time I've laughed with him since before Mom died. It makes me light, almost like I'm floating.

When the laughing dies down, Dad sighs. I see the war waging inside him, but finally he says, "Yeah. Of course you guys can hang out. You don't mind if I get your cell number from you, Christian?"

He shakes his head. "Absolutely not."

"Good." Dad nods. "That's good."

I can see that he's still nervous when I say, "I'm going to walk Christian out. I'll be right back."

When we get to the front door, I close it behind us. "Thanks for that. I really appreciate it."

"No problem. All I did was let you feed me pizza."

"I'm sorry about the freak-out...with the...you know." *Kiss! It's a kiss, Brynn. You can say it!*

"It wasn't a freak-out. All you did was say no."

In that moment, I wonder if there is another boy in the world as amazing as Christian Medina. Maybe it was being raised for so many years by two women and with only a sister. All I do know is he's incredible, and I wish I could be as together as he is.

"So, we're going out as friends, huh?"

I nod, embarrassed to look at him. "For now," I add at the last second, because if I can get my head straight—if I can mend my heart—I don't think there's another boy I'd rather date than Christian.

As Christian walks by me, his hand brushes mine slowly. And I let him. Savor him. I don't go back inside until his door closes.

When I do, Dad's sitting on the couch. The urge to just walk upstairs is there. Not that I want to, but it's just habit now. We don't spend time together like we used to, but I stop myself.

"Thanks, Dad. For understanding. For letting me hang out with Christian."

Tears pool in his eyes when he says, "I love you, Brynn. I know it doesn't seem like it, but I'm trying."

"I know," I tell him. And really, I do.

• • •

"Jason, you're going too fast. Please slow down."

"Come on, you trust me, baby, don't you? You know I love you. I won't let anything happen to you." He smiles at me and I feel it. Feel like he will protect me and like he loves me.

"I know. I love you, too."

"That's my girl." As soon as the words leave his mouth, he pushes harder on the gas pedal. The car goes faster and faster as we take turn after turn. Tires screech. Jason laughs as my right hand grips the door.

"Jason, I'm scared."

"I thought you trusted me. You said you trusted me. No one in my life trusts me. I thought you were different."

Another fast curve. "I am! I'm different. You know I believe in you."

"Prove it," he says as he goes faster. I bite my tongue to keep quiet. Not to ask him to slow down. The bitter taste of blood fills my mouth, but I tough it out. Tough it out for Jason.

He looks at me and smiles and that's when I feel the love from him. Then his door opens. He's laughing as he jumps out of the car and I slam into a tree.

Just like that, I'm awake. It's been so long since I had a dream like that. My heart races, and I feel like I could throw up.

Things with Jason had been bad, but not that bad. He didn't take my feelings into consideration. He used my need for acceptance against me. I see that now, but he wasn't the cruel, vicious man he is in my dreams.

But he could have been. One day, he could have

been, and I don't know that I would have tried to stop him. That's what scares me the most. I'm sure Max wasn't mean to Emery at first, either.

Pushing into my slippers, I grab my phone and go downstairs. It's silly and ridiculous. It's two in the morning, but I trust Brenda and know she won't mind my text.

I need to talk.

I'll be right there, mija.

"I'm sorry," I say as soon as she steps outside.

"No reason to be." Brenda grabs the chair off the porch and brings it to the fence. I do the same with one of ours and we stand there, on either side of the fence looking at each other.

"I had a dream...about Jason. He's my ex-boyfriend. He lied to me." My words are just the tip of the iceberg, and I have a feeling she knows that.

"I'm sorry. I know how hard that can be. How hard all relationships can be. Even for adults, we struggle with them. It's even tougher for people your age."

We're both quiet for a minute. I'm not surprised when she opens her mouth and says the real reason I called her out here tonight. The reason I'm scared. "You're going out with Christian today."

I nod. "I like him and I'm scared to. I don't want to like another boy ever again." Tears start their descent down my face, picking up speed and going faster and faster.

"Come here, *mija.*" She holds her arms out to me over the fence and I fall into them. Let her hug me the way Mom would have.

"I miss my mom so much," I say into Brenda's neck as I cry harder. She shushes me as she strokes my hair and hugs me. When she pulls away, I want to cry harder, but realize she's climbing over the fence. Christian's mother is climbing over my fence and then I *do* cry harder, happy tears mixed with sad ones because it makes my heart feel good to have her.

She wraps an arm around me and we walk. I'm crying and she's shushing. She leads me right into my house. Doesn't freak out that Dad might wonder what the heck she's doing here. All she's thinking about is me, and she sits on the couch and I lay my head in her lap and cry more. Cry for the Mom I miss. For the boy I hate. And for the boy next door. The first boy I danced with. The boy who called me beautiful. The one I'm scared to love.

When my eyes won't cry any more tears, I let them close. Brenda doesn't stop touching my hair. She doesn't get up to leave. Just lets me lie there.

"He wasn't always bad," I say, not sure why I feel the need to say anything good about Jason. It's true, though. If he had been horrible from the beginning, I probably never would have fallen for him.

"I'm sure he wasn't."

I pause before saying, "He picked me flowers sometimes. And he made me a playlist full of my favorite songs and another one of songs that reminded him of me." We laughed sometimes, too. I'll never know if any of those moments were genuine, but they'd felt that way to me.

"I miss my mom," I tell her again.

"I know you do, sweet girl."

Right before I fall asleep, I say, "You remind me of her." Then I let my world go black.

· · ·

"Brynn?" The sound of my dad's voice jerks me out of sleep. I'm still on the couch. Still with my head in Brenda's lap as she sleeps with her head against the back of the couch.

"Dad...I..." Freaked out. Lost it.

"*Hola.*" Brenda stirs. I sit up and she stands and holds out her hand. "I'm Brenda. Christian's mom. I wondered if we could have a moment alone in the kitchen."

I'm not even scared of what she'll say. I trust her. I know she'll say it better than I would.

Chapter Thirty-Three

Now

"You'll call me if anything goes wrong, right?"

"Yes, Dad," I tell him for the millionth time.

"If you don't want to go, you can change your mind."

"I know." How do I tell him I'm tired of changing my mind? That I *need* to find a way to do this. It's just Christian. It's just a coffeehouse. It's not a big deal.

"Brenda said... Is that the first dream about Jason that you've had, Brynn?" His voice is low.

I think about lying. Almost do, but stop myself. "No. But they've been less lately." Even though it's the truth, a bit of guilt still weighs me down, since it's not the whole truth. Dad's being cool. He's letting me go out with Christian. I don't want to jeopardize the progress we made by telling him about talking to Jason. I don't even want to think about how he would react.

He closes his eyes and I know it's because he's

hurting. "Why didn't you tell me?"

Because I can't. Because you don't believe me. You've never said you believe me. "It's…hard."

Tell me I can. Tell me you want me to. Tell me you believe me. That you just trust in me like she would have.

But he doesn't. And the doorbell rings. "I'll call you later, okay?" I tell him. It's silly that Christian insisted on coming over to get me, but kind of sweet, too.

Dad hugs me. "Have fun and be careful."

I tell him I will, and then I take a few deep breaths before going to see Christian.

. . .

"Gummy bear?" Christian asks as we drive down the freeway. Even though he's been back for months and I've seen him eat a hundred bags of them, it still sounds so odd.

"Sure." I smile at him and wonder if it's the first one I've given him since I've been in the car. It's shame if it is. I made a vow this morning. As I remembered all those tears I shed with Brenda and how I let her hold me, I promised myself I wouldn't ruin this day. That I'd have fun and nothing would change that. Not even Jason.

This day will be the best.

"How'd you find this place?" I ask as we drive.

"I've played there before. Went for coffee, saw the stage, and there you go."

"Are you playing today?" I ask.

He shrugs. "Nah. I wouldn't want to do that to you."

"Do what?"

"I know you just want to be friends. We're almost on a date. If I play for you in that kind of environment, you'll have no choice but to fall for me."

"Ha! Whatever!" I smack his arm. What he doesn't know is it would take less than that to make me fall for him.

The hour goes by quickly. We talk about classes, homework, parents, the upcoming dance at school. My heart trembles when that topic comes up because dances are so closely tied to Mom. How important they are to me, and embarrassingly, what is often expected after them. But the subject drops quickly and before I know it we're pulling into the parking lot of a cute little coffeehouse. It looks like it belongs in Seattle or New York. Like a place that's dark inside where people have poetry nights. I've never been somewhere like this. I feel jittery excitement at the thought of being here with Christian.

We head inside and I'm even more impressed. It's not like the chain coffee shops you go into. The furniture is old and mismatched and the little round tables slightly dinged. The stage is small. There's a patch on the curtain, but it doesn't look old. The place has charm. It definitely reminds me of somewhere Christian would spend time.

"I love it," I say.

"Yeah? I thought so. I have pretty good taste, ya know."

We go to the counter and I order a vanilla latte. Christian

gets a regular coffee. "Who comes to a coffeehouse and gets regular coffee?" I ask him.

His forehead crinkles as he looks at me. "I'm thinking a lot of people, Bryntastic."

"No one I know."

"You know me."

My stomach bubbles. "I do."

We get our drinks and sit at a small table in the corner. There's a guy on stage with his guitar on his knee, singing. He has a good voice, but not nearly as good as Christian's. We drink our coffees and listen to the music. After a few songs the guy leaves the stage and a girl with dreadlocks comes on, carrying a guitar and a harmonica.

She's incredible. I watch Christian lose himself in her as she plays and sings. He studies her. Watches her fingers move. I have a feeling if I were to talk to him, he wouldn't hear me. And that's okay. I like seeing him like this. When she takes a break, I tell him, "I used to get like that with my pottery, too. So totally lost in it that I didn't notice anything going on around me."

"Sorry. I didn't realize I was spacing out." Our table is next to a wall, and Christian leans against it. There aren't too many people here and they aren't paying any attention to us. Most of them have their eyes on the stage, waiting for the girl to play again.

"Music was big in helping me deal with shit. It's almost like it transports me to another world, ya know?" he says. His voice is low, so no one else hears, but loud enough for me.

"Yeah. I get it." And according to him, he found it

because of me.

"That's why I think you need to get pottery back."

"I know." I try to take a sip of my coffee and realize it's empty.

"I'll go get another one," he says, and before I can tell him he doesn't need to, Christian is on his way to the counter. The girl starts to play and sing again, this mellow, relaxing beat that makes me want to lose myself as though I'm the one playing.

A couple minutes later, he returns.

"Will you tell me about it? About Angelica?" I ask. Christian pauses with his coffee cup close to his mouth and I add, "You don't have to. I know I'm not one to talk. I haven't told you about anything."

"That's not true." He sets his cup down. "You told me you lost your mom while you were making pottery. That everyone thinks you lied but you didn't. Those are big things."

I nod, because they are.

Christian sighs, but then says, "My stuff isn't really a big deal. I mean, she was freaked about my parents getting divorced. It made it even harder on her because she didn't get that Mom was in love with Sally."

"What about you? Was it hard on you?"

Christian shrugs. "It was shocking as hell. I was confused, but I think being younger helped me. I was stoked as long as I still had my mom around and was able to get away with more because they didn't want to upset us."

I shake my head, but I'm smiling. "Boys."

"Whatever works." He looks at the girl singing for a minute and then back at me. "It was hard. Dad was pissed. Hurt. He kind of took it out on all of us and just dropped off the face of the earth for a while. As you know, we moved to deal with it. It was harder on Angelica, though. Like I said, girls are *loco* and they're hard as hell on each other. While the guys at the new school thought it was cool I had two moms, the girls gave her crap about it. They teased her about being a lesbian and made big deals about changing in front of her in gym. Shit like that."

"I bet that was tough," I whisper. My friends might not be friends with me anymore, but it's not like people are teasing me.

"But Angelica had us. Mom would have done anything for her. She would been at the school every day or taken her out. Whatever Angelica needed, but Angelica never said anything to Mom. I didn't get how serious it was at first. Didn't see it was a big deal, so when Angelica asked me not to say anything, I didn't."

Emery's words play in my mind.

"She lost weight and Mom noticed. She still said she was fine. I got pissed because my sister was so sad all the time. Mom was worried and I didn't get why Angelica couldn't just tell the people at school to fuck off, ya know?"

That sounds so much like him. Christian's one of the most caring people I know, but he doesn't always get it. Doesn't see that what's easy for him might not be easy for all of us.

"So that began the cycle. Angelica started to act out. I started to get in fights to…I don't know, pull the attention away from her or something. It's crazy how things catch on in school. The people who didn't give a shit about it before suddenly did because they saw it bothered her. They saw her as a weak link and it made everyone attack. I wasn't going to be that weak link, and I wanted to do anything to make it so Angelica didn't look like one, either."

"You love her."

"She's my sister." He takes another drink. "So Mom realized what was going on. The school was calling about my fighting all the time. It had been going on for a while. We moved again, and then Angelica just didn't want to be friends with anyone. She didn't want to get close and she started to get depressed. Mom had a really hard time. She just wanted to fix her. It was hard for her that she couldn't. Angelica just got more depressed and I got more pissed. Mom didn't want me to get as bad as Angelica so she stuck me in classes for my anger. The guitar was better for me than anything else.

"Next thing we knew, Dad was in the picture again and Angelica was going to live with him."

Wow...how sad for them all. And just because of who his mom loved.

Love is such a powerful thing. My whole life I've been looking for it. I felt it from my parents, talking about it with my mom. Thought I was in love with Christian and then Jason. And Brenda's loving Sally is what tore their family apart. "That breaks my heart. How sad for all of you."

He nods, but doesn't say anything else. We listen to

the music a little while longer and finish our drinks before he says, "You about ready to go?"

I nod and we get up to leave. We talk a little on the ride back to town, but not too much. Our earlier conversation changed the mood, and it's both good and bad. I'm glad Christian told me that part of him. I respect him for being able to do it. He's transparent in a way, like he walks around completely open and letting the whole world see inside him, while I'm completely closed off. Sealed up tight. When I think about what I see when I look inside Christian, I know I like it. He isn't perfect, but no one is.

"Can we not go home yet?" I ask him.

He looks over at me. "Definitely. What do you want to do?"

"Listen to you play." If it's like every other day I've gone anywhere with Christian, he has his guitar in his trunk. It's a part of him. His therapy and his passion. How cool that those things can be one and the same.

"I know the perfect place." He drives until we get to a park. It's not the kind kids play in, but a big, open space far enough from the main street that you can't see the traffic. In the center is a little white gazebo.

"It's chilly outside, but I have another jacket in the back if you want it."

I nod and Christian gets me the coat, which I put on over my sweater. He's wearing his typical nineties Christian fashion with a T-shirt and a long-sleeved shirt underneath it.

He grabs the guitar out of the trunk and then we head over to the gazebo.

"What do you want me to play?" he asks.

"Whatever you want."

So he does. He plays songs I don't know. Songs that are his and then a couple of other people's. Christian's voice is beautiful. It sings to my soul and makes my hands yearn to be covered in clay so I can match my passion with his. So I can lose myself the way he does.

With each song he plays, I think about the look in his eyes as he spoke about his family. The freedom in them, the honesty, and I want that feeling.

I want it more and more and more.

One of his songs ends and he opens his mouth to start another, but I know if I don't speak right now, if I don't open my mouth and say it, I never will. "I met Jason not long after my mom died."

Christian's eyes widen, but he doesn't speak. He sets his guitar next to us and looks at me.

"He told me I was beautiful. He called me *his beautiful* and it was so close to what Dad said about Mom that I thought it was destiny. How stupid is that?" I shrug. "I mean, there's more to it. I was lonely and missing Mom. I guess I thought he could fill something in me that I'd lost."

"You respect your parents. You love them. I think it's normal to try to get what they have."

"Not when you totally lose yourself in it."

Like he always does, Christian speaks the truth. "No, not then."

When I start to talk again, the words come out easier than I thought they would. Actually, it's like they're pushing their way out, tumbling and fighting one another to find their way out of my mouth. "He fed me lines and I fell for them. I can't believe I fell for them. He said he had a bad home life and wasn't supposed to date. We'd meet at what I thought was his brother's house, which I later found out was his. He wanted me to keep our relationship a secret and I did... Only Ian had started dating someone else and, I don't know, I didn't want to feel left out, I guess, so I told them about Jason, but said I didn't want anyone to meet him."

The words are like acid on my tongue. They make me feel stupid. So incredibly stupid. Was I really the kind of girl who would fall for that? Who felt left out because everyone was dating someone other than me so I had to brag about Jason? Had to say I didn't want anyone to meet him?

The thought makes me nauseous.

Am I any better now?

"I know you heard the rumors."

"Like I said, I don't give a shit about rumors. I want to hear it from you." And then he pulls out his gummy bears and I reach in the bag and grab one. It's silly. So silly, but it's comforting. Somehow, it helps.

"I...I got pregnant. I thought he loved me. He was the only boy I'd ever been with."

Christian's features visibly tighten.

"When I told him, he wanted me to get rid of it and I couldn't. There were never two people in the world who loved each other like Mom and Dad—and they tried for a baby forever, both before and after they adopted me.

How could I get rid of mine? I'm all for a girl's right to choose, but I wasn't choosing. *He* was. And that's when I found out who he really was. That he played for the Storm and he was twenty-three. But I didn't know. I swear I didn't know, Christian. Everyone thinks I did because I wouldn't let them meet him, but I didn't."

He curses and pulls me to him. I let him hug me, take comfort in his arms as I cry. I hate all the tears I've shed since Mom died. She was all about happy, and that's what she wanted for me. But the tears feel good right now, too. Almost cleansing, and I need to be cleansed of my past. Of Jason.

"He said he would tell everyone that I lied about my age. The crazy thing is, he didn't even have to—they all just assumed it because I'd kept the relationship secret. No one asked me if I was telling the truth. My lies about not wanting anyone to meet Jason came back to haunt me. It just made everyone think I *did* lie to Jason and that I knew."

Christian squeezes me tighter.

"Even my dad. He's never said it, but I know he wonders. How can he think I would do something like that?"

I feel Christian shake his head from where my face is buried against him.

"This is one of those times I'm going to sound sexist, but I don't think it's that, Bryntastic. Your dad's a guy. He feels like it was his job to protect you. I think he looks at you and thinks he failed."

His words give me a kind of comfort I never would have

expected. I don't want Dad to think he failed me, but I don't want him to doubt me, either.

"You think so?"

He nods.

"Is that how you feel? About your mom and Angelica?" The way his blue eyes darken is the only answer I need. "Christian, it wasn't your fault."

"I know that. I do. Sometimes it's just hard."

We sit there for a few minutes and I let him hold me. I know I should pull away, but I don't. I can't make myself and I don't want to. I'm comfortable close to him. I deserve to be comfortable. To hug a boy or go out on a date or whatever else I want.

"Hey...I have an idea," he says, breaking the silence. "It could maybe get us into a little trouble if we get caught, but I'm down if you are."

My reflex is to say no, but I don't. Because I don't *want* to. Without even asking Christian his idea, I agree. We drive to a store, where Christian buys three eighteen packs of eggs. I'm feeling a little confused, but I go with it. Call me crazy, but I'm pretty sure egging will be involved and though I'm not sure what brought that on, I'm trying hard to go with the flow here.

It's dark by now, but not too late. Christian drives, and I'm curious where we're going, but when he stops on the side of the road, I realize the answer is in front of me.

A billboard.

With Jason's face on it. The boy who overcame the hard past. The one who took so very many things away from me.

It's crazy because I can't even tell you if the sign is

new or not. It's one of those things people just don't pay attention to. I'm not into baseball. It's not something I would have looked for, and maybe Jason banked on that.

Anger pushes me to grab the eggs. I slam the car door behind me and storm closer to the sign. Christian's behind me, but I don't wait for him. In this moment I don't care about anything but taking this one little step toward claiming my life back from Jason.

I set the eggs down, open the first package, and throw one as hard as I can. It smacks Jason right in the forehead.

It fires me up in the best possible way. Like happy energy pumping through me. So amazingly wonderful that I actually start to shake. Adrenaline surges through me as I throw egg after egg at Jason. Some of them miss, but it's okay. In this, I'm beating him. I'm telling him how I feel.

I'm taking my life back.

There's no fear of getting into trouble. It would be worth it because tonight, I will win. Tonight, Jason's going down.

"Good shot," Christian says as I lob another one.

When I pick up the last egg from the carton, I look at it. Look at Jason. "I'm taking my life back," I tell him as I let the egg fly through the air toward his face. I know it's not that easy. I know I won't walk away from this night magically better, but my vow means something to me. It's me opening the door toward the maze of finding my way back to my life.

As soon as the egg crashes against Jason's face, I jump into Christian's arms. He catches me and hugs me. When

I start to laugh, he does, too. I feel so…free. I know I'm walking through that door and finding my way home again.

The laughter dies down and I look at him. We're close. So very close that all I would have to do is lean forward to kiss him. To take another step. He said he wouldn't try again and I know he won't. Christian is always honest, so if I ever plan to kiss him, I'll have to be the one to do it.

Yes, no, yes, no, yes, no.

My phone rings, making the decision for me. It's Dad. I know it is, because no one else calls me. The moment is broken.

"I…I better get that. My dad will freak out."

Christian nods and lets go of me. My feet hit the ground and I answer Dad's call. Tell him I'm on my way home now and then hang up.

We're walking back to the car in the dark when Christian stops me. "I'm sorry that happened to you. And thanks for telling me."

I feel like I'm glowing. Think about kissing him again, but settle on saying, "Thanks for today. And the eggs. Thanks for everything, Christian. I wouldn't be able to do any of this without you."

He smiles as we continue walking back to the car and mutters, "Yes, you would."

And I think maybe he could be right.

Chapter Thirty-Four

Now

It's a couple days before Christmas break. Things have been kind of busy. My "date" with Christian was right before Thanksgiving. Christian, Brenda, and Sally went to spend a week with Sally's family for the holiday, so I didn't see him the whole time.

But we texted.

I don't care that it's silly to be excited about something so small, but I am. God, Dad used to tease me so much for my crazy texting skills before everything happened. Mom did too. It feels like another step toward claiming my life back.

I haven't had any dreams about Jason. Things are still awkward and strained between Dad and me. I don't know how to cross that bridge, but I think we're getting better. We made Thanksgiving dinner together, which was a huge step for us. No sauce, but that's okay. We had a turkey, potatoes, and all the other trimmings, and it almost felt like it used to.

The only thing off is Emery. She hasn't been at the center as much. I tried to see if she wanted to hang out one time, but she said no. Which I guess shouldn't mean anything. It's not like she *has* to hang out with me; I just hoped she would want to. Hoped I didn't make her mad when I bugged her about Max, but I must have. It wasn't my business and I should have known that.

As I park my car at the center today, I'm determined to talk to her. To remind her that I trust her, the way no one trusted me. That I won't bug her about Max anymore. She said she wouldn't see him and she won't.

That is, until halfway between my car and the center, I see his multicolored vehicle off to the side of the lot. My heart begins racing as I keep walking.

She promised.

Not my business.

What if he hurts her?

What if someone had stopped Jason from hurting me?

I can't see him very well because he's leaned so low in the seat, his car almost hidden. On reflex, I jog the rest of the way to the center. Emery isn't in the main room. I keep checking, walking from room to room until I find her in the empty art room. She's sitting in a chair, her feet up on another one, with her back to the door.

"Emery?" I close the door.

"Hey," she replies.

"What are you doing?" I walk toward her. When I step up beside her, she looks at me. I gasp at the sight of her purpling eye.

"Oh! It's nothing. I ran into the corner of an open cabinet in the kitchen. Can you believe that? My foster mom felt so bad for leaving it open while we were cooking."

It sounds like the truth. I could see it happening. It *did* happen to Mom once. I was there. Dad was making sauce and left the cabinet open and she ran into it. He felt so bad and kissed it for her, telling her how sorry he was. How beautiful she was. His beautiful lady.

But there's a sinking feeling in my gut that doesn't feel right. It's off. If there's one thing Dad taught me, it was to trust my gut.

"You did that with your foster mom."

"That's what I just said, right?" She's getting irritated and part of me wants to shut up, but I keep thinking about that car in the parking lot.

"You're not seeing Max though, right? You said you weren't seeing him." There's accusation in my voice and I know how I'd act if I were her, so I'm not surprised when she rolls her eyes at me.

"Yes, *Mother*. I'm not seeing him. I'm smart enough to keep away from someone after he hurt me."

Though that's not true, is it? Not that she's not smart, but she's seen him since he hurt her before. She saw him at the movies and to tell him the baby was a girl and who knows when else. Unless she means since he hurt her again.

"Don't act like you're perfect. Remember, I know you saw Jason, too."

"But that wasn't my choice! I didn't *meet* him and I haven't seen him since then. Max is outside right now. What did he do to you?" I reach for her, worried for her. I can't take my focus off her black eye. He *hit* her. He had to have.

Emery jerks away. "He's here? You saw him?"

I nod, trying to see if she really knew or not. "Yeah. Just now."

"Did he say anything to you?"

I shake my head.

"What the hell is wrong with me?" Emery asks before covering her face with her hands. I don't think she's crying. At least she isn't doing it loudly enough for me to hear, but it doesn't stop my heart from breaking for her. For hurting and reaching out to her. Our situations may have been different, but I get it.

I kneel down beside her. "Are you okay?"

She pulls her hands away. "I don't know. I really don't know anymore."

I put my arm around her, but Emery pulls away. Pushes to her feet. "I don't need you to baby me, okay? I can handle this myself. I can handle Max."

The flip in her personality feels like a slap. Standing, I turn to face her. "He *hit* you, Emery."

"I know that. You think I don't know that? This is his fault. Not mine. Don't try to blame me."

I let her words run through my head. Repeat them. Dissect them. I don't want to blame her. This *is* his fault, I know that. "I wasn't trying to say it was your fault."

"Or maybe it is. I'm the one who gave him another

chance, right? I thought he loved me. He's the father of my baby, Brynn." She sits back down. "I just wanted someone to love me."

Her words sound eerily familiar. They could be mine. They *are* mine.

"He promised he wouldn't do it again. He's been so sweet. I thought he changed, but now I see it was a lie. It's always a lie. They're nice in the beginning, aren't they?"

If red wasn't my favorite color before, it definitely is now.

Red hair…red dress, and now red cheeks. I never knew blushing could be so damn sexy…

Ah. There it is. Love that blush.

My beautiful.

I love you.

I love you.

I love you.

All Jason's words in the beginning. All lies.

"Jason lied to me, too." My words are soft, weak.

"I'm so tired of it. Tired of being taken advantage of. I'm never going to trust anyone again, and I can promise you I'm not letting Max anywhere near me. God, what's wrong with me? I can't believe I let a guy hit me."

"What are you going to do?" I ask her.

Emery tosses her hands in the air. "What can I do? I'm just going to stay away from him. Seriously this time."

Her words make me pull back slightly. She's said this before. She's promised to stay away from him, yet she's sitting here with her eye angry and purple. Jason bruised my insides. Max is doing the same to her, both inside and out. "That's what you said last time, and now you're sitting here with a black eye. Even if you really do plan to stay away from him, he was *outside* today. That doesn't mean he'll stay away from you."

"What do you mean *if I really do plan to stay away*? I just said I would, didn't I?"

"You said that before, too!" My voice is too loud and I try to lower it. "I know it's hard—"

"Yeah, I know you do. When did you tell your dad about your ex's call? Or that you saw him?"

I close my eyes, knowing she has me there.

"That's what I thought."

"Emery…" I don't know what to say. "I just want to help. I'm worried about you."

She sighs and some of the anger seems to seep out of her. She stands. "I know I'm kind of being a bitch right now. I'm just… I have a lot on my mind. If you want to help, just be my friend. Trust me and be my friend and keep your promise not to tell. I can't depend on my parents or Max, so just let me be able to count on you."

She walks out. I fall into the chair she just left, totally lost on what to do.

• • •

My hands are shaking when I pull into the driveway at home. Instead of memories of Jason haunting me, I have pictures of Emery's eye. The knowledge that her ex has hit her and I know about it. I know and no one else does.

And I'll be betraying her trust if I tell anyone.

How am I supposed to handle that? What do I do? He can't hurt her if she doesn't see him. She said she won't see him again. And she's strong. I've seen that, so I should believe her. That's what friends do. My friends didn't believe me and I was telling the truth. I would hate to betray her trust if there's not any chance of her seeing him again.

He was outside today...

But she didn't know. She didn't want him there, which should count for something. All I wanted was for my friends to believe me. If I don't do the same for Emery, I'm hanging her out to dry.

My cell beeps, making me jump. "Oh my God. I'm losing it."

I pick it up to see a text from Christian.

Im now a stalker. Jumped your fence. In the pottery room.

My lips beg me to smile, but the nausea churning in my stomach makes it impossible. My fingers move to tell Christian I can't. That I need to be alone. But I feel this little pull to him, too. The urge to watch him play and share gummy bears with him. Spending time with him is starting to feel like my new normal, and though I want nothing more than to be excited about that, I can't fully muster it up right now.

I also can't tell him no.

Dropping my backpack inside the foyer, I go through the house and right out the back. When I open the door to the room, I see Christian sitting on the small couch with his guitar next to him.

"I thought you could try to make something again if you want. Or I could give you another lesson— Hey, what's wrong?" Christian pushes his hair behind his ear so it doesn't hang in his face.

I want to tell him. To tell someone. I don't know what to do.

"I…" Owe Emery. But do I owe her by telling or not? Right and wrong are all mixed up and blurred inside me.

"Sit down. We'll play. That always helps."

I sit next to him, so grateful I have someone here. That I have *him* here. I don't know if Emery is going to want anything to do with me after everything that's happened and that makes my chest ache.

"What's wrong?" Christian asks again. "And don't say nothing. You can say 'I don't want to tell you,' but I know it's something."

Leave it to him to cut right to it. "I got into a fight with Emery."

He nods but doesn't go any further. I wish he would. That he would just ask me or poke and prod until I let the words come out. Maybe it will be okay if someone forces me. Because I think I want to tell him, or I should tell someone.

"She…" I begin, but stop the words there. Emery is my friend and she asked me to trust her. I should, I think. All I wanted was for someone to trust me before. "Never mind."

He turns sideways on the couch so he's looking at me.

His guitar is in his lap and he's absently letting his fingers stroke the chords.

"You can tell me, you know?"

"It's not mine to tell."

Christian nods as if he understands before he starts playing again. It's a good twenty minutes before either of us speaks again.

"This probably isn't the best time to ask you this," he says, "but, hell, who knows. Maybe it is. I'm going to be gone most of Christmas break so I'm going to do this now."

Curiosity fights to be the primary emotion pushing to the surface. "What?"

There's no pause. No preparation. Christian just blurts out, "I want you to go to the dance with me."

I actually *feel* my face pale. My skin gets itchy. My mind rushes through all my memories. Memories of Mom smiling when she told me the story about her and Dad from their dance. About how she fell in love with him there. The way I felt with Christian at our dance in the seventh grade. How happy it made me, and how connected I felt to Mom and Dad's romance because of it. Dances are connected to so many happy memories for me.

Until the dance that caused my stupid fight with Mom.

That night was the beginning of *now*. The now that is nothing like before. That led me to Jason, who taught me the opposite of everything Mom thought love should be. Sometimes it's ugly and it hurts. Sometimes it's a lie.

Just like Max and Emery.

I look at Christian and everything inside me starts to break. To hurt and want and feel the need to run at the same time. I don't want him to be a lie. I don't want him to hurt me. Going to that dance gives him the chance to let me down, and I don't think I can handle that from him. To taint the happiness of what we shared at our first dance together.

I never expected Jason to hurt me. Emery never expected it from Max. That means Christian could do the same. People's kindness doesn't come with guarantees.

"Go to the dance with me, Bryntastic. I like you. I want…I don't know, more than what we are."

More. What kind of more? The kind Jason wanted? Diana and Ellie both planned to have sex with their boyfriends after a dance. It's just what people do. I can't give Christian that kind of more.

"You can do this," he says.

No I can't. I was mad at her over a stupid dress for a dance when she died.

His simple words knock me over the edge. Hurt me, though they don't have the right to. Because I thought he *wanted* to go to the dance with me. Not to *fix* me. "I'm not your sister."

His eyes narrow slightly as he looks at me. "I'm pretty sure I'm aware of that."

"Then why are you trying to fix me? Trying to save me won't change things with her." I push off the couch, Christian right behind me.

"First of all, you don't know what you're talking about.

Going to the dance has nothing to do with Angelica, and second, stop lying to yourself. It's not working on me. You know damn well this has nothing to do with my sister. You're just scared. God, Brynn, you're scared of *everything.*"

Whipping around, I let all my anger come out. "You know what? Screw you, Christian! We can't all be like you. I can't just push away the past, pretend it never happened and stroll through like nothing's a big deal the way you can!" I thought he understood. I thought he cared. My whole body aches, hurts from the inside out.

"What are you talking about? That's not what I mean."

"You might not have meant it, but that's what you do. You talk about what you read and what you think people should do as though you have all the answers. We can't all be as strong as you. We can't all just get over it."

"You think it was easy?" Christian raises his voice. "I had to work for it. I thought you had it in you to work, too."

It's always a lie. They're always nice in the beginning. Emery's words fuel my anger because they're true.

"By going to the dance with you? That's the answer? When you only want to save me."

Christian shakes his head and grabs his guitar off the couch. "If that's really how you see me, then I don't know what I was thinking wanting to go to the dance with you. *Dios.* I told you I had to work up the nerve to ask you to dance when we were kids. You were the one I missed when we left. I thought I saw something different in you.

Hell, I don't know what I thought, but obviously we've never been on the same page."

Christian pushes around me and opens the door. "I never wanted to fix you, Brynn. There's nothing to 'fix.' And it's not like I believed going to the dance with me would save you. But I thought you might want to. I thought you might be ready to fight for your life back. Even if it isn't with me."

Without another word—without even looking back at me—Christian walks through the door, closing it behind him.

For the second time today, I'm left stunned. Unsure of what happened, and unsure of where to go from here. Lost and alone, just like before.

Chapter Thirty-Five

Now

The next couple days before Christmas break are torture. They're even worse than those first days at school at the beginning of the year. Not because no one says hi to me—people do. Ellie and Diana still don't talk to me, but to everyone else, I'm old news. The whole situation is in the past. Something they're starting to forget, but I can't let myself enjoy it. I'm trapped in a bubble, alone where no one can reach me. That's exactly how I feel. I miss Christian. I miss his laugh and his jokes and his guitar and gummy bears.

I miss my friend.

And I also miss the feeling of his eyes on me. The bubble in my stomach and the warmth that spreads across my skin when he touches me. Which means I was falling for him. Falling for another boy when I swore I never would again. That knowledge should make me ecstatic that we're not talking, glad I dodged the bullet, because Emery was right—they are all nice in the beginning. But it doesn't. It leaves me feeling even more alone. Like the bubble got thicker, or maybe like it's made of some kind of bulletproof glass that protects me against feelings and friendship.

Why? Because it's safer to pull away.

But safer doesn't feel very good anymore.

Emery weighs on my mind. I sit in the center every day after school waiting for her to show up. Waiting for an answer to come to me about what to do. To tell or not to tell?

God, I miss Mom. She would know what to do. She would help Emery, but she's gone and I'm alone. Obviously I'm not good at fixing much of anything.

Maybe Dad could be here… Maybe Christian would have been, too…

Going to another dance is a betrayal to Mom, though.

I'm drowning in my loneliness again. In this dark room that I can't find my way out of, all the air getting sucked out around me.

Emery responds to my texts, but they're just short, clipped answers that she's fine. Spending time at home and hasn't felt like coming to the center. I have a feeling she means she hasn't felt like being around me. I'm the one who pushed her when for all these months, I haven't wanted anyone to push me.

Irony sucks.

• • •

"You were quiet at Nona's yesterday." It's the day after Christmas. We always spend Christmas with Dad's mom. We have for my whole life. We'll have sauce and she'll laugh her loud laugh and talk about the good old days growing up in New York.

I used to love it. Yesterday, I didn't let myself. Surprise, surprise. I'm seeing a pattern here. "Yeah."

"Brynn." Dad leans against the couch where I'm sitting, pretending to watch TV. "Did something happen? Christian hasn't been around."

It's strange hearing that come out of Dad's mouth. Before he didn't want Christian here, wanted me to avoid any guy as if they were the plague (or Jason), but now he's concerned because Christian *hasn't* been around? "They're gone for the holiday." Which means I don't even have Brenda—not that I'd feel right going to Christian's mom after everything.

"Before that..."

"It's fine."

"Are you sure? You can—you can talk to me, you know."

It's what I've wanted. What I've been begging for from him for so long, yet I can't make myself say it. Don't know what to even tell him. God, I'm tired of being so weak, but I have no idea how to change it. There should come a point where realizing something is the key— where it's all that matters and once you catch on to something, it all gets better. Instead I'm sitting here with this knowledge and can't force myself to figure out what to do about it. "I'm fine." I push to my feet.

"Brynn—"

"We have breaking news!" A reporter on the TV interrupts the show I wasn't really watching and catches my attention. "We're at the scene of a major accident that happened earlier today on Highway 301. Reports have come in that local baseball star Jason Richter was driving the vehicle at high speeds when it went off the road and hit a tree."

Major accident. Jason Richter, Jason Richter, Jason Richter.

I never would have noticed that name before, but now it's engraved into my memory. Accident. Jason's been in an accident.

My dreams flare up in my mind, making me dizzy, and my legs go weak under me. I collapse, but Dad's arms wrap around me, catching me. I'm not sure why this is hitting me so hard, but there's this loud fuzz in my ears that's only broken by the reporter.

The image of Jason that last time I saw him hits me. His mint and cigarettes when he stepped close.

"According to police, the vehicle was traveling at high speeds when it lost control on one of the curves. There was a female passenger in the vehicle with him, but due to her being a minor, no name has been released yet. Both occupants of the car were dead at the scene."

Dead.

Dead.

Dead.

They're both dead. Jason is dead. A girl is dead. *Due to her being a minor…*

Another girl, just like me.

The fuzz takes over again. I don't hear anything else. Just my pulse mixing with the noise and throbbing in my head. The cries ripping out of me with so much strength, they tear me apart. A girl I didn't know has died with Jason. He could have lied to her like he did me. Maybe she thought she loved him and he loved her. Maybe she just *trusted* Jason like he always told me to do. The way I *did*. And now because of that, she's dead.

"Shh. It's okay, *dolcezza*. I have you. I'm here. I have you." Dad repeats the words over and over as the tears keep coming. I'm holding him so tight, my nails dig into his skin, but he doesn't pull away. Doesn't do anything but comfort me. Tell me he loves me and that everything is going to be all right. A weird thought pops into my head and I try to remember if I hugged him like this when Mom died. If I cried this much and let him hold me and tried to hold him, too.

"She died... She's dead." I don't know if I'm talking about Mom or the girl. Both, I think. A wreck flashes behind my eyes but I see me. See blood on my face as Jason's in the car. But it's really her. Another girl, but I can't see her because I don't know who she is.

I cry until I can't cry anymore. Until my eyes hurt from all the tears. The living room is dark, night having come, but Dad hasn't pulled away, not even to turn a light on. The TV is going in the background, making flashes of color dance on the walls. I manage to tune out the sound, try to focus on the blurry, dancing blues and reds.

I let Dad cuddle me and rock me in his arms. I realize

then, I'm not crying for Jason. Not really. Did I want him to die? No, but I don't think I can shed any more tears over him, either. Not over the boy who thought he could use me. Who called me to be a jerk and was so hurtful the last time I saw him.

I'm crying for the girl in the car with him and wondering if Jason told her all the same lies he did me. For Mom because I know the last thing she ever would have wanted was to leave Dad, to leave me. For Emery, her baby, and her struggles with Max. Angelica, Christian, and Brenda. I'm even crying for myself, too. For the girl I used to be who is now gone. For the one I became who is so broken. And for the girl I maybe hope to be one day.

I don't stop until I can't hold my eyes open any longer. Dad sits on the floor, his arms tightly wrapped around my body, rocking me, until I fall asleep.

Chapter Thirty-Six

Before

"Have you ever done something you regretted? I'm not talking about something small. I mean, life-altering regret. A mistake that hurts other people but you can never take it back?" I nuzzle Jason when he wraps his arm tighter around me, holds me close, making me feel like he needs me the way I do him.

It takes him a few minutes to reply, which is strange. Jason is smart and well-spoken. He never has to work to put his words together. "I have…lots of times. Every time I do it, I tell myself it's the last time. That I'm going to be smarter, be *better*, but it's not always that easy."

His reply is so different from anything I've heard from him before. I try to sit up, but he holds me to him.

"Do you wanna talk about it?" I ask.

"No, you don't want to hear about that."

His father must really be horrible. I know he's hit

Jason a few times. Know he drinks, and I wonder how much more there is. I hate to think of the anger and rage Jason tells me he lives with. "It's not your fault." That I believe. Jason can't control how his father acts.

He gives me a humorless laugh. "That's one of the things I love about you, Brynn. The way you believe in me, the way you trust me. It makes me feel like I'm invincible."

"I love you." I pray my words help. That they make him feel better. No matter how strong Jason is, no matter how strong anyone is, we all need love.

"You really do, don't you?" His voice is soft, almost needy.

"You know I do."

"Good… I want that, Brynn. Tell me something about when you were younger. Something cool you used to do with your family. I like listening to your stories."

So I do. I tell him about a surprise picnic Mom and I made for Dad once. We got so excited about keeping it a secret and actually blindfolding him so he didn't know where we were going that we forgot the food. I tell him about Dad teasing Mom and that we all split a candy bar she had in her purse for lunch.

Jason is quiet the whole time, stroking my hair as I speak, making me wish he had stories like that to share with me, too.

"Thanks…" He pauses, then continues. "Go to sleep, Red. I'll be sure to wake you before you have to be home."

Jason rolls, tucking my back against his chest. I do what he says, close my eyes and let darkness swallow me, wondering if he's doing the same.

Chapter Thirty-Seven

Now

The sun shining through the living room window wakes me up. Dad's arms are around me as he snores softly. I'm curled up next to him, leaning all my weight on his side as he sits on the floor. He slept all night like this, for me. The thought comes out of nowhere and I wonder what else he would do for his daughter. If he would do anything for me.

I look up at him and his eyes flutter open. Suddenly it's like the words are impossible to hold back. They're slamming against the wall inside me, taking fists and hammers to them, just so they can break free. Finally, *finally* they're ready to fly. "I didn't know. I swear, I didn't know about Jason. I didn't lie about my age. He told me he was seventeen. He said he loved me. I just wanted him to love me."

"What?" Dad moves, making it so I sit up, looking at

him. Concern tilts the corners of his mouth down, his eyes filled with sorrow. "I know you didn't lie, *dolcezza*. Do you think I don't believe you?"

I look at the floor, trying to take his words in, and maybe hide, too, but Dad won't let me. He's tilting my head up so I have no choice but to meet his eye. "I believe you. I've always believed you." Mom and I have both always known, Dad says what he means. When he wants to, I'm not sure there is anyone in the world who can speak with as much conviction in their voice as he can.

He believes me. He's always believed me.

I actually feel those words start stitching me together again. The more I look at him, see truth and sincerity holding me with his eyes, the faster the stitching goes. It's like I was ripped in half, broken, and I'm slowly being put together again. "You believe me?"

"Of course. You're my daughter. I will always believe you."

His daughter. *His.* Even after everything, he doesn't wish he didn't have me. "Then why…" I almost stop, but realize I want to keep going. I can't let myself hold back anymore—hold things in. "Why didn't you tell me that? I needed you to say it."

He closes his eyes and takes a deep breath. I hate that I'm hurting him, but maybe this is the way to heal us both.

"I've really failed you since your mother died, and for that I will never have enough words to tell you I'm sorry. It wasn't because I didn't trust you, Brynn. It was because

I couldn't trust myself not to fail you. I let your mother down already, and then I failed you both when I didn't protect you."

A mixture of emotions swirls around inside me, like clay on a pottery wheel or paints being stirred with a brush. The part of me that wishes he could have saved me, blending with the one that knows he never could have. I'm not sure anyone can really save someone else. We have to do it ourselves.

"It wasn't your fault," I say. "No one could have saved me but me."

Tears wet my dad's eyes. He pulls me to him, squeezing me tightly. So very tightly. "I love you, *dolcezza*. I should have been better. I should have paid attention to you, instead of losing myself. I owed you. I owed your mom. We both loved you so much."

I shake my head. Speak into his chest. "I sat in my room making pottery while she died. She told me she wasn't feeling well, but I didn't listen. I was mad at her because she wouldn't take me shopping for a dress to wear to the stupid dance. I went out in my room and didn't take care of her and she *died*! At least I could have made it so she didn't go alone."

Dad's voice is maybe the firmest I've ever heard it when he says, "No." He again makes me look at him. "Don't you do that. It's not you're fault, Brynn. Do you hear me? You couldn't have saved her. You couldn't have known. She hadn't been feeling well for a couple weeks, but I didn't push it. I didn't think anything of it, either. And who knows if the fact that she hadn't been feeling well had anything to do with the aneurysm, but I will regret that until the day I die. Still, we couldn't have known, okay?"

I can't stop myself from listening to him. From believing him. The strength is back in Dad. The determination. And it reminds me of who he'd been before she died. It's impossible not to let his words be truth.

I thought last night I'd cried all my tears, but I didn't. This time we cry them together. Hug and tell each other we're sorry. He says he loves me and I know he does. And we're okay. I know from now on, we'll be all right.

When the tears finally dry, Dad tells me, "I have something for you. A memory gift."

I thought he'd forgotten. When I didn't get one yesterday, I'd thought we wouldn't do it without her. My heart races at that. This was Mom's thing. Her most favorite thing in the world.

Dad stands before helping me to do the same. He goes to his room and comes back quickly with a red-wrapped package. The paper goes quickly. Mom use to tease me for being impatient. She unwrapped her gifts slowly so she could savor it. Me? I ripped right in. A part of me always believed the quicker you got to something, the more amazing it would be. When it's almost open, I wonder if maybe she was right. If I tried to open my packages too fast, wanting too much, when I should just savor every moment.

So the last piece comes off slowly. I gasp when I see it.

"It's more my memory than yours," he whispers.

I actually have to grab the wrist of the hand holding

the gift so I don't drop it. It's a picture. One of Mom I
don't remember seeing before. And it's me, I'm guessing.
There's a swaddled baby in her arms, the biggest smile
I've ever seen on her face. We're outside, the sun bright.
Wind flies through her hair, making her look like a movie
star on set.

She's incredible. She's happy. She's beautiful.

"That was the day we brought you home." Dad stands
up and walks over to me. "You were her world. She never
wanted anything as much as she wanted you, Brynn. She
was heartbroken when we couldn't have a baby, but then
she found you and she told me she knew that everything
that happened was to lead her to you. That she was meant
to be your mom and it made all the pain worth it. Being a
mom to you was all she ever wanted."

Tears fall freely down my face now. They splash
against the glass of the picture, but somehow none of
them hit her.

"She was so beautiful," I tell him, trying to talk
around the ball in my throat.

"*La mia bella signora.*" With his finger, he touches her
through the glass.

"I loved her so much," I whisper.

"Me too, *dolcezza*. And I love you, too."

He does. I know he really does.

"I love you, Dad."

We're quiet for a minute before I ask another
question. "Do you think it's normal to be a little sad
about Jason? I mean, not because I still care but—"

"Of course it is. You're human, Brynn, and you have a

big heart. Death is always sad. Especially…"

"Because of the girl. What if that had been me?"

"It wasn't."

"It could have been. And maybe that doesn't matter. What does is that she's gone. I'm scared… I'm scared it's my fault. Because I didn't press charges." Or I didn't tell when I saw him or when he called me. Who knows if those things would have mattered, but maybe the attention would have made Jason more nervous. Maybe it would have kept him from trying to take advantage of someone the way he did me.

Dad sighs. "Then it would be my fault, too. The right thing to do is never completely clear. We just have to try our best. And that doesn't mean it's your fault."

I think maybe he's right. When I thought I was in love with Jason, I would have done anything to be with him. Maybe his age wouldn't even have chased me away. Not if he really loved me. That's not a good thing, but it's an honest one. "People aren't all good or bad, I don't think." Not me, Jason, Christian, my friends, my parents. None of us. We've all done things that are wrong and things that are right. In the end, that's part of being human. Some of our actions are just a little worse than others.

"No. I can promise you they're not."

I think about everything that's happened since we lost Mom. How he pushed me away. How I pushed my friends away before, and now I've pushed Christian. Christian was right. I'm not taking my life back. I'm not fighting. Jason is still winning. And maybe… Just maybe he wasn't all bad, either. It's not something I will ever know. But maybe he just wanted to feel loved and didn't know how to find it the way he needed to. Just like me. He's responsible for his actions, and I'm responsible for mine.

Maybe if I could have been stronger, he wouldn't have been in that car. Or that girl wouldn't have been with him. Maybe she would still be alive, maybe not. There's no way of knowing. It could have been the first day they met, or he could have been tricking her the same way he did me. Either way, I refuse to stand by anymore. Refuse to let people get hurt because I wasn't strong enough to *do* something. Even though Jason is dead, I want to fight, for myself, for others, to be happy. To see all the beautiful in the world and to find it in my own. Not to wait for someone like Jason to give it to me.

I can be my own beautiful.

"I have to go," falls out of my mouth.

"What? Where?" Dad sounds panicked.

I walk away and he follows me. "To the center. Emery never told me where she lives, but she could be in trouble. She's been seeing her ex-boyfriend when she's not supposed to, and he's hurt her."

A little flash of something I can't read blips in his eyes. Pride maybe? "I'll go with you," he says.

We get ready and go to the center. The counselor is surprised to see us, but leads the way to her office. Dad holds my hand as I tell them about Emery and Max. She might hate me for it and though it will hurt, I can't regret this. I know in my heart it's the right thing to do. For Emery. For her baby.

Valerie thanks me and says they will be in contact with not only Emery's foster parents, but Max's probation officer.

"You did the right thing. He's dangerous. You could have just saved your friend's life. Hers or her baby's," she tells me.

"Thank you."

I'm scared for Emery. Scared for our friendship, but for the first time since losing Mom—maybe the first time in forever—I feel like I'm becoming the person I'm supposed to be.

"Valerie?"

"Yes, Brynn," she replies.

"Maybe we can plan an extra session. I need... I want to talk."

Dad squeezes my shoulder.

"Absolutely, Brynn. I would love nothing more than to listen."

Chapter Thirty-Eight

Before

"Christian moved. I can't believe he just *left* and didn't even say good-bye." I cry into the phone with Ellie. Mom and Dad aren't home. It's their anniversary and they went to dinner and a movie. I know if I call them, they'll come home, but I don't want to ruin their night.

"I'm so sorry, Brynn. Boys suck."

"I know it sounds stupid, but I thought maybe we would be like Mom and Dad…"

"It doesn't sound stupid. I'm going to get cookies and I'm coming over, okay? I'll tell Diana to come, too."

"Your mom said you couldn't. She said they're having a dinner party."

"So? You're more important than their stupid parties. They have them all the time. Even if I'm here, she'll forget about me within five minutes."

"But you won't have a ride."

"I'll ride my bike. We're best friends, Brynn. That's what best friends do for each other."

Forty-five minutes later, Ellie and Diana show up at my house, sweaty from their bike ride, and with cookies in hand.

We run up to my room and all jump onto my bed. We relive my dance with Christian and then take turns making up reasons he had to leave. That his parents dragged him away even though he didn't want to go. He was massively in love with me and was currently crossing the country on foot to make his way back.

Even though I cried earlier, now I'm laughing. That's what these girls do for me. They make me happy and they're always there when I need them, just like I will always be there for them.

It's less than an hour later when Ellie's mom calls and asks if she's here. I hand the phone to my friend. One of my best friends.

"Ellie? What do you think you're doing? I told you to stay home." Her mom is yelling so loudly, both Diana and I can hear her.

"It's important! My friends needed me."

"I don't care. You get your butt home right now or you're grounded for a month."

"Fine!" Ellie yells before hanging up.

Then she does the craziest thing… She climbs right back on the bed and pops another cookie into her mouth.

"Ell, you have to go! You're going to get into trouble." I stand.

"You guys are here for me more than they ever are,

so I'm going to be here for you."

"But it's not that important. I'm just being a baby over a stupid boy."

"Boys are very important." Ellie laughs. I roll my eyes and she continues. "I'm staying. That's what friends do, right? We make it better."

I can't help but smile. "I don't want you to get into trouble."

"I'm staying regardless. I guess that means we need to have extra fun so it will last me the next month!" She laughs and we do, too. We eat the whole package of cookies and put makeup on in silly ways just to be able to laugh and tease each other. And even though Ellie does get grounded for a month, she says it was worth it. Diana would have done the same. And I would have for them, too.

Always.

Chapter Thirty-Nine

Now

I text Ellie and Diana to meet me at Ellie's house. Her parents will both be at work, even the day after Christmas. They're like that. They always work. It's one of the reasons Ellie used to like being at my house so much.

I raise my hand to knock, but Ellie is already pulling the door open. Diana sits on the couch and gives me a small smile. Just seeing them, being open to them, all my emotions push to the surface. These were my best friends. I loved them. They held my hands at my mom's funeral. They danced with me in the girl's bathroom and cried with me just because Christian Medina asked me to dance. We pinkie-swore to be friends forever and to tell each other everything. I miss them...

And I want them back.

"Hey," I say. As if on cue, they both say hi at the same time. Ellie and Diana sit on the couch, Diana pushing her dark hair out of her face. I can't stop my feet from wanting to move, but I won't let myself pace. Holding still, I lean against the fluffy chair across from them and say, "I was lost, when she died."

It's amazing how much you can take in after an announcement like that. I see Ellie's hands start to tremble. She wrings them together, tries to shake it out. Diana's eyes dart to the ground, but then they look back at me and I think I see a "thank you" in them. Maybe this is what they wanted all along. Maybe we just needed to talk. For me to meet them halfway, or at least to show them I needed them. I glance at Ellie, who always felt so cast aside by her parents and wonder if maybe she felt like when Mom died, and I didn't introduce them to my boyfriend, I was casting her aside as well.

"I know I pushed you guys away—"

"We *get* that. You lost your mom, Brynn. We knew you were hurting. All we wanted was to be there for you," Diana says. It hits me, how much better this all could have been if I would have let them be by my side. It's so easy, *so easy* to lock yourself up. To push people away because you think the pain isn't as much if you don't have to acknowledge it, but that's not true. It makes the hurt a million times worse not to share it with those who care about you. And there's always someone, I think. I found Emery when I thought I lost my friends. Or Brenda, the people at the center. There has to be someone.

"I know that," I continue. "I do. It's like, my brain knew these things. I wanted to open up to you, but I didn't know how."

Ellie adds, "You always used to talk to us. We told each other everything."

My eyes begin to pool with tears. "I just missed her so much. She was incredible and she made me special by choosing me, and I felt so much guilt for not saving her. Or being there for her the way she was always there for me."

The words are freeing somehow. I thought they all broke free with Dad, but there were more, locked in a cage inside me, begging to escape. Pleading with me to open up because there's no way to be free from inside that cage.

Ellie looks at me, her blue eyes watery. "She was amazing. We all loved her. You know…I wanted her to be my mom, too. I almost felt like she was. She was always there for all of us and she made everything so much fun. I know it's not the same, but I felt like I lost her too… And then we lost you as well."

I shake my head. "I was only lost for a little while, but I found my way back."

Diana speaks next. "Your mom was incredible, but she didn't make you special, Brynn. You did that yourself. We're your best friends. We love you."

At that the tears start to leak from my eyes. "I love you guys, too."

"It hurt to have you push us away," Diana whispers. "We'd always been a team and though we understood, it sucked. And then when you started talking about this new boyfriend you didn't want us to meet, it was like you didn't care. You'd moved on and forgotten about us. We weren't good enough to be there for you, when we loved her right along with you."

When Ellie's parents fought, she talked to Mom. When we needed a ride somewhere, we asked her. Diana started her period for the first time at our house and my mom was there. I should have realized it hurt them, too. That they felt like I left them, as well.

"And even after everything happened…" Ellie shifts. "You didn't want to see anyone after the baby, which again, we get. But then all these rumors started to go around and you didn't answer our calls again. We came to your house that day and I know we were angry but you didn't even try then. It was like you didn't care anymore."

"No." I shake my head. "Never. I could never forget about you guys. I didn't know how to deal with it. I know that's not an excuse, but it's the truth. I was lost without Mom and then Jason…I thought he loved me. He told me he did. It was all a lie."

"It was like we didn't know you anymore. We tried so hard to reach out to you after your mom that it was hard to keep trying after Jason. You could have tried, too."

And I know they're right about that. It was another way I didn't fight. Another way I just folded in and accepted everything. I didn't make sure the world knew what Jason did or make sure people knew I didn't lie. I became a bystander in my own life and let everyone else take the blame for not coming to me. "You're right. I know you're right and I don't have an excuse. I wish I did. The only thing I know to do is try to move forward. To fight for our friendship now because I love you guys.

You've always been my best friends."

Their breaths hitch at that...and then they part, putting space between them on the couch, and I know what they're saying. After all these years, I can read them like that.

My legs shake as I walk over and sit between them. We hold hands and I continue to talk.

I tell them everything about Jason. His lies. My feelings. And I even admit to being embarrassed by him not wanting to meet my friends and lying about it. No, I never should have told them it was me who didn't want Jason to meet anyone. But I was lost and finally felt I had something that was mine.

"I wish things could have been different," Diana says. "We missed you, Brynn."

"I missed you guys, too. So much."

We're silent for a minute, and then I add, "I know I pulled away first...but you guys aren't innocent either. The way you treated me. I don't think I deserved that."

"You're right," Ellie says.

"I'm so sorry," Diana adds. "Maybe we can try to start over... Go slowly."

My heart bounces. "I would love that."

"All of us made mistakes. I'd like to try to get our friendship back, too." Ellie looks down.

It's not perfect, but it's a start. I need to prove things to them, and them to me. The fact that we're all willing gives me hope.

I listen as they talk about some of the things they've been doing the past months. Then I talk to them about

Christian and tell them I have a new friend named Emery I hope they can meet one day.

Each word is a cleansing breath. A compression on my chest bringing me back to life again.

And I can't wait to live.

When I finally get up to leave, both girls stand, too. Diana holds out her pinkie first, then Ellie, and finally me. We link them all together. "Always," I say.

"Always," my friends whisper right beside me.

Chapter Forty

Now

The day after I visit Ellie and Diana, Dad's at work. I slip on my bunny slippers, grab the picture of Mom and me, and head straight to my pottery room.

My hands shake a little, but I ignore it. I fight through it as I set the picture down so it's facing my wheel. "I'm getting this back for me, Mom. I'm doing it for you."

I'm on autopilot as I get everything together. It's as though I blink and then I'm sitting in front of my potter wheel. Wetting my hands in a bowl, I touch the clay as it spins round and rough. I savor the feel of it on my fingers and let my mind *free* the way I always do when I create.

My movements are natural. A part of me that will always be there because Mom helped me find it. I mold and sculpt. Each movement of my hand and easy spin of the wheel is my fight. My way to get my life back. My way to create my own piece of beautiful.

• • •

Christian comes home on New Years Day. Stalker-ish, I know, but I've been watching for their car. I should probably give him some time to rest or unpack, but I can't stop myself from going straight over. He cocks his head at me when he sees me coming and leans in the doorway.

"Are you here for my mom?" There's no real anger in his voice, but I can tell he's upset. I respect that he's not the type of person who is going to continue to chase someone when they've cut him off at every corner, like I did.

"No," I tell him. "I'm here for you. Can you come with me somewhere?"

"Brynn—"

"Please. It's important."

He nods and turns to tell Brenda he'll be right back.

"Is that Brynn?" she asks, and I smile at the sound of her accent. I missed her.

"Yeah," Christian says. When his mom comes out, Christian heads to my car as though he's giving us time.

"I heard that you spoke to Valerie about Emery, *mija*. I'm very proud of you."

Stepping forward, I wrap my arms around her and give her a hug. Brenda squeezes back. I know that if I ever need to talk, she'll be there.

"It took a lot of bravery for you to come forward like you did. The right thing. It's not always the easy thing to do, but you did it. I hope you're giving yourself credit for that," she tells me.

After I pull away, I nod. "I am...and I have more to tell you. About Jason and everything else. Maybe we can talk soon?"

She puts a hand on my shoulder and grins. "I would be honored. Any time, okay? I'll make you breakfast again and I'll try not to burn your mouth this time." Brenda winks.

"I'd love that."

She nods toward Christian. "He's waiting for you."

Without another word, I climb into my car and Christian does the same. We drive to the park with the gazebo where he took me on our one and only date. And it was a date. I'll admit that now. I hope someday, we can go on another one.

Christian sits on the table in the middle and puts his feet on the seat as I stand in front of him. No preparation. No warning. The words just come out of my mouth. "Jason is dead."

His eyes widen, the shock evident on his face. "Shit. I'm sorry. I didn't know. Are you okay?"

I think there are people in this world who are just *good* people, not perfect but *good*—and Christian is one of them.

"I'm trying to be. I *will* be. He had a girl with him. She was a minor. She's gone, too." I will always wonder about that girl. I don't know her, but even though we've never met, she'll own a piece of my heart. "Who knows if he was using her the way he used me. I think so, but we'll never know. I can't stop myself from wondering if I could have stopped it. If I could have been stronger, if I would have fought, if things could have ended differently for her. Even if I didn't have a good case, more people would have known about it. It might have made that girl think twice."

Christian shrugs. "Maybe, but maybe not. Like you said, we might never know. Regardless, it's not your fault."

"Who knows if it is. All I *do* know is I don't want to question it anymore. I don't want there to be a possibility."

He gives me his half grin. His hair is hanging around his face and he's cute. So freaking hot. I like him. And it's okay. It doesn't make me weak unless I let it, unless I make myself *need* him. And he's not automatically like Jason, either.

"You were right the other day, Christian. I wasn't fighting. I've completely given up on everything since I lost Mom and I'm not doing that anymore. I'm taking my life back."

Another grin.

"I'm sorry for not trusting you. Or for not admitting… that I like you. That I've liked you since I was in seventh grade. I cried in the bathroom because you asked me to dance, Christian Medina. After Jason, it was all so scary to admit, but I'm not going to let myself be scared anymore."

"Hey. It's okay. I—"

"Wait." I hold up my hand. "I need to get this out. You weren't innocent, either. I get wanting to be strong, but you have to realize not everyone deals the way you do. You put a lot of pressure on people and I understand that it comes from a good place, but you don't cut anyone any slack. We're all different."

He nods at me. "You're right. I talked to Mom over Christmas break. She let me know that girls aren't the only ones who are a little *loco*. Apparently I can be, too." He stands. "I'm sorry, Bryntastic."

We're standing close. So very close I can see every color in his eyes. I can see how deep they go on, and that makes me smile.

"So…you've liked me since the seventh grade, huh?" He winks.

"Did I say that? That's not what I meant." I take a deep breath, getting serious again. "I wanted to go with you to the dance, but it was hard for me. I should have told you this before, but dances are very connected to my memories of Mom."

"Well, that makes me feel like an asshole. I wish you would have told me."

"Me too. I'm tired of holding everything in. And…" I take a deep breath. "Christian, will you go to the dance with me?"

He smiles. A big, huge, real smile that makes my heart go wild.

"Are you asking me on a date or are we going as friends?"

My heart speeds up even more. My palms sweat. I'm scared and excited, but can't wait to do this. I answer him with something other than words. Pushing up on the tips of my toes, I kiss him. Our lips press together in a series of kisses, but I retreat before I let my tongue dip into his mouth. He tastes sweet like gummy bears. He kisses as smoothly and with the same skill that he plays guitar.

My arms wrap around his neck and Christian's around my waist. It's the same way we danced all those years ago. He deepens the kiss. Pulls me closer, and I try to push even closer to him. It goes straight to my head and my stomach and I think I just feel him *everywhere*. Christian Medina. The boy I used to talk to Mom about. I know she would be happy for me now.

When we pull away, I press my lips against his one more time, just needing to be close to him again. "I'm asking you on a date."

"Yes. I am so saying yes." He kisses me again and I get even dizzier than the first time. I touch the hair that I've admired for so long and sweep my tongue across his and wonder if there is anything better in the whole wide world than kissing this boy.

"I have something for you." I grab my bag and pull out my gift for Christian. The first piece I've made since Mom died. He takes it from me, traces the guitar patterns, and the pictures of a couple dancing and the— "Bears?" he asks.

"Gummy bears."

Christian leans forward and his lips press to my forehead. "It's incredible. You're really talented."

"Thank you."

He looks at it again. "It's beautiful." A pause. "You're beautiful."

It didn't take him saying it for me to know it.

Epilogue

I stand in front of the mirror in my bedroom. My hair is down in long red curls that took forever to do. I have makeup on, but not too much. Just right, I think. Mom was always very particular about makeup. She told me less is more and that it shouldn't take away from natural beauty. I'm not surprised that she was right.

I run a hand down the front of my dress, which is a beautiful shade of red, too. It bums me out that I got rid of all my old red clothes because of Jason. Never again.

"You look hot. Stop staring at yourself." Emery steps up beside me. I shake my head at her.

"You're crazy."

"I'm funny."

She is. We both know it. "I wish you were going with us." I turn and lean against my dresser.

"Eh." She shrugs. "I'm a lot of things, but a high school dance crasher isn't one of them."

"You wouldn't be crashing. I could have gotten you a guest pass."

She doesn't reply to that. Instead, she walks over to my bed, sits down, and kicks up her feet. "I probably shouldn't do much dancing. I always loved it, though. We'll go sometime. Once the baby comes, things will be different." There's a sad edge to her voice. A few weeks ago, I probably would have ignored it, but now, I won't. Walking over, I sit beside her.

"Are you scared?" I ask.

She pauses, taking a couple deep breaths before she replies. "A little. I mean, who expects to give birth to a baby at our age? And knowing that I'm giving her up..." Another pause. She wipes her eyes. "I know in my heart it's the right choice. It's the best thing for my little girl and for me, but it's scary, too. Scary and sad."

I put a hand on her leg to comfort her. It's not something I would have expected to be able to do. Once I told about Max, I was so scared she wouldn't want anything to do with me. It was a few days before she showed up at the center again, but when she did, she came right up, sat with me, and invited me to go see a movie with her.

We went the next day, and then we went out for ice cream a couple days later. This morning she came out to my pottery room with me and drew while I worked on a piece. I like that we share a love of art.

We haven't talked about Max. She knows I told. The look is always there in her eyes, but I think her asking me to that movie was her way of saying it's what she really wanted me to do all along. I know how easy it is to feel something—to need it, but not be able to put it into words. I am glad to have been her voice.

It's amazing sometimes how much easier things are if someone takes the choice out of your hands. I'm sixteen. I don't want to worry about the big stuff. I have time for that later.

Right now, I just want to be young and have fun.

And I know one day, she'll be able to be her own voice.

"That's understandable…being scared. I think you're being a great mom, though."

She cocks her head, her eyes wet. "But I'm giving her away. How does that make me a good mom?"

I think about my mom and dad and about the woman who gave me away. I don't know anything about her. Never wanted to, but I know she did the right thing. I know I was meant to be a De Luca girl. Meant to dance with Mom and do pottery and hear her stories about love. Mom and Dad were my destiny, and the mother who birthed me made the best choice for me by giving *me* a chance to find *them*.

"Because you're making a hard decision, one that people might not understand, but you're doing it because you know it's best for her. I think my mother would have said that's what being a mom is about. That beautiful kind of love. Doing what's right for someone else, even though it will hurt you."

I gasp when Emery leans forward and pulls me into a tight hug. My arms wrap around her, embracing her back.

We don't talk for a few seconds, and them Emery pulls away. "Thank you," she tells me.

I smile at her. "No problem."

"No...not about that. Well yes, about that, but also about Max...for telling. I wouldn't have had the guts to do it, but I know I needed to get away from him."

It's the most perfect thing she can say to me. I squeeze her hand, trying to show her how much those words mean to me. It's so hard, not knowing if you're doing the right thing. Not knowing where betrayal lies and just wanting the best for someone else. Right and wrong isn't always clear. Or maybe it is, if we really take the time to look. From now on, I'm looking.

"I didn't want to betray you, but I wanted you to be okay."

"I am. Or I will be." Before I can keep the conversation going, she adds, "What time are you leaving?"

I look at the clock beside my bed. "Christian should be here any minute. We're meeting Kevin, Todd, Ellie, Diana, Ian, and his girlfriend for dinner and then heading over. I'm nervous. This is the first time I've done something with my friends in a long time." We've been talking, but we're kind of taking it slow. Tonight is a big night in more ways than one.

It will be the first time I've seen Ian outside of school since we talked, too. Clearing the air with him was something I felt I had to do. He was more hurt than I realized when things fell apart after Mom died. Ian and I were so back-and-forth and up-and-down, but what I didn't know was that he'd sort of gotten used to that. I didn't realize he cared more than he showed, and even though he's the one who dumped me, he thought we'd get back together. It's not that he loved me, but I was comfortable, and breaking up for good pulled him out of that zone he was used to.

There's a soft knock on my door. Glancing to the right, I see Dad standing there. "Christian's here."

Emery nudges me and I stand. "You guys will be great," she says.

Dad walks over and touches my hair. "You look beautiful, *dolcezza.*"

"Thanks, Daddy."

"Your mother would have loved to see you right now."

I close my eyes and could swear I feel her. Her sunshine on my skin and her smile in my heart. "She sees me," I tell him and know it's true.

"I think you're right."

Emery and I follow Dad out of my room. Christian is standing by the door in a black suit. His hair is loose around his face like always and those too-blue eyes are pinned right on me. My heart does a somersault.

"I told you he was gorgeous," Emery whispers.

"He is," I reply.

Dad takes a million pictures before asking Christian to come over for dinner the next night. That Dad and I are making sauce.

Christian and I drop Emery off at her house, where we make plans to meet up in a couple days. She's going to come over and draw while I work on my pottery.

Afterward we head out with our other friends for dinner. The only interaction between Ian and me is a quiet hello but it's something. It's a start.

There are a couple awkward moments as we are all navigating friendship again, but there are more laughs, girl trips to the bathroom, and I can't help but remember the last dance we all went to together. Where I cried in the bathroom because I thought I was in love with the boy who's sitting at a table waiting for me right now.

We go to the dance and that same boy wraps his arms around me and we move together with much more skill than we did in seventh grade. He whispers in my ear again that I'm beautiful, and his sweet, sugary scent is so familiar.

It's funny how life moves in a complete circle sometimes. There might be lots of bumps in the road and maybe even a few cliffs, but it's a journey, and sometimes it can bring you to the most wonderful places.

I don't know if Christian is the love of my life, but that's okay. I know he makes my heart beat faster and I don't want to kiss anyone else but him. I know he's sweet and kind and has a wonderful heart. I can't imagine my life without him and I'm not sure I'll ever be able to.

I know we have a long road ahead of us and possibly more bumps and cliffs along the way, but whatever it is, all we can do, all anyone can do, is deal with it. Try to grow from it.

That's what I'm doing. And if I fall again—because we all get scraped knees at some point—I'll get back up. Because I'm worth it.

We all are.

Acknowledgments

I have to give a huge thanks to my editor Stacy Abrams. She helped this book become what I always hoped it would be. Thanks to my family for dealing with me when I'm in "crazy writer zone" and to everyone at Entangled for believing in Brynn and her story. And to my readers, as always, I owe so much to you. Thanks for the continued support.

If you enjoyed Searching for Beautiful,
don't miss Nyrae Dawn's
OUT OF PLAY
co-written with Jolene B. Perry

Rock star drummer Bishop Riley doesn't have a drug problem. Celebrities—especially ones suffering from anxiety—just need a little help taking the edge off sometimes. After downing a few too many pills, Bishop wakes up in the hospital facing an intervention. If he wants to stay in the band, he'll have to detox while under house arrest in Seldon, Alaska.

Hockey player Penny Jones can't imagine a life outside of Seldon. Though she has tons of scholarship offers to all the best schools, the last thing she wants is to leave. Who'll take care of her absentminded gramps? Not her mother, who can't even be bothered to come home from work, let alone deal with their new tenants next door. Penny's not interested in dealing with Bishop's crappy attitude, and Bishop's too busy sneaking pills to care. Until he starts hanging out with Gramps and begins to see what he's been missing. If Bishop wants a chance with the fiery girl next door, he'll have to admit he has a problem and kick it. Too bad addiction is hard to kick... and Bishop's about to run out of time.

Read on for a sneak peek!

Chapter One

Bishop

Bishop! Bishop! Bishop!

The chants from the crowd won't stop rattling around in my head.

Bishop! Bishop! Bishop!

I stumble from the car to the front door, catching my foot on the step and slamming into the side of the house. The world around me blurs. It always does after a show.

Look, it's Bishop Riley from Burn!

Left, right, and left again, I look over my shoulder like the paparazzi are still behind me, their voices mixing with fans that haunt me. What kind of rock star can't handle crowds? It's pathetic. *I'm* pathetic the way I let the anxiety practically swallow me whole.

Just get inside. I need to get inside, and then it will all go away.

I wave my personal guard back into the car before grasping the handle, desperate for quiet. But as soon as I push the door open, it's like I'm back on stage again, everyone wanting a piece of me. People are everywhere, closing in. No one's supposed to be here. She promised. Maryanne fucking *promised* there wouldn't be a party tonight.

I shove my way through the people crowded in her living room. The crowd's screams during my drum solo overtake me, wipe away the high I get when my sticks slam down on the drums. No one's staring, but it feels like they're climbing inside my skin, gnawing from the inside out.

I need Maryanne. She said she had a surprise for me, and it sure as hell better not be this party.

Someone hits me on the left, scoots around me on the right. Each touch amplifies the screaming in my head, the vice twisting around my throat. I flex my hands, wishing I had my drumsticks.

"Bishop!"

I cover my ears, but then I realize it's Maryanne calling my name.

She bounces over to me, a big-ass smile on her face. "Come with me!" She's yelling, but I can still hardly hear her.

My feet tangle again as I go up the stairs and follow Maryanne down the hallway. With each step, the vice around my throat gets tighter, flashes of the show tonight playing in my head.

10,000 people.

Burn! Bishop! Burn!

It mingles with the phone call from my asshole dad. He

wants more money, he always does. It's the only way to get him to leave us alone. I squeeze my eyes shut, everything becoming too much.

We slip into one of the rooms…and it's quiet. Blissfully fucking quiet, the noise of the party muted by the walls. I turn on Maryanne, hating the way my hands shake. "You better have something good."

She holds up a pill bottle and grins.

My mouth goes dry. "What is it?"

"Come and see." Laughing, she backs away. As soon as I step toward her, she tosses the bottle at me. When I get the lid off, I toss the pills in my mouth and grab the beer Maryanne hands me to wash them down. Pills and beer gone in three seconds flat. Gone the way we used to be before I had the money to pay Dad off, when he would find us in whatever new town we moved to so we could escape him. Only the pills make me feel a whole lot better than leaving did.

Maryanne trails her fingers down my stomach. "How many did you take before you got here?"

"A couple. I only had a few with me, though."

"Here." Maryanne hands me her beer, and I down that as well.

It doesn't take long for the edge to start drifting away, for the vice, the voices, the hands grabbing for me to fade.

My cell rings.

Shit.

I pull out my phone, knowing I'll get hell if I don't answer. People are always checking up on me.

"Where'd you disappear to?" Blake, my band's lead singer, asks. "I thought you were coming over."

The room is spinning. How the hell does a room spin? I fall onto the bed to see if that makes it stop. Nope. My body tingles all over. It's such an incredible feeling. So much better than the hands ripping at my skin during a show or the chanting trapped in my head.

"B.R.?"

Oh, right. I'm on the phone. "Paparazzi wouldn't stop following me," I say. "I had to ditch them." *True.* The word sounds funny, so I keep playing it over. *True, true, true, true.*

"You could have ditched them and still come over. I thought we all decided the band would hang together after the show tonight."

We did? Little bits and pieces try to form in my brain, but struggling to figure them out takes too much concentration. Blake's trying to kill my buzz. I'll be damned if I let that happen. The spinning starts to slow down, and I'm pissed about it. The dizzy was way better than dealing with him. "It's not that big a deal."

My upper teeth brush against something on my bottom lip, and it startles me. But then I realize it's my lip ring, and laughter starts pouring out of me. I don't want to stop. I don't remember the last time I laughed this hard—the last time I let loose with people who weren't in my head.

Burn! Burn! Burn!

It's more than our band's name when they yell it like that. It makes me feel like they're burning me alive. My high starts slipping more…

I want to grab onto to it. Find something else to take to make sure it doesn't go away for the rest of the night.

"Bishop, you need to take this shit seriously. I can only cover for you so long before—"

Wait. "Cover for me? What the fuck does that meant?"

"Mean."

Mean? What is he talking about? The spinning slows to a stop. He's giving me shit for something all of us do. *They're* going out tonight. There's no difference if I do it with or without them. And at least I have an excuse. They don't feel like they're going to lose their shit on stage like I do. Not that I'd ever tell any of them that.

"Bishop," Maryanne whines. "You're ignoring me. I don't like to be ignored." She falls onto the bed next to me and runs her fingers down my chest again. My heart picks up. *This* is what I'm in the mood for. Not Blake's shit.

"Is that Maryanne?" he asks.

Bishop Riley! Burn, Burn, Burn!

My buzz is sizzling away...

"Gotta go." I hang up the phone and drop it on the bed...floor, I don't know and don't care. Maryanne's skirt is short—so short. "What'cha want, B.R.? I know you want more."

Do I? Yeah, I do. Just a few minutes ago, I was laughing. It takes the stress away so I can be happy.

I think she bats her eyelashes at me, but I can't tell. Maryanne gets up and walks over to the dresser. A bottle of vodka flies at me, which I almost don't catch. With a slow smile, she pulls out two more pill containers. The stress immediately seeps out of me, just that easily. I deserve to party once in a while. I'm tired of people telling me otherwise. I don't know anyone who doesn't let loose sometimes. Who doesn't need help relaxing after the crazy schedule we keep? The rest of the time, I just maintain. We all have to maintain.

For once, I want to do more than just maintain.

I get up and grab one of the bottles out of her hand, don't bother reading it before trying to twist off the top. It takes me three tries to open the stupid thing, but I finally get it before shaking whatever's left into my mouth.

"B.R. What about me?" Maryanne swats my arm, but I ignore it. I'm so tired of getting shit from everyone. Tired of feeling on edge all the time, like my own heart wants to eat me alive. I just want it all to go away. After fumbling a couple times, I finally manage to open the vodka before I down some, pills and all.

What feels like a second later, my legs go weak. The spins pick up again, but it feels like my head and not the room. Maryanne starts laughing and dancing around. I try to watch her, but a sheet keeps dropping over my eyes.

The room lurches. I fall to the floor. Maryanne's laughing, and I'm fighting to talk, but nothing comes out. Something tries to crawl up my throat. That stupid sheet drops down again, but it doesn't go away this time. Why won't Maryanne take it off? She keeps laughing... laughing...

Soon, there's nothing left.